I0544994

Jak Barley-Private Inquisitor

and the Temple of Dorga, Fish-Headed God of Death

Dan Ehl

Published by Rogue Phoenix Press
Copyright © 2011

Names, characters and incidents depicted in this book are products of the author's imagination or are used fictitiously. Any resemblance to actual events, locales, organizations, or persons, living or dead, is entirely coincidental and beyond the intent of the author or the publisher.

No part of this book may be reproduced or transmitted in any form or by any means, electronic or mechanical, including photocopying, recording, or by any information storage and retrieval system, without permission in writing from the publisher.

ISBN: 978-1-936403-26-4

Credits

Cover Artist: Christine Young
Editor: Brian Young

Printed in the United States of America

Dedication

To Barb Ehl

Chapter One

Attacked by a horde of tin mining trolls, I was tied to a tree, beaten unconscious with pickax handles and left for dead on the floor of my loft. At least that was one possible explanation for the condition I found myself in this morning--though nocturnal patrons at the King's Wart Inn might tell a different story of ugly inebriation and wretched overindulgences in vices frowned upon by the dour, dwarfish priests of my troubled childhood.

No matter what wicked act took credit for my fevered brain and palsied body, it resulted in an ill-favored day and a nastier attitude. The sulfuric smell lingering in the air, like that of rotting eggs, did not benefit my traumatized stomach. I watched the laboratory testings and spastic antics of the hunchback with little enthusiasm.

"I would say that the owners of the spilled seed and lock of hair are one and the same," alchemist Olmsted Aunderthorn announced with finality as he held the glass vial up to one of several small openings cut through the limestone wall to the rear of the laboratory.

Dust motes flittered like gnats in the shaft of light pouring from a window in the shape of a two-headed carp. The ray went nova in the blue liquid of the vial and exploded into shards of primary colors that danced across the pitted walls, ratty furniture, and shelves of dusty jars containing aborted creatures, pickled eyeballs, shrunken organs and scaled parasites looking like grotesque, armored dew worms. I squinted in puzzlement, momentarily distracted by the light show, wondering how such refractions could be discharged from a round object.

"You do not seem overly elated about the success of your latest case," observed the alchemist as he wiped his free hand on a greasy apron.

Olmstead might be a top-notch metaphysicist, but he maintained the personal hygiene of a corpse-scavenging dog. He stank worse than a dead, bloating cow in August. All he lacked was a buzzing plague of flies and they only remained truant because of a minor potion that also warded off gnats, lice, and mosquitoes.

"Yes, well one can only be so elated with proving the corpulent baker of Nostrine Lane has been in the bed of a kitchen wench. Especially when Baker Grensen is such a loutish old fart and his wife such a pretty thing, though apparently soon to be a rich divorcee. Will your findings stand in the King's Court?"

Olmstead peered closer at the glass tube and shook its contents.

"Our bodies are more than just meat, Master Jak Barley," the alchemist replied peevishly at my lack of confidence. "Though modern metaphysics cannot yet see or measure this vitality, there is an essence of life force all living tissues carry. Think of it as the magnetic power displayed by the iron needle of a ship's compass. The life force also flows invisibly, but through our flesh rather than iron. When a part is separated from the rest of a stem, body, or trunk, this emanation seeks to rejoin the divided corporeal specimens.

"In this tube is a sampling of the seed taken from a blanket off the maid's bed. I have also inserted a hair from your client's husband. Though we cannot see the life force, we can observe its effect in this liquidous compound. The stronger the attraction between specimens, the bluer becomes the formula. Samples that are of no blood relation will remain in a clear solution. Those of distant kin will slightly tint the vial. Sisters, brothers, children and parents--these will murk the liquid even more. But the samples taken from the same organism will have this result."

I backed away as the alchemist waved the dark blue vial in my face then gingerly grasped it and wrinkled my nose. The bitter smell made my afflicted stomach recoil even more.

Olmsted absentmindedly reached into a nearby jar, withdrew something green and popped it into his mouth.

I grimaced even more and said, "You just ate a pickle."

The alchemist's eyes bulged and he quickly spun to examine the container of live nose grubs. He turned back and leveled an accusing eye at me. I know how much he hates pickles.

"Well, I guess you can send the report when you have finished the parchment work. Just charge it to my office."

"Humph-h-h," he snorted. "Not bloody likely, Jak. Not until I see the flash of silver."

"Olmsted, are you saying you do not trust my credit?" I spoke in as deeply hurt of tone as I could muster.

"What credit? You still owe me for that work on the missing spice trader, and I hear you are three months in arrears on your rent."

I gave the alchemist an amiable slap on the back, only to jerk my hand away when I realized what I was doing. I maintained a strained smile as I furtively wiped my palm across a nearby rag.

"I will have more than enough to pay these petty debts once the baker's wife settles her bill with me, but I will not be able to give you a copper pfenning without this laboratory report."

"Well..."

I knew he would relent. How could he refuse his own half-brother? Father might not have been a very good parental figure for his numerous offspring--a downright miserable one since he did not remain to see even one of his many scions actually birthed--but he did leave behind an expansive network of kinship for his whelps that transcends the usual social and economic barriers of a provincial capital like Duburoake. He was impartial when it came to pretty women, whether they be scullery maid or duke's daughter. His current whereabouts and state of health remain a mystery since many good fathers and husbands of the berg still nourish ill feelings. No doubt he fled to a far realm to ply his talent among a less suspecting populace.

The alchemist's laboratory was in the guild section of Duburoake and hanging in the air was the stench of wet sawdust, rotting animal hides awaiting tanning, coal-burning forges, and workmen's sweat concentrated like the collected essences for some noxious perfume.

The cobblestone alleys are wide enough for freight wagons to pass in opposite directions, but the sidewalks are little more than narrow ledges. They are raised just enough to be above the street rivulets of slop thrown unceremoniously from the second-story windows of cramped and squalid apartments. One always keeps a wary eye cocked upward when walking these streets. At each corner are steppingstones spaced to allow wagon wheels to pass between them, while offering pedestrians safe fording above the sewage. It is not my favorite neighborhood.

That is not to say my third-floor office and loft are situated on snob knoll. The neighborhood was once comfortably middleclass made up of prosperous burghers and elder yeomen who retired to town to let their sons take over the farmsteads. Not so anymore. The Dwarf Wars forced thousands of Frajan refugees to flee their dank mountains and many made their way to Duburoake. They now cram a 10-block area. Once comfortable townhouses are now roughly divided into warrens of cramped lodgings sheltering families of old and young Frajans.

I could tell I was nearing my office just by the gradual change in the appearances of sausage hawkers, street urchins, beggars, and vegetable peddlers. The city of Duburoake, like the rest of the nation of Glavendale, is composed of various peoples who arrived in waves through the centuries, blending until an array of looks can be seen in the market places--from black to yellow hair, blue to brown eyes and pale to black skin. But none are as ashen as the Frajans with their white hair, faded blue eyes, and bleached skins. They were often called spooks in jest, if not open derision.

They now swirled about me and an occasional sharp glance met my own gaze. They tend to keep to themselves even after twenty years and look upon strangers with distrust.

I heard the commotion before I turned the corner. Two teamsters were beating a downed horse, the large beast having collapsed to its front knees as if begging for mercy. The wagon it pulled was overloaded with white-crusted barrels of salted herring. One of the two freight haulers, a pudding-bellied man with sloped shoulders and watery eyes, half circled the mare as he unceasingly flicked at it with a braided wyvern-hide whip. The other, shorter and with a hairless crown shaped much like a volcano, sporadically slapped the horse's haunches with the flat of a barrel stave.

I could have walked by if the horse had not looked up as I passed. Its large, dumb eyes were filled with more quiet misery than I believed any man or beast could survive. I faltered and came to halt. The horse continued staring at me. It was of the giant mounts bred to carry armored knights. The animals are sold cheaply once they become too old for the harsh rigors of battle. They mostly wind up as this one, half starved and pushed beyond their limits by spiteful simpletons. The poor animals are often left where they drop and usually find their way to neighborhood stew pots.

"Outa me way," snarled the shorter of the teamsters as he elbowed me to the side while making his way around the horse. He had the pinched, close-set eyes of a rodent and his sparse, long whiskers lent themselves well to the impression.

The pinhead truly raised my ire. I do not seek quarrels, but I hate bullies such as the two cretins now before me. But they did present a quandary. Either of the burly shippers could stomp me into the ground. The oaf who shoved me wore large jagged rings on his sausage fingers-- the type that inflicts scars similar to the blemishes running down one side of his face. Add to that his steel-toed brogans that were more likely used in brawls than for guild safety and I knew I faced a man-version of the pit dogs that fight at the wharf--so I pulled a stave from the wagon and smacked him on the back of the head. He collapsed silently to his knees before pitching onto his face. It took but a few seconds for the other teamster to notice his cohort's mysterious swoon.

"Hey, what happened to me mate?"

I paused as if surprised he was speaking to me then kneeled to closely examine his partner. "I believe he naps."

"What? A nap? He ain't taking no nap."

"No? He appears to be heavily into slumber."

"Ooh, my head."

I had not cuffed the brute hard enough. He was climbing to his knees and rubbing a growing knot. "Yah hit me. Wot did yah hit me for?"

"Are you mad? Why would I hit you?" I exclaimed in feigned astonishment.

"Yah hit Kried? What did yah do that for?"

"Obviously Kried still suffers from his collapse. I suggest you find a blood letter as soon as possible in case his brains are addled--the loss of a few pints to a leach would do him good."

I was now facing two severely nettled teamsters. Fists the size of hams clenched convulsively as they towered over me. Spittle flew from the half-dazed hauler as he tried mouthing accusations. A small crowd was gathering. It was getting ugly.

"Stand where you are," I spoke in my best voice of command. I drew forth my brass identification badge showing I was bonded and licensed by the Duburoake Royal Council of Public Safety as a private inquisitor. "You will do best if you cooperate with this investigation. Or perhaps you would care to taste of the Duke's famous hospitality? I believe I can reserve a room for you."

They stopped in mid-step when I flashed the badge, both licking their lips nervously at the sign of authority in my hand. I hoped they could not read.

"What investigation?"

"Animal brutality. The Duchess has ordered that the beasts of Duburoake no longer be ill treated, such as you have been doing with this poor, dumb animal."

"By Ubick's five eyes, we was just beaten the horse. It would not move, the lazy animal. Wot was we supposed to do?"

I meaningfully eyed the overloaded wagon and turned back to the duo. "I believe you may also be in violation of weight limitations. Could I see your freight permits?"

That put the oafs on the defense. I could tell by their sheepish visages that they were hauling without proper tax stamps and royal warrants. They looked nervously at each other. The big one abruptly turned to the horse. It had risen shakily to its feet and watched as if following our conversation.

"To hell with dah horse. We was just doing our jobs. Yah is going to hafta talk to the yard overseer about this. We'll go get em."

I watched in surprise as the two hastily took down the street and disappeared around the corner. I turned to look at the horse. It stoically returned my gaze.

"You are in luck that the drivers did not know you are only a ferret," a silver voice tinkled behind me. The crowd was drifting away, but a slim Frajan girl remained, arms crossed in a haughty pose. She stood with the cocky assurance of a rathskeller bouncer at closing time. "Is not it a high offense to masquerade as a city warden, ferret?"

"Private inquisitor, it is, Jennair, not ferret."

"What are you to do with the horse?"

"Horse?"

"The horse, me sweet but dim simpleton," the girl said as she stepped lightly off the curb and picked her way carefully to the animal. "If you do not claim it now, the mare will be butchered before you have gone two blocks."

"What am I to do with a horse? I was only teaching those rude dolts some manners. I make it a gift to you."

Jennair smiled. "No doubt me mother would delight in the arrival home of such a pet. Do you believe it will fit under me bunk at night?"

Her laugh was contagious and I could only smile back. It is hard to frown around Jennair, or not gaze appreciatively at her lithe figure and sweet, open face. There is a tint of blush to her cheeks missing from the other Frajan maids, a heritage from our father. It was not the first time I had cursed the fate which made the beautiful Jennair my half-sister. It was because of our kinship that the Frajan community let me keep my loft and office. Most native Duburoakians gradually moved from the neighborhood to other parts of the city as the parochial immigrants moved in. Their cliquishness commonly translated into downright rudeness to those not Frajan. They suffered my presence because of Jennair. That my father had been able to seduce a Frajan maid spoke more of his prowess than any other conquest.

"Here, help me with the harness. Those dolts will be quickly back with another horse in fear that more than this nag will be missing from the wagon," Jennair ordered as she began working at the buckles. "Do not tell me you were just arguing with those teamsters. I know you stopped because of this suffering beast, Master Jak. You have too soft a heart for that of a ferret. You like to pose for your ruffian tavern friends, but I know you better."

"Private inquisitor, Jennair. I am a private inquisitor."

The brief rest aided the nag. It had quit its shaking. Though its ribs showed much too clearly, a look at its teeth and legs showed a horse that had more than a few good years left. The teamsters were not only brutish and mean; they and their master were stupid for overtaxing the beast to the point of almost killing it.

"There, she is ready to go," Jennair proclaimed as the last clasp was freed and the harness slipped to the ground.

I eyed the horse. It was a wasted mountain of skin and bones.

"What am I to do with it? Its feed alone will impoverish me, let alone the cost of shelter." My protests followed Jennair's back as she returned to work in a small milliner's shop. "How do I get it home? I doubt the beast can go three blocks."

The next moment it was just the horse and me. We silently scrutinized each other before I finally sighed and turned homeward. Maybe I could fill out the poor animal and make a few coppers. I needed no lookback to see if the mare followed. The echoing clomps of her tub-sized hooves were enough.

I like Frajans, but they act as if they have icicles up their arses. They remain behind an imperturbable facade, an aloofness that sets them apart from the rest of the more demonstrative Duburoakians. Therefore it was no surprise that those on the street made a point of not gawking at the lone pedestrian followed by an immense and malnourished war steed. I, in turn, acted as if I were completely unaware of my equestrian shadow, smiling and nodding at the occasional fishmonger or street vendor. It gave me a certain delight knowing that there had to be some puzzlement behind those cool exteriors.

But I was the one with the dilemma. I reached the limestone structure and had yet to figure what to do with the horse. I looked with longing at the third-story window of my office. Above it was a smaller hexagonal portal that marked my attic loft.

"What be with dah horse?"

"What horse?" I asked as I turned to face Hebron, the kettle mender and knife sharpener. He was one of the few non-Frajans to remain in the neighborhood. I attributed that to his unmatched ability to not comprehend the most direct insult.

"Dah horse behind yah."

"Behind me?"

"Aye, dah horse behind yah."

I made a great show of slowly turning and reacting with surprise as I looked up into the weary face of the mare.

"By Saint Quantumous, it is a horse!"

His gaze darted back and forth between the mare and I. "Yah is jesting. Yah knowed dat horse was behind you."

"Yes, Hebron," I sighed. "I had a suspicion she was behind me."

"What are yah to do with it?"

"I guess the first thing should be to feed the poor creature. The mare was left for dead by two teamsters."

"I 'ave ah cousin who stables. He will feed dah horse for yah."

"Hebron, I thank you. Please take the mare."

"Dat will be 'alf ah mark."

"Half a mark? That is outrageous. What does your cousin use as feed, wine-soaked rice and bread?"

"Dat will include a couple night's lodging. Yah cannot let dah animal in dah streets overnight. And I need it up front," Hebron added.

I fished in my pockets, feeling mostly lint until I drew out a few phennings and a lone mark. The pot mender eyed the coin suspiciously before handing me back half in smaller coin. I hoped the baker's wife was prompt with her payment.

I was heading to the stairway door when Hebron's shouting brought me around. The horse was trailing me to the entrance as if it wished to follow me inside.

"Whoa, my lady. You must go with Hebron if you wish to eat," I said while patting its nose. "I will see to your quarters when I have finished other business."

I do not usually converse with dogs, cats, rats, king's guardsmen, or horses. I was surprised not to feel simple-minded, but an awareness I imagined in its eyes made my remarks feel not that preposterous. It appeared to understand me, turning away and pausing as if waiting for Hebron to lead the way. I watched as the odd twosome strolled down the street.

At least my headache was easing off. I climbed the wooden steps two at a time until I came to the third floor and its narrow, high-ceilinged hall. My neighbors were a tax consultant, solicitor, astrologer, palm reader, and barber who also pulled teeth. As honest tradespeople, we frowned upon the lawyer as the only disreputable scoundrel among us.

Chapter Two

Lamana was waiting with a frown, the heavy treading up the stairwell announcing my approach well before I opened the door. My part-time receptionist tended toward surliness the longer her monthly compensation went unpaid. She is taller than me--lean, dark of hair, and acts meaner than a Rwenian dragon. I like to think it is just an act.

"You are late. Crogs said you are on the street if you do not have the rent by moon's quarter."

"Curse my luck. I was so hoping to visit with our benevolent landlord. Of course you offered the old boar my deepest regret at missing him?"

"You have a client in your office," she answered, ignoring my attempt at wit.

"A client?" I quickly lowered my voice. "Why did you not tell me we had a client?"

Lamana sniffed and turned back to reading her horoscope. I inspected my dark gray tunic while vainly attempting to smooth out the deeper wrinkles. Hurried scrapings with my thumbnail finally dislodged a small remnant of yesterday's ox tail soup. The tunic did not look too bad since I had slept only one night in it. Running fingers quickly through my hair, I next took a deep breath and let settle about me what I hoped was a professional air.

The client presented a slim silhouette against the stained-glass oval window depicting the slaying of Dragon Gorgli. Long ago, the room had been a study for a well-to-do merchant and its window was the pride of my office. The figure turned as I entered. She was something to view-- garbed in a tight swath of burgundy material the texture of rose petals, though her figure was a step beyond the budding stage. Her smile slowly soured as I intently studied her in silence.

"Have you seen enough?" she finally snapped.

I had not. The silence was a ploy I routinely used on new visitors to my office. Disconcerted, they often spilled more information than they planned. It also gave me a chance to gain an optimum first impression.

This time I had a difficult task in completing a professional survey. My gaze kept returning to green eyes partly obscured by a waterfall of lustrous black hair, or to the swell of her breasts partly exposed by a very low neckline. She presented the hybrid impression of an expensive hooker and a young elfin princess. The look suited her--very much.

"You wish to keep our visit a secret, you have recently come into a great deal of money, part of your morning was spent with correspondence, you recently lost a loved one and as a child you had a pet dog named Samathannon that was lame in its left leg."

She stared at me in disbelief, a common reaction to my sharpened skills of observation.

"How did you know? I told no one I was coming here. Have you been following me?"

"Just the keen deductions of a trained private inquisitor," I assured her as I crossed the room and seated myself behind an oak desk given as payment for finding the driver of a hit-and-run dog cart. "Please, have a seat."

"How could you tell all that from just meeting me?"

I laughed as if slightly bored. "As with a stage illusionist, a private inquisitor seldom reveals his methods. Let us just say that I observe obvious signs an untrained eye will miss."

Her look was still one of doubt. She was not aware that I had breathed a secret sigh of relief when my deductions proved correct. Last week I told a portly gentleman that he had once received a gut wound during a fray with Farpathian hill bandits then learned that my no-longer-to-be client was a pregnant v'Landgren.

She ignored the chair and seated herself at the edge of the desk, leaning until her red lips were level with my eyes. They filled my sight and formed the words, "You must be a wonderful inquisitor to have such lore at your beck. Will not you please reveal your secrets?"

I felt an enthrallment and cleared my throat. "I based my deductions on several observations. There is fresh sealing wax on your sleeve, therefore you have been writing letters. You wanted our meeting a secret since there is no carriage in the street below my office. You obviously ordered the driver to return at a given time.

"Several massive gems decorate your fingers, yet your nails are short and the hands still retain traces of manual labor. Hands with such signs of wealth would not normally know rough work; therefore your good fortune is of a recent matter. Though you are not wearing black, a trace of nettle incense, the fragrance used in Anvadran temple services for the dead, still faintly clings to your hair and dress, therefore the recent loss of a loved one."

"As you see," I continued, "once explained, my deductions suddenly plunge from the realm of wonder to a more mundane plane."

"What about my dog?"

"Just a lucky guess. But enough about me. What about you, my Lady...?"

The mysterious woman looked about the room as if suddenly doubting the wisdom of seeking aid in such a seedy section of Duburoake and from such a dubious appearing private inquisitor.

"Selladora," she answered softly and looked intently into my eyes.

I did not gasp or go slack-lipped like a clubbed carp, but I did start at the name. Before me was the infamous Selladora, who began her childhood as an orphaned singer with a traveling troupe of musicians then to recently meet and marry Tgnatys, the richest guildmeister in Duburoake.

Tongues would normally wag at such an alliance, but the fact that Selladora was a beautiful woman and Tgnatys the ugliest of trolls made the gossip even tastier.

"Welcome, Lady Selladora. How may I serve you?"

"Find my husband's murderer."

"I, ah, was under the impression that your late husband died of an unfortunate accident during a feast at your manor," I replied cautiously. "Did not the Duke's own physician declare Master Tgnatys choked on a chicken bone?"

"My husband detested chicken."

"Might not he have sampled a plate?"

"In the library? My husband would not eat among his precious tomes."

She was a woman of blunt speech and sharp wit. I felt as if I were before a cabal of high inquisitionists for Dorga, the Fish-Headed God of Death. She used her brief answers as a probe, closely searching my face for the smallest reaction. The Lady Selladora was not your usual young widow.

"Are you saying that after slaying your husband, an unknown assassin inserted a chicken bone in his throat?"

"I am not saying it, my husband is."

"Your husband? He made a dying statement?"

"No. He was dead when I found him."

I was confused--a state to which I believed Selladora was purposely leading me. I smiled and forced myself to relax. Leaning back in my chair to maintain the illusion of a confidant private inquisitor, as well as to distant myself from those magical lips and green eyes, I considered several possible tacks.

I finally sighed and spoke, "I am afraid you have succeeded in thoroughly baffling me, Lady Selladora. Are you saying your husband has been revived?"

She slid off my desk and returned to the window to gaze upon a street painted an array of colors by the stained glass.

"No, my husband is still dead, but his specter remains. Each night his cries echo in the halls along with those of the shades of earlier inhabitants. Tgnatys was a stout troll and his spirit is terribly irked at his untimely end and lack of vengeance. The terrified servants have fled, no guests will visit after sunset, and I find myself becoming a hermit."

"I beg your indulgence, but it sounds as if my lady is in more of need of an exorcist than a private inquisitor."

She spun, her control finally cracking as she angrily retorted, "I know the common prattle of the streets paint me a scheming wench who married for money, but I loved Tgnatys."

"I did not..."

"Yes, you did. The folk of Duburoake believe that poor Tgnatys was ensnared by my comeliness. Do you know that a troll's idea of beauty more fits some squat, meaty scrubwoman with gnarled fingers and bulbous nose? He married me in spite of what you see as beauty. He loved me as a person. And I loved him, despite what the idle clucking of old hens say. He was a kind and generous person. Exorcism is out--I will not have him chased from his home like some errant bat. I want found the villain who killed Tgnatys so his soul may be freed. If you do not desire to work with a woman shameless enough to marry a troll, I will not take any more of your time."

"Please, I did not say that I would not take your case, Lady Selladora."

I quickly stood and pushed back my chair. She stopped at the door as if debating whether to stay or leave.

"You will help me find my husband's murderer?"

"Of course, that is my trade. Who did your husband's ghost say committed this act?"

"He did not. The killer caught my husband unaware. He has no memory of his actual death."

"Have the Duke's constabulary been contacted about your husband's appearance and his claim?"

Selladora laughed bitterly. "They try to act as if it is the hysteria of some witless woman, though I know it is because they fear to dig too deeply. Our guests were the most genteel of Duburoake's citizenry. Better the unexplained death of a presumptuous troll than to implicate someone with the power to halt a constable's career."

"I will need to speak with your husband's shade. What about tomorrow tonight?"

"He does not appear until midnight."

"I am used to odd hours. I will present myself slightly before midnight."

Selladora opened the door and stood framed for a brief moment. For the first time I saw her with a smile devoid of bitterness. "Yes, I was corresponding this morning, but the wax on my sleeve is from the candle I wrote by. And that which you took for funeral incense is a very expensive perfume. Good day."

I am going to have to quit explaining my deductions.

Chapter Three

It was a quiet afternoon in the King's Wart Inn. I stood at the bar nursing a cheap ale since I was still low on funds. A thick fog of incense hung in the air, burned to cover the body odor of the great unwashed masses. Many of the inn's clientele were not that fastidious about bathing on a regular basis. It was a humdrum time to be in the inn, but there were inferior ways to kill the half-dozen hours until my date with the widow.

"I hear you are looking into the troll's death."

I turned to see Examiner Hald, one of the Baron's constables. He wasn't in uniform and wore a worn and nondescript tunic favored by royal agents in the mistaken belief that they will blend in with the disreputable denizens of such inns as the King's Wart. Their greased-back hair and meticulously shined boots always give them away.

"News travels fast."

"Fast enough for me to advise you to go back to shadowing wayward husbands. You are out of your league with this one."

"You are thinking of buying a new dwelling, probably in the Gevonish area, and you skipped breakfast this morning.

"Slash the rubbish, Barley. I am serious."

"Your worry comforts me. Could I ask why my aiding a grieving widow is any concern of yours?"

Hald paused to make a quick sweep of the bar. No one was within listening distance and none of the patrons cared to be--they tended to dissolve into the shadows when a warden made an appearance. Cill, the inn's owner, stood behind the bar washing mugs and trying not to scowl too deeply. Having lost numerous customers to the Baron's dungeon, she was inclined to frown upon such visits.

"I am not for discussing such matters in a den known to harbor brigands and swindlers. Let us just say it does not pay to look for trouble where there is none to be found. The troll choked on a chicken bone. To suggest otherwise would be an embarrassment to those who are friends of the Baron's. You can only create a scandal where none exists."

"That is not how Tgnatys' shade views it. He claims he was murdered."

"Shades," Hald said a low voice dripping with disgust. "When could you believe anything one of them would say? They are a crazed lot. The woman needs an exorcist rather than a ferret."

"Private inquisitor, Hald, not a ferret. I am a private inquisitor," I corrected him.

"You will not be if your license is plucked."

"Is that a threat?"

"Barley, just drop it," he sighed. "I am warning you for your own good. Did you not learn your lesson with the Duke's son's case? I cannot always be there to get you out of trouble."

I took another sip of ale and studied the constable. He was of a slight build like myself, with the same brown hair and black eyes. We could have been brothers, at least half-brothers, which of course we were. Only he wore a perpetual gloom inherited from his mother's side.

"Thank you, Hald. I appreciate your worry. If the troll actually died from a chicken bone, that will be my finding. If not, well, since when has being a friend of the Baron's been enough to place one's self above the law?"

Hald sighed again. He does a lot of that when speaking with me.

"I did not think you would listen, but I have tried. I must go now."

Hald started to leave then paused as if bound by some invisible thread he was straining to stretch and break. He finally surrendered and shook his head at his own weakness. "All right, I give up. How did you know I was thinking about moving to Gevon and missed breakfast?"

I smiled enigmatically.

"Come on. You know how I abhor it when you speak thus and will not explain."

"Procure me an ale and I will divulge my secret," I answered, having no shame when it came to cadging a free drink.

Hald rolled his eyes and threw a copper coin onto the bar.

I waited until I had the brew firmly in hand before answering.

"Hev told me. I saw her and the babe at the market square this afternoon."

My half-brother smiled lamely and spoke one last time, "Just be careful in your assertions. These people you may mix with are not your common drinking cohorts."

Hald turned without another word and headed to the door. I looked about me. Thank Dorga, the Fish-Headed God of Death, that Tgnatys' dinner guests were not some of my common drinking cohorts. I counted highwaymen, assassins, blackmailers, and extortionists among the regular crowd at the inn. I rued the day I might be called to a case involving some of the loathsome scoundrels that frequent the Wart.

I stopped by the stable to see to the horse's well being. It stood contentedly in a stall to the back of the paddock. I reached over the half door to pat a nose level with my forehead. There was grain and hay in the trough. It appeared Hebron's cousin was giving me my money's worth.

"There he is. That's dah one."

I turned to see the two ruffian teamsters of yesterday's meeting.

"A fellow told us you are not a real constable, just a ferret. We come to get our horse back."

It was the pinhead, speaking much more clearly than right after his unfortunate fall. A goose egg still perched proudly on the top of his volcanic crown.

"Sorry, you abandoned the horse as dead. By rights she is now mine."

They advanced menacingly. There was no doubt they meant

business and me without even a barrel stave. The pudding-bellied knave grabbed my collar and jerked me forward. I continued the momentum and slammed my forehead into his nose, crunching cartilage and causing the teamster to release me with a howl. His partner also yelled and pulled an exceptionally evil-looking dirk from his belt.

The dim interior of the stables was thrown into mayhem with a loud crash and hay dust exploding into the air. The horse was rearing and its front hooves came down on the stall door with the thunder of a hundred sledgehammers. She was no longer the down-and-out mare I'd seen harnessed to the wagon. There was fire in her eyes as she stepped over the shattered boards and advanced on the surprised dual. The horse reared again, towering above us like some maddened demon. Her scream was that of a banshee.

That was all it took to send the two teamsters frantically scrambling out of the stable. I was a little more than shocked myself. I watched the pair vanish and nervously turned back to the enraged mare. She was watching the panicked flight of the scoundrels and seemed content with their escape. Her formidable head swung around and she appraised me with one large eye the color of walnut wood. I couldn't help but flinch when she took a step toward me, but she only pressed her muzzle against my cheek for a brief second then butted me gently several times on the shoulder. They were obviously meant affectionately, but the taps sent me staggering back.

I didn't mind. I was just relieved that the horse was not in some uncontrollable fury in which she couldn't recognize friend or foe. The attack had triggered old battle training and she was prepared to defend her new master against all comers. Too bad horses aren't allowed in the King's Wart Inn.

I stood on tiptoe to scratch behind her ears and led her back to the stall. I was going to have some explaining to do about the door. But rather that, I thought, than suffer the fate the two teamsters had planned for me.

~ * ~

"And this is where you found the body?" I asked as I scanned a long narrow hall lined with exotic hunting trophies. A cavernous marble fireplace dominated one end of the room, its interior immense enough to burn whole tree trunks. Carved figures of nubile young girls sported naked in the stone waves.

I eyed the massive head of a direpoodle, a ferocious canine that stood six foot at the shoulder and once terrorized area peasants before becoming the favorite quarry of royal hunts. They now flourish only in the rugged mountains to the west. The sole reason the gentry does not pursue the beasts to extinction is because the mountains are also home to a very nasty breed of yellow vampire. I wished the direpoodles were still about to thin out the swelling number of spoiled nobility, who in their blood lust tromp through the sparse crops tilled by poor peons, sending arrows at anything that wasn't wearing a collar, mooed, or oinked. Even then it was not uncommon for some poor cow or pig to drop dead of mysterious punctures.

I was wishfully imagining what the Duke's youngest son would look like in the dagger-lined jaws of the direpoodle when Selladora answered, "Yes, I found him by the billiard table."

"They were here when Tgnatys bought the mansion," my client added when she noticed my gaze. "The previous owners, Vendel Hyst and his ancestors, were noted huntsmen. The founding patriarch, Purjyn Hyst, was a bastard son of our king's great-great-great-grandfather and the whole resulting Hyst tribe was a pretentious lot. Some of the remaining bloodline had a fit when the family estate was bought by a troll."

"I am surprised they sold it."

"They were not happy with it leaving their hands, but Vendel Hyst is a luckless gambler indebted to the kind of people who lack sentimentality in such things," she continued as she walked to the fireplace and stretched her slender fingers to the fire. "Not that he had an easy time selling the place since the mansion is crawling with the restless spirits of his ancestors, most notably that of the famous Purjyn Hyst. They say he was a great warrior and it is his statue that stands at the main gate of Duburoake.

"The whole lineage must have been a vile stock since only those who die violent deaths or lead truly evil lives find their spirits still trapped among the living, and yet a veritable horde of Hyst shades linger here like beggars around a temple. Their rustlings and wails did not bother Tgnatys--he being a staid troll. I wanted to have them exorcised, but my husband was intrigued with the mansion's history and would not let me. I believe the only reason they have not since tried to harry me from their home is that they are a lecherous lot. I can feel them staring at me every time I disrobe."

It was the first time I could empathize with ghosts. I forced myself to consider the matter at hand instead of imagining what the lady would look like unclothed or the way the flickering light played across her lovely face. It was nearing midnight and an ominous chill was pervading the flagstone-floored study. Such great residences are impressive to look upon but lack in the simpler amenities of even my humble loft. Their airy wards, lofty ceilings, winding halls, and multitude of rooms like chambers in a hornet's nest offer the cold comfort of a government building.

And there was something more than the normal indifference of such buildings that chilled my soul. I had closely studied the palace after entering the unguarded grounds and while following a winding brick lane to the massive front doors. The domicile appeared to have been built upon the foundation of an even older structure. The lower rock slabs were the gray of weathered bones of something more ancient and disproportionate in size to the rest of the smaller building stones. The footing of the mansion reminded me of the monolithic edifices that stand abandoned in the Cythnian Desert, those evil megaliths where the oppressive memories of unspeakable, bloody rites can still be heard in the whispering sands that drift among the abominable temples.

I detected a continuation of that unwholesome vein in the later addition. Though plainly of human origin, the upper dwelling retained a subtle perversity that echoed from the alien shorings. The patterns of windows and the shadows thrown from columns and arches suggested unwholesome and tortured visages. Even the seemingly conventional room we now occupied pricked at the edge of my consciousness, causing a morbid uneasiness because of the slightly skewed lines of the room that only seemed abnormal when glimpsed from the corners of my eyes. The unimaginative troll might have failed to notice the depravity of the mansion, but I was amazed Selladora could stand to live alone in such a malevolent abode. I hoped there would be no call for me to visit the cellars.

I shook myself from the reverie and asked, "You are sure none of the guests left the dining hall after Tgnatys came to this study?"

"I am sure. We were all seated at the table being served by our two remaining maids when Tgnatys left to retrieve the latest rare book he had acquired. He wanted to show it to Bishop Yonlun. I went looking for him when he did not return."

I found myself cradling my left elbow in my right palm while twisting my mustache with the remaining hand. It was a stance I unconsciously took when contemplating unpleasant thoughts. If all the guests and servants have each other as alibis, that left only Selladora as a possible suspect. The riches she inherited provided a plausible motive.

"I did not murder my husband," Selladora spoke, once again seeming to read my mind. "I know you find it hard to believe, but I loved him."

"Ah, I am sure you did." Her outburst flustered me.

"I have inspected the entire dwelling and have found nothing out of the ordinary other than several unmarked graves in the wine cellar," Olmsted interrupted our discussion, entering the room so quietly that neither of us had noticed his entrance.

"What?" Selladora and I both exclaimed in unison.

"Oh, they are no concern of ours. I believe them over 100 years old."

I brought my half-brother along as a consultant. Throwing the extra work his way took some of the heat off my late payments. He even bathed and wore a semi-clean smock and leggings for the occasion. I thought it would be difficult to break his lengthy avoidance of soap and water, but he readily agreed when he heard we would be visiting the domicile of the beautiful Selladora. She accepted his presence with surprising ease.

The trail was cold and important clues lost. The body was already entombed, the study cleaned, and the witnesses dispersed. I had contemplated asking Selladora to invite the guests back for another feast so as to reenact the evening and question each of them in the original settings then decided that it was a foolish idea with little merit.

I would be depending upon some clue from Tgnatys' ghost. I admit I was a bit nervous at the prospect. I have always felt uncomfortable with shades, even as a child when one of my playmates was a tot who drowned several dozen years before in a pickle vat. He displayed a nasty disposition and twisted sense of humor that I believed he possessed even in life--which most likely accounted for his not continuing on to wherever spirits are suppose to proceed. Too many times I was wakened in the dead of night by his cold clammy hands. That was the first time I called upon Olmsted's talents, well developed even when we were children. My hunchbacked half-brother trapped the malevolent phantasm in the body of a scum trout and we fed it to a particularly sullen neighbor lady who later puked up a bright green discharge. My step-father would have beaten us both if he had not also loathed the old bat.

I decided to make one last tour of the mansion before the spirits arrived and I excused myself. I was not looking forward to the arrival of the phantasms.

Chapter Four

Selladora had a lot of housekeeping to finish. The Hysts must have been pigs. There were deep layers of grime on a row of armored suits lining the hall outside the study. I thought their number a bit pretentious when one considered the family members were noted for buying their way out of military service, preferring to pay the younger sons of impoverished lineages to take their places. I stopped at the top of a magnificent marble staircase that curved its way far below to the atrium like some frozen mountain rapids. Portraits of elder Hysts trailed the staircase downward--their piggish eyes seeming to follow me with malevolence.

I froze at the muffled sound of footsteps. The ghosts were early. At least they were not as boorish as to be clanking chains and wailing. I stepped into the shadows of a suit of armor, though I was unsure if spirits needed light to see. Just thinking about the dead made me feel the glacial hands of my childhood tormentor. The footsteps were coming down a darkened hall. Hairs rose on the back of my neck.

A dim shape slowly took form. The figure solidified into that of a wasted-looking creature bearing a slight resemblance to the villains in the paintings. I hoped it would pass by and leave me undetected, but it spied me and let out a frightened yelp. If the only good Hyst is a dead Hyst, then it was obvious this Hyst was still very bad. I leaped upon him and wrestled the rogue to the floor. Our struggles brought Olmsted and Selladora from the study.

"Master Hyst," spoke my client in surprise. "What are you doing here?"

I hauled the rogue to his feet and held him by the scruff of his neck. I released the wretch when it appeared he would give us no trouble and the dolt stood in a state of pitiful dejection.

"I..., I was only here to see my family manor once more before you strip it of its noble trappings. I hear you are planning to sell them to common scrap mongers."

A frightful moan echoed down the hall and set my nerves on edge. Vendel Hyst shuddered and nervously licked his thin lips.

"Is that your husband?" he asked Selladora.

"Why?" I asked and again grabbed him by the collar. "Do you have some reason to fear his shade?"

"No, no, most certainly not," he said while squirming in my grasp. "I was on excellent terms with the troll."

"I am afraid that would be one of your vulgar forebears, Master Hyst. Tgnatys would never make such a racket," Selladora spoke coldly. "May I ask how you entered my home?"

"Ah, you left the door open. I do not mean to be rude, but I did not image you would rob me of one last visit and no one answered the door. My man, what are you doing?"

I was searching him and pulled a brass key from a vest pocket.

"The realty guild agent told me I had all the keys," Selladora spoke in a vexed voice as she snapped the key from my hand.

"I forgot I had an extra."

"Which means this rascal could have entered undetected on the night of your husband's death," interjected Olmsted.

The accusation brought a light of terror to the little man's eyes and he squirmed even harder.

"No, no. I have not used this key until tonight. You cannot blame me for the troll's tragic death."

Anything else he would have said was drowned out by louder wails. Down the dark hall a gleaming form convulsed like a bag of rats.

"That sounds like my great-great uncle Hemost Hyst. You would do well not to displease him by treating me harshly."

"Humph-h-h," snorted Olmsted. "Have no worry there. That phantasm is only a fourth or fifth level apparition. It can do no more than shriek and warble. But I brought these in case of a more serious encounter."

Three gold rings lay in the palm of his hand. I picked one and held it up for a closer examination. Several vipers coiled about the band to enter behind a misshapen skull, there to leer from empty eye sockets. Strange runes blurred and wavered when stared at too intently.

"What are these cheerful baubles, friendship rings?" I asked my half-brother.

"Cfxzyth bands, cast in dim lairs to ward away such spirits that lurk these halls."

That explained the strangely fashioned skulls. It was how the rat head of a Cfxzyth would appear stripped of meat. I wondered that such loathsome creatures would fear mundane specters. I nervously rolled the ring between my thumb and fingers.

"We should return to the study where my husband usually makes his appearances," Selladora spoke.

Master Hyst was not eager to meet Tgnatys' shade and I dragged him along. We entered the library to find my other client standing directly on the spot where Selladora said she had found her husband's body. We followed the lady's lead through the study and stopped several feet from the glowing outline of the troll. The shade's energy was potent enough for me to make out his dimly glowing features. Trolls always look gloomy, so it was difficult to tell if he was even more upset with his present state.

Selladora remained silent so I took the lead. "Good evening, Master Tgnatys. My name is Jak Barley. Your wife hired me to discover the culprit behind your death. I would like to ask you a few questions."

It was a first for interviewing a ghost and I felt very awkward, rolling the ring in my hand while waiting for a response.

"Ask."

"It takes much energy for a new apparition to speak," Selladora apologized for her husband's curtness.

"Did you not see or hear anything unusual before your death?"

"No."

"Did you know of any hard feelings your guests might hold against you?"

"No."

"Do you think Hyst, here, might have killed you?"

"Such a creature could not have caught me unaware."

His form dimmed as he made the effort to speak a full sentence. Hyst visibly relaxed in relief at the shade's answer.

"Do you have any thoughts on who might have murdered you?"

"No."

"Were you expecting any guest who did not make an appearance?"

"No."

This was not going to be easy, I thought, then a bolt of genius struck me.

"Have you asked the other specters if they witnessed the event?"

Everyone of flesh and blood tensed while I leaned forward eagerly awaiting his answer.

"They will not speak to a troll."

Damn, I cursed silently. A possible horde of witnesses and they had to be a bunch of bigoted ghosts.

"Olmsted, can you summon all the spirits that I might question them?"

"Jak, I am a metaphysicist, not some mumbling conjurer," he answered in an offended voice.

"Cut the dragon turds. I know you dabble in anything that catches your curiosity, licensed or not. I will not report you to the magician's guild."

Olmsted sighed and his brow wrinkled as he searched his memory for an appropriate incantation. My hunchback half-brother might wear the appearance of an ignorant oaf, but his probing mind bore no such impediments. He closed his eyes and whispered in an unintelligible chant so favored by snotty wizards. I believe they use such arcane mutterings just to impress us laymen when simpler words would suffice. They are worse than solicitors. I was glad my half-brother followed a more scientific line of work.

The flames in the fireplace boiled and bathed us in a strange blue light. A wind roared through the study and slammed shut the doors. About us erupted a half dozen ill-shaped apparitions that howled in anger. They whirled about the room like a pack of blood-crazed direpoodles. Repeatedly they rushed us three trespassers, but our rings held them at bay. One shade blazed with a greenish-yellow light that easily out shined the others.

"There would be Purjyn Hyst," my brother pointed and shouted above the screams and shrieks of the very annoyed spirits.

In their rage, the ghosts finally turned on their own descendent and lifted Vendel Hyst from the floor, throwing the poor wretch into the fire. He quickly scrambled out with his clothes smoldering, only to be hurled across the room to become impaled on the horns of a mounted Quelian Steppe Ox. He hung lifeless and limp on the beast's horns, the moth-eaten creature finally taking vengeance upon the family that killed it.

In my surprise I dropped the protective ring and watched in shock as it rolled across the stone floor. The entities howled insanely in maddened glee and rushed to surround me. I made a frantic dive and landed with outstretched hands inches from the rolling ring. I felt glacial hands grab my ankles and begin to draw me back. I kicked with the desperation of a man who knew he was being dragged to a gruesome death. The hold was momentarily dislodged and in a frenzy I scrambled after the ring. My hand clutched it just as I felt the return of frigid claws. The spirits barked in pain and frustration before releasing me. I lay stunned on the floor until Selladora rushed to my side and helped me to my feet.

Olmsted was again chanting, the power forcing the abhorrent

family to congregate in one corner of the room where they shrieked their indignation. I carefully placed the ring on my trembling finger.

"Well, that surely brought them," I said while endeavoring to regain the cool air of a private inquisitor.

We turned to the pitiful body that was once Vendel Hyst.

"I suppose we are going to have another shade to deal with," I tried pronouncing jauntily, though my jest came out a bit quivering.

"It will take at least three days before his spirit is orientated enough to form into a visible manifestation." Olmsted's practical observation did much to calm my nerves.

"Can you make these spirits answer my questions?" I asked my brother.

"At least an hour is needed for them to stew within the confines of the incantation before they will submit to our wishes."

"And they cannot escape?"

"They are imprisoned until I release them or morning comes when they become powerless."

I sat at a study table in relief. Before me was a dusty tome. Elegant penmanship announced the history of the Hyst clan. I opened it to the exploits of a Varbillian Hyst, dead for over 180 years. Though the words were couched to make the rascal's financial plunderings seem a virtue, his deeds were anything but heroic.

"I suggest we retreat to more pleasant surroundings while we wait," offered Selladora. "There is cold ham and warm beer in the kitchen."

It was tempting, but I had an idea and wanted to search further through the library. The two left and I continued pouring over the monograph. The Hoyt clan boasted a number of scoundrels and villains, beginning with Purjyn Hyst. The hour passed quickly and I pushed away a pile of books as Olmsted and Selladora returned. Both seemed refreshed by the break, with the lady even smiling.

"I am ready for the questioning," I told my half-brother with a confidence that comes with solving a difficult puzzle. "Ask for Purjyn

Hyst--great warrior, former slave merchant, and wife beater."

The query was directed to the seething mass of evil spirits. To the side floated the greenish light of Selladora's husband.

A reddish shade visibly wavered as it answered, "What do you want, malodorous scum?"

I announced with a wave of my hand, "I present your assassin, Purjyn Hyst."

There was unexpected silence then the shade that had spoken railed against its invisible confinement, cursing and shouting threats that clearly incriminated itself.

Selladora looked at me in amazement. "How do you know this ghost killed my husband?"

"Elemental, my dear lady," I replied modestly then turned to the culprit. "You are the same Purjyn Hyst who was the lone member of this stock to actually take part in battle?" I asked.

"I was a mighty warrior," it answered in a scornful tone.

"The same Hyst who was terribly wounded in battle with a troll, surviving long enough to return home and die?"

"He cravenly struck me from ambush."

I turned to Tgnatys' shade. "Purjyn's shade must have seethed with rage when his family estate was sold to a troll, the same breed that ended his debased life. He flung some object to knock you unconscious then choked you with a chicken bone so as to make it appear as an accident. He feared exorcism if his villainous deed was discovered, an act my half-brother will now be glad to perform."

Tgnatys opened his mouth as if to speak, only to begin gently fading away. His last expression was one of peace. A low sob from Selladora brought me around. She stood gazing sadly at the spot of her husband's last presence. Olmsted put a comforting arm around her and she pressed her head against his shoulder. It would have been a touching scene if I hadn't wanted to be the one to so soothe the beautiful woman. Selladora had actually loved the ugly troll, who was no more uncomely than my half-brother. It appeared she liked the strong, ugly type.

"Come with me as I fetch articles needed for the exorcism," he gently told her.

They were completely oblivious to me as they walked from the room.

"You ignorant knave," shrilled the guilty spirit. "You are more simple-minded than that ox that my witless descendant now hangs upon."

"Smart enough to discover the perpetrator of this crime," I answered with a smile, having a hard time not gloating on my for-once excellent deductions.

"You pompous fool," a gaunt, fleshless face sneered as it momentarily solidified in a swirl of dark red light. "Yes, I killed Tgnatys, but not for any petty vengeance. The nosy troll was planning to show my private diary to his dinner guests."

I did not like my deductions suddenly shattered. "Why would you kill the troll for simply showing your diary?"

The shade remained sullenly quiet, as if angered that it had spoken.

"Come," I found myself almost whining, "admit I was right."

It continued to pout.

I walked to the study desk and sorted through a pile of books I had not yet examined. A tell-tale shriek came from the ghost as I picked up a felt-covered book. I began leafing through the pages to the continued shrilling of the ghost. In a cramped script the former shade's self had written of his private life. It appeared this Hyst was not the brave warrior our city history made him out to be. His successful battles were more like shameless attacks on helpless women and children, with strategic withdrawals whenever there were armed enemy about.

"I never cease to be amazed that people will transcribe such secrets," I spoke while leafing through more pages. "So, that troll ambushed you?"

"He struck me as a coward from behind."

"It is hard to strike a foe in any other spot when they are running away," I muttered as I scanned the pages dealing with the final encounter.

The observation put the shade in ill humor. Its screams rattled the windows and I apprehensively felt to see that the ring was still firmly on my finger.

Continuing to thumb through the book, I stopped at another interesting passage. I began laughing.

"What do you find so humorous, you simple-minded stooge?"

"I see where you liked acting the part of a groveling slave to domineering Elf women clad in leather."

Another page showed he had a fondness for dressing in his wife's clothes and being called Glenetta. The infamous Purjyn Hyst, legendary warrior, was a coward and simple debaucher of the ilk still sporting among a number of cellar taverns on the east side of Duburoake. No wonder he did not want his diary shown about the troll's dinner party.

I would be lying if I said I was not a bit dejected. Once again I did not get the girl or solve a case based on correct deductions.

I looked where the face had last been in the churning mass of evil light and said, "I will make you a deal. You keep quiet about my mistake and I will not tell of what I have read."

The shade grumbled and blustered, but I knew it would agree. We both had reputations to maintain and it seemed to fear exposure more than exorcism. I crossed to the fireplace and tossed the book among the coals, where it burst into oily flames.

Through a tall and narrow window of the study shined the moon still hanging high above the trees. If I hurried I could make the closing hour of the King's Wart Lodge. I was in dire need of the solace offered by a very tall ale. I might even leave a message assuring brother Hald that no scandal would come from my investigation--old or new.

But, I said to myself as I descended the marble stairway, I was going to have to learn to stop explaining my deductions.

Chapter Five

The old man cowered under the menacing gaze of the Ghennison viper mage after his feeble attempt at improvisation. He knew his words rang hollow even as they left his mouth. The two stood in the doorway of a tidy cottage at the edge of the village green. To the pawn of this incomprehensible game, the gaunt magician towered in his conical hat like the skeletal mast of a plague ship, his voluminous sleeves the wind-starved sails.

"You say your nephew is dead, killed by a crag boar four months past, even though the mountain beast would be in hibernation during that time of year?" the sorcerer asked with a voice as fluid as a spilled pitcher of spit-warm olive oil. "How can this be? You would not be lying to me, now, would you?"

"Please, your masterful. I am just a grounds keeper. My nephew has been gone for over a year in the Queen's Guard. I have not heard from him since he was home after his primary training. I would know, being I am all the boy has, him being an orphan."

"And yet you tried convincing me the boy was dead," murmured the wizard as if he were thinking out loud to himself. "Now why, do you surmise, would you do that?"

"I worry about the boy, that is all."

The old man paled as the wizard extended an index finger like a spider about to prod a trapped fly. The nail was a shard of yellowed ivory and filled his vision as it languidly approached. He felt dizzy and his vision blurred as the question echoed malevolently in his head.

"Where is Elfshold?"

"On his way to the capital of the kingdom of Glavendale, to Stagsford."

The elderly gardener couldn't believe his own lips were betraying his young nephew. He fought the bewitchment to deny his traitorous tongue but could only sputter unintelligibly as the effort sent tremors through his scrawny, bowed frame.

"Thank you so much for the information, old man. That was just what I wanted to hear. Now let me repay you."

A passerby walking beneath the moonlight would not have been able to perceive the going ons in the darkened doorway, but they would have heard the low, tortured moan that sent the rats scurrying in terror. The wizard had gently brushed the old man's nose with the tip of his talon and a spark leaped to devour the gardener. A column of black, oily smoke engulfed the figure and invisibly roared upwards into the night sky. Soon only an unctuous stain and unsavory odor spoke of the irretrievable passing of a man.

~ * ~

It was a squalid lodge in an equally wretched village peopled with miscreants, thieves, and black guards, yet even an unpretentious traveler as myself expects some peace for sleeping. Earlier it had been a drunken chicken plucker still reeking of rendered poultry fat and sporting loudly with some brazen tavern tart. And now an insistent knocking next door was beginning to fray my nerves. I was trying to rest after a hard day on the road--plagued by rain, wind, and an unfortunate intestinal problem most likely blamed on a rank leg of mutton. I should have known not to eat at an inn only slightly less greasy than the mule tenders of the caravan.

"I will shrivel the blackguard's testicles 'til their size would be an embarrassment for even the cooties inhabiting this berth," Olmsted Aunderthorn grumbled.

The rustling of the straw mattress was followed by the protestations of old floor boards as my half-brother rolled from our bed and crossed the room. He cracked the door and I scowled when a sliver of light slipped through like an unwelcomed fly. I shut my eyes and waited for the hunchback to release a torrent of profanity at the inconsiderate lout. Instead, there was only the muffled sound of the door being carefully closed and the alchemist tiptoeing back to bed.

"Are not you going to tell that dolt to cease that racket?" I asked in surprise. "I thought you were going to boot some buttocks."

"Sh-h-h-h," Olmsted ordered in a whisper while crawling back under the blankets. "We do not want to mix in whatever business be in the hall. There is a Ghennison viper mage and two Glavendale warriors at the door of our luckless neighbor."

"You are crazy. Viper mages do not visit hovels such as we frequent. I will put an end to this obnoxious intrusion if I have to kick the drunken dog turd down the stairs."

Olmsted croaked a plea as I rubbed my eyes and tried navigating across the dark room. I stubbed a toe on one of his boat-of-a-boot and cursed. My half-brother again hissed a warning. I ignored his blubbering and flung open the door.

"What the...?"

I stood bare foot, hair mussed, and mouth agape. Just several yards from me stood a Ghennison viper mage and two Glavendale warriors, all now turned to my door and staring in serious displeasure. Even without the conical hat the wizard was tall. He had an unhealthy yellow complexion like that of a fading bruise--and a reek of mold and dank caverns. A guard looked as if he were about to bark a rebuke when the door they had been beating upon flew open.

"What the...?"

I assumed the ominous trio elicited similar responses wherever they went. I looked at my neighbor with pity. He stood in a state comparable to my own--that of obviously having just risen from bed. I guessed him to be middle aged, with a black mustache that hung past his chin. Olmsted was still hoarsely begging me to shut the door.

The wizard gave my neighbor but a brief glance and said scornfully, "This buffoon is not who we seek."

"Who, dunghead, do you think you're calling a buffoon," the man grumpily answered in an unfamiliar accent. "You got a lot of insolence calling anyone a buffoon, dressed in that clown getup."

It was not an expected reply. I involuntarily retreated a step into my room, but couldn't completely tear myself from the unfolding drama. The King's men looked outraged then fearful as they turned to see how their companion was reacting--which wasn't good. Ghennison viper mages are known for their arrogance, evil tempers, and as loathsome students of the black arts. This is an unfortunate combination of personality traits and talents for those who come under the scrutiny of the notorious magicians.

The wizard's eyes erupted into burning coals as if fanned by the insolence. He reached out with a finger that more closely resembled a bird claw, but it came to an abrupt halt as my foolish neighbor seized the mage's wrist.

"Beat it, Bonzo, and take your two girly boys with you. I'm trying to get some sleep."

An ear-splitting shriek erupted from the wizard and he thrust his free hand at the foolhardy stranger while mouthing a fierce curse. I frantically closed my eyes and shoved the heels of my hands into my ears. It is dreadfully painful to hear the dead language of the even deader Xlantians spoken by a human tongue. The following discharge of light seared its way through my closed eyelids and sent me staggering against the doorframe. The hall was flooded with the stink of seared meat and hair.

I could hear Olmsted's lumbering tread behind me as I forced open my eyes. The hall was filled with noxious black fumes that made me lightheaded and stung my watering eyes. Strong hands gripped my arms and tried pulling me back into the room. I struggled reflexively and jerked free to see the smoke thinning. A greasy patch of charred cloth and crumbled bones lay on the hallway floor. It looked worse than the meals they call food at the King's Wart Inn. Two frightened faces looked down at the incinerated mass and to each other. The King's guards were bewildered by the sight. Instead of the expected cremation of the stranger, it was the Ghennison viper mage who was blasted into ashes and oil.

My neighbor opened his mouth to speak. The soldiers fell over themselves to escape before he could utter a word and their footfalls could be heard pounding down the stairway well after they were out of sight. The amazing event had the opposite effect on me. I stood frozen in my doorway.

"I could have warned the cretin, but he probably wouldn't have listened," the stranger said in a matter-of-fact voice. "I hope they clean the mess up before I leave in the morning. I hate looking at crap like that before breakfast."

"W-what did you do? That was a Ghennison viper mage. They are invincible. Even the lizard wizards of Jhrstlik fear them."

"The mightier they are, the faster they burn," the stranger replied solemnly as if importing some great wisdom, then stepped back into his room and shut the door.

Olmsted hesitantly craned his head out the door and gasped when he saw the stinking mass--greasy scraps in the muck still bubbling and smoking.

"Amazing," my half brother said in a husky voice. "I have never heard of a Ghennison viper mage bested at his own trick."

I shoved him back into the room and bolted the door against the unpleasant reek.

"I must speak with the man. Such a thing has never been documented. The editors of The Journal of Modern Metaphysics will be begging me for a paper."

"Forget it," I snapped. "He did not look like he was up for a professional discourse. Anyway, you are an alchemist, not a wizard. Leave that stuff for the big boys."

Olmsted drew himself up and huffed. He gets that way when he thinks I am demeaning his avocation.

"I will have you know is a 'big boy,' Master Jak Barley. More so than that of a ferret. While most wizards practice magic haphazardly through rote and superstition, an alchemist studies the phenomenon by scientific experimentation. Someday sorcerers will be looked upon as the hacks they are and alchemists will receive the prestige they deserve."

"It is private inquisitor," I reminded the hunchback, also a bit defensive of my own discipline. "Aye, that is great, Olmsted, but for now Ghennison viper mages and their ilk can still crisp you and your colleagues. Why not wait until dawn to speak with our neighbor when he is in better humor?"

He grudgingly acknowledged the wisdom of my counsel, but grabbed my arm when I pushed open the lock.

"Where are you going?"

"I'm going to check on Jennair. The row might have frightened her," I said as I slid out the door.

I looked back to see my half brother leaning into the hallway and staring at the nasty debris. He looked like a dog that has been ordered not to sniff around something hit by a wagon. The door opened on my third knock and I viewed the nose and one eye of my half sister through the narrow gap, as well as one fist clenched to a sheet she had wrapped about her nubile body. Once again I cursed the fate that had made the comely Jennair my half sister.

"What be the matter, Jak? Cannot you get to sleep without your cloth bunny toy?"

"Just checking. Wanted to make sure things were well," I said, not wanting to distress her if she wasn't aware of the peculiar incident down the hall. I purposely blocked her view of the smoldering corpse.

"How thoughtful, but I will not be able to rise early if you do not let me sleep."

"Good. See you come morning."

I reached my door just as a young lodger came rushing around the corner. He was thin and bore the air of a man with a great burden upon his shoulders. At his hip was a curved blade with a hilt wound with fine silver wire, though the sheath was worn and plain. He faltered when he saw the molten mage on the floor. His face drained as pale as his hair and he looked as if he were about to swoon.

"W-what is that?"

"What?"

"That," he choked out the word.

"Oh, that. My friend drank too much of the grape and was indisposed. He tends to do that."

"But there are tatters of a Ghennison viper mage's cloak among the disgorge."

"Aye, he will eat anything when he is drunk. It is an affliction he suffers."

I shut the door on the bewildered young man. I was too tired to explain the matter. It wasn't until I crawled under the blankets and was fearing the bed to be louse ridden that I wondered if he had been the man whom the mage had been seeking.

~ * ~

Kaiserhelm squats at the knees of the Megaoulas Mountains like a skinless, bleeding toad and grows fat on the caravans that come and go through the only tolerable pass for 120 miles. The whole village, from the cobbled streets to the squalid houses, temples, and warehouses, are all made of bricks from the surrounding red clays of the foothills. Constant rains keep Kaiserhelm glistening like the raw skin under a broken blister and washes down sluggish streams of odorous, scarlet water that ooze across the streets like the spilled blood of some murdered giant.

The villainous innkeepers and peddlers are well versed in fleecing the provincials who excitedly anticipate crossing the mountains for their first views of the fabled wonders of East Glavendale and to gawk at the royal city of Stagsford and its abominable temples. I looked in contempt at a group of pilgrims excitedly jabbering like children as they waited for the latest convoy to begin its trek through the perilous crags and gorges. I stood apart from my fellow travelers so as not to be thought one of them.

Being a proud West Glavendale native of Duburoake, I believed my smaller port city was just as intriguing and urbane as the royal metropolis. Better, since it didn't have in residence our pig of a king who is noted for a number of sordid habits and vile entertainments best left for the thoughts of those with baser imaginations.

The only reason I was traveling to Stagsford was because of the annual private inquisitor's convention that would begin next week. Olmsted accompanied me to lead a symposium on "The Detection and Conviction of Brigands, Embezzlers, Highwaymen, Swindlers, and Assassins through the Modern Science of Alchemy."

Jennair had her own reasons she kept close to her bosom, though from a hint I believed it dealt with distant kin now residing in Stagsford. The Frajan refugees were scattered across the world and had sought havens in many cities.

I impatiently searched for the cloud-obscured sun and wondered where my traveling companions were, last seeing them leave to visit the many odd shops that beckoned the gullible tourists and pilgrims. Olmsted had been in a snit after missing our mysterious neighbor this morning and volunteered to accompany our half-sister in hopes of spotting the stranger. I pulled the oilskin cloak tighter against the drizzle and turned to the twisting alleys of commerce in search of my friends.

And there were a number of odd stores. Clumps of people huddled under colorful tarps draped over the shops and booths. Here were beakers of holy water from the Ginht River, used as protection against the dangers of travel--though more likely drawn from a well in back of the stalls. I passed a narrow quarter filled with books and scrolls. Maps of strange lands marked with foreign runes covered the walls.

I stopped at a ramshackle hut selling an assortment of cosmetic aids for those injured in battle. Wax ears of a variety of sizes and hues lay in a long row. I paused to more closely examine a cleverly fabricated dwarf ear and observed that its artfully projecting inner hairs were boar bristles. There were also noses of many shapes, carved from wood, ivory and pink quartz--as well as cast silver for the jauntier of casualties.

I jerked back in surprise when my gaze met that of a singularly blue orb--a glass eye that was a perfect specimen of the art. I stared in amazement at the jewel-like article. The iris was amazingly realistic and gleamed in a way I imagined to be a teary stare of lost love or yearning. Its melancholy pervaded my being and only the impatient cough of the tradesman tore me away from the glass marble.

I felt quite foolish minutes later as I slid the velvet purse into my tunic pocket. I couldn't believe I had purchased the glass eye and might have seriously puzzled over the acquisition if I hadn't spotted Jennair and Olmsted wading through the sodden crowd. I groaned in agony.

"What is that ridiculous hat and blouse you are wearing?" I asked my half-brother.

"Like it?"

"What is there to relish? Only simpletons and blockheads wear those."

"You be quiet, Jak. Me thinks Olmsted looks quite dapper," defended Jennair.

My brother was wearing one of the foolish felt caps sold to simple-minded laborers and farmers on their first pilgrimage. Shaped as the triple-crowned peak of Jyrse Summit, it sported the words, "Me Survived Masgarth's Pass." His tunic proclaimed, "Me Brother Acquired A Sacred Relic And All I Got Was This Feeble-minded Tunic-- Kaiserhelm."

I had been reluctant at first to travel with the hunchback because of his history of bad grooming, but he surprised me with his change of hygienic habits now that he was betrothed to the Lady Selladora. But the hat and light surcoat were as bad as yellow and green teeth.

I sighed and shook my head in resignation. "We best get our mounts since the caravan will be leaving shortly. I have them saddled and loaded."

One thing I can say about the trip--I was traveling in style on the back of a giant war steed. Though the two months of stable care had almost ruined my purse, I had to admit the once-starved mare now impressed my fellow travelers on their runt ponies and mules. She was big boned and heavily muscled, having been bred to carry the great weight of fully armored knights. Her brown coat now gleamed like burnished hazel wood, thus I named her Hazel.

"Did you spot the man?" I asked as we weaved through the teeming corridors to the stable.

"No, but I must find him," he grumbled. "Tell me, my little ferret, since you boast of your powers of observation, what was last night all about?"

I was afraid he would ask that, a tough bit of gristle I had chewed at most of the morning. The stranger who bested the loathsome mage was an enigma. He spoke a curious dialect, used strange idioms, and wore a mishmash of clothing that pointed to no particular land or city.

"I believe we witnessed a hired Ghennison viper mage sent to seize or execute an individual. Such wizards are not retained by common thugs, so he was on an errand for someone of great wealth and power. The two accompanying royal guardsmen reveal that this master must be a member of the Glavendale nobility. Their mission was not some subterfuge or covert plot since they moved about boldly."

I paused in my narration until a squad of royal cavalry passed us.

"The stranger is not a magician," I continued. "He wore no rings, charms, amulets, fetishes, or talismans of power, nor occult tattoos. He did not even recognize a Ghennison viper mage, something no wizard could fail to do, no matter how distant his or her land."

"Then how did he defeat the sorcerer?" protested Olmsted.

"Good question, but you are the alchemist. That is a problem for you to answer. There was also a young man who passed our door soon after the confrontation. Even he is a riddle. He had the bearing of a soldier and carried a blade much grander than the inferior scabbard that enclosed it. His plain clothes were of cloth made from the looms of Ayers, that small state to the north of Glavendale. He also spoke with an accent common to the Ayers and the other small East Mountain provinces that are fiercely independent.

"I believe he was the mage's quarry. He blanched at the sight of the wizard's remains, which is to be expected, but he responded differently than most coming upon such a scene--promptly looking about as if he feared other enemies to be in hiding. Though his carriage was that of a soldier, he did not have the hands of a lowly peasant trooper accustomed to scrubbing barracks or hauling supplies. Still, he did not have the appearance of someone dangerous or important enough to warrant a Ghennison viper mage. It is a puzzle."

"Humph," grunted Olmsted, not impressed with my observations.

"I can tell you that the young man and your stranger are both headed to Stagsford and once were to be members of our caravan. I doubt, though, that they will still be going."

My half-brother eyed me with suspicion. "How do you know this?"

"I have my ways."

Explaining the deductions behind my conclusions tend to make listeners presume the inferences are simpler than they are. A private inquisitor who reveals his observations secures no respect.

Therefore, I didn't tell Olmsted that I had seen the two guardsmen of last night riding at the forefront of the horsemen who had just passed us. They were headed to the village commons where the Stagsford caravan was readying to leave. That meant they suspected their quarry, who I believed was the young man, was headed toward Stagsford, as that train was the only convoy currently in Kaiserhelm. Our innkeeper also told me, after pocketing a few pieces of copper, that our strange neighbor spoke of also going to Stagsford. Since the two witnessing guardsmen to last night's cremation would soon be searching through the caravan, I doubted either the stranger or youth would risk making the trip.

That thought stopped me in my tracks. I had also been seen by the two guards, who might just collar me since I had viewed their humiliation.

"What is wrong, my dear but simple half-brother?" Jennair asked. "Why have you stopped?"

I was continually amazed how she could turn off her Frajan lilt when she felt like it. I explained about the guards and we halted under a tattered awning to mull over the problem. Jennair suggest we meet the caravan once it left the village, but Olmsted argued that such a rendezvous so soon after a search would make the caravan master suspicious.

"This is the time to use your vaunted powers of disguise you so like to boast about, me Jak," offered Jennair once again in Frajan. "Have not you bragged of changing appearances with just a few turnabouts so as your own mum would not recognize you?"

It was true. I had scored quite well in disguises during my apprenticeship under Phen the Razor. A credible disguise did not necessitate elaborate wigs or costume but a shift in gait, expression, and manner, and a sweep of the comb to rearrange the hair. I knew my half-sister was baiting me, but I took up her challenge.

I snatched Olmsted's ugly hat and turned my back to the two. A kerchief was withdrawn from my pocket and I tore off two strips. These I inserted between cheeks and gum to fill out my face. Next, I drew my hair back from my face and pulled it into a pony tail, tying it with the remaining bit of cloth. I dropped to my knees and rubbed my fingers into a clump of the red Kaiserhelm clay I find so repugnant and lightly smeared it into my mustache and eyebrows. The hat went on next and I tucked my pony tail out of sight.

Before turning, I let my limbs go loose and imagined myself a hamlet oaf, my face twisting into the mindless leer I had observed on too many of my fellow traveling companions.

"Holy Murgford," I said facing them, "I hope Stagsford is as fine as they say."

"I thought you were going to put on a disguise," Olmsted remarked dryly.

I raised my hand as if to knock his head and he stepped back chuckling. "If only the lads at the King's Wart Inn could see you now."

"Do not mind him, I think it is a very brilliant transformation," Jennair said, "but I think you need to cover that tunic. They might recognize it."

Jennair was holding up a blouse she had purchased at a nearby stand. I groaned. The tunic carried a crudely inked likeness of a shock of barley and a mug. Above it were the large letters announcing "Karl's Ale." Only complete dolts wore such brew advertisements on their garb, but I shrugged my shoulders in capitulation and slipped into it.

I was lucky that Hazel recognized me despite the pretense. The mare had become quite taken with me and would not suffer the touch of a stranger. She nuzzled me in welcome as we paid the stable master. I hoped the guards would take her for an exceptionally large plow steed. Jennair and Olmsted were both riding hardy mountain ponies leased from the caravan master.

A shakedown was going on at the caravan just as I predicted. The caravan master stood by sullenly as the guards ransacked the wagons looking for hidden passengers. A veteran of many passages through the mountains, he was puzzled as well as irritated at the unexplained inspection. We rode our horses to the wagon of a merchant we'd paid to haul our belongings and waited as the guardsmen worked their way back.

I was surprised when the stranger in the room next to ours boldly ambled up on his horse and looked at me in surprise.

"It's a good look for you."

"What?"

"Your getup, quite dashing."

"I do not know what you are talking about," I answered nervously as the guards approached us. "You must have me mistaken for someone else."

"Oh, I get it. You're in disguise," he laughed when he saw my anxious glance toward the soldiers.

I frowned murderously at him and turned to stare blankly to the front, hoping he would go away before he drew attention to us. I did not want to be seen talking to the man when he was spotted by the guards. He chuckled again and continued sitting nonchalantly in his saddle, showing no concern as a guard leaned from his saddle to lift a corner of the canvas covering our wagon.

The soldier continued past us, followed by the two guards from last night. They gazed past me with no recognition, but paled when they recognized the slayer of the Ghennison viper mage. One of their horses began to fidget as if it could feel its rider's consternation. It was plain that they did not know how to handle this stranger who boldly stared back at them.

"Are you looking for me?" he asked the guards in an amiable voice.

The shorter of the guards cleared his throat to speak then thought better of it. The killing of a Ghennison viper mage is no small feat and the deed had clearly intimidated the two.

"No," answered the other after a strained silence.

They laid their heels into their mounts and hurriedly continued down the caravan.

"Nice boys, but a bit nervous," the stranger observed. "Is it you who they seek?"

"Me? Hardly," I answered now that the guards were gone, though still piqued that he'd seen through my cover. "But I was afraid they might want to question a witness to last night's incident. The King's Guards can be over enthusiastic in their queries and I have not the distinction of terminating a Ghennison viper mage to moderate their eagerness."

"Since we are to be traveling companions, I believe I should introduce myself. Lorenzo Spasm."

"Jak Barley."

I cautiously reached out to shake his offered hand. I examined his face and guessed him to be in his late middle years. There was nothing exceptional in his visage, but there was a shrewdness behind his brown eyes that belied his casual demeanor. He was lanky and his black hair, with traces of gray, hung to his shoulders.

I tried guessing his origins through his facial features, but it was impossible. His narrow nose could be Gevonish, but the brow and cleft chin were more that of the Brisbon sea folk. His high cheek bones and brown eyes suggested Elfin blood. Still, there was some nagging familiarity I couldn't pin down. I didn't even try to place such a barbaric surname as Spasm. And like yesterday, he was wearing a mishmash of clothing. This mongrel was a complete enigma.

He smiled as if reading my perplexment and turned to Olmsted. "I believe I have the honor of meeting an alchemist."

"How did you know?" my half-witted brother blurted out.

"You have a singular variety of chemical stains on your tunic, as well as singed cuffs as if you are more intrigued by the results of your investigations than to paying heed to the Bunsen burner--all the marks of a dedicated metaphysician."

Olmsted's smile countered my scowl. I forced an indifferent expression when I noticed Jennair smirking at what she must have perceived as petty jealously on my part. In reality, I was frowning at his simplistic deduction that any dimwitted stable boy could have produced.

Even as tolerant as I have become due to my occupational exposure to derelicts, thieves, and ne'er-do-wells, Spasm's next gesture shocked me. He took Jennair's hand and kissed it, an act one traditionally performed only with married women or widows. That he had the courage or stupidity to execute it with a Frajan maid was all the more astonishing. I tensed and waited for my half-sister's renowned temper to flare at this presumptuous act. Instead, she smiled brightly and nodded her head before saying her name.

"Excuse us sir, but we must be readying for the journey," I replied more curtly that I intended. I could still feel Jennair's taunting smile.

"Oh, perhaps Master Spasm would care to travel with us. I have many questions I would like to ask the gentleman," Olmsted interposed. He ignored my covert scowl.

"Why yes, tedious travel is always lightened by good company," he answered

The traditional ox-like bellow of the caravan master drew everyone's attention. The lead animals and wagons began moving and we watched as the far front started off. It would take several minutes before the back legs of this long caterpillar could move.

It appeared the stranger was going to accompany us despite my obvious disapproval. Soon my half-siblings were speaking with Spasm on a first-name basis. The only heartening development was that we were finally moving and could at last leave the stinking confines of Kaiserhelm.

The edges of the hamlet were shamelessly littered with large placards announcing the last food stands for 9,000 leagues or inns at Stagsford with special pilgrim rates. I shook my head in disbelief. My stepfather had taken our family to the capital when I was only a lad and none of this blatant mercantilism was then evident. That and constant fights with my half-brother Fedward were about the only things I remembered of the trip.

Just beyond the town began the twisting upgrade that would mark the first half of the trip. Our highway was narrow and bordered a rapids of churning water and monstrous boulders, the pass barely wide enough for two oxen carts to pass each other. The massive walls of black granite soared straight up to disappear into the perpetual cloud cover draping the mountains like an old crone's colorless hair. The vibrant green lichen covering the black stone produced a surprisingly pleasant effect. It reminded me of the expensive tile used in the bathhouse of the Duke's daughter.

I drifted forward to escape the newcomer's prattle and with a studied nonchalance, examined my fellow travelers from the corner of my eyes. There was a troupe of jugglers, puppeteers, contortionists, and ventriloquists hoping to find fame in Stagsford. They appeared to be a merry lot and I decided I'd have to visit their evening fire before the journey ended. That there was a striking red haired fortuneteller among them didn't make their company any less appealing.

Beyond them traveled a monger with three goat-drawn carts of fetid Mayday cheese. He was dressed in the traditional cheese peddler burlap pants and tunic.

I could smell the strong cheese even through its wax casings. Legend has it that a shepherd lad's spring tete-a-tete with a village girl took them to one of the small limestone caves that pock the hills of Ward Jasper. The shepherd returned to his flock after their secret rendezvous but forgot his humble lunch of coarse bread and cheese wrapped in waxed paper at the cave.

Months later, the lad sought shelter from a surprise summer storm and found himself in the same cave. His hunger grew and he spied the forgotten repast. Unfortunately, mold had consumed his bread and even marbled the cheese with thin veins of blue fungus, creating a staunch rotting smell.

Hunger finally overcame his reluctance to eat moldy food and he nibbled a corner of the cheese. To his delight, the shepherd discovered the plain cheese had taken on a wonderful flavor. The cheese is now widely sought as a delicacy, despite its odor.

Next in line were three tall, slender wagons especially fabricated to navigate the narrow mountain passages. Painted in bright reds and yellows, they bore fanciful carvings of crag demons to scare away evil spirits. The wagons were clinched together and pulled by a team of 12 woolly mules. Far up the line was a small contingent of soldiers, including the two from the night before.

I then drew abreast a knot of followers of Dorga, the Fish-Headed God of Death, whom I considered more odious than the cheese monger. Stagsford abounded with abhorrent sects and cults that honest folks shunned, but few were as loathsome as the ominous rumors hinted that these devotees and their diabolic priests to be. It was said all neophytes had to ride a goat naked and blindfolded while drinking the blood of an infant before entering the sect.

I was distracted from my covert observations by one of the dolts passing as a caravan guard. He had the swollen face of a turnip and rode his mount with an annoying ponderous swagger. Little good this ragtag collection of oafs would do if we were seriously set upon by brigands.

He stopped his spiritless bag of bones square in my path, forcing me to pull in the reins of Hazel before she ran the poor creature down. I didn't like the way he enviously eyed my mount.

"That is a pretty stalwart horse for a country lad to be riding," he said with a sneer. "Are not yah afraid of falling off and hurting yahself?"

"Funny, I was thinking the same thing when I saw the two of you."

"Are yah trying to jest?"

"Of course not, fine sir. I apologize if I gave that impression since I would never fight an unarmed man in a battle of wits."

"That is better. But yah speak mighty fine for a bumpkin. Maybe I ought to teach yah how to act about your betters. I be Fishwetter, the greatest swordsman alive."

"I think you are not aware of to whom you are speaking, Pantswetter," I snapped, growing impatient with the lout. "I happen to be one of the most respected private inquisitors in Duburoake and am trained in five forms of deadly combat, including Kim Chee. I could shove your bulbous nose into your obviously ineffectual brain with the flick of my right hand while tearing your heart from your chest with the other."

"Hah, if that ain't a good one," the guard snickered, his piggish eyes disappearing into the greasy folds of his face. "Is this how ferrets dress, then?"

"That is private inquisitor, you..."

Damn. I looked down at the tunic and remembered the disguise. I'd forgotten I still wore Olmsted's monkey suit and now realized why he was eying me with such disdain. I could hardly blame him. Still, the dullard wasn't doing anything to ease my foul mood. I moved to lead Hazel around the guard, but he pulled his own mount sideways to block me.

"What say I do yah a favor and trade horses before you hurt yahself?"

I eyed him with my most severe gaze, knowing the effect was

probably lost under the triple-crowned peak of the Jyrse Summit cap. He wasn't impressed. I knew the caravan master would frown upon having one of his men stomped into the ground. I could feel Hazel tensing under me as she caught my mood. Just knowing she would trample the oaf at the slightest signal made it easier for me to retain my temper.

"I think not. Now why not be a good fellow and let me pass?"

His grin made his face even uglier, if that was possible. He put his hand on his sword and was about to speak again when a voice broke from behind me.

"Does your master know you are harassing his charges? I would think he would take a great interest in hearing how one of his men torments paid customers."

I twisted in my saddle to see the mysterious stranger directly behind me. He and my cohorts had ridden up during the conversation with the guard.

"I can take care of myself," I spoke with little gratitude.

"I'm sure you can. Especially while mounted on that battle steed. I was thinking more of the health of our illustrious protector."

The guard gazed at Hazel as if seeing her for the first time. I believe until then that he thought of her as just a large plow horse. He looked into the grim eyes of the mysterious stranger and grew nervous.

"Just having a bit of fun," he mumbled and wheeled away.

I fell back into place alongside my traveling companions.

"Making friends?" Jennair asked coyly.

"Actually, I was setting you up with him as a suitor. I worry about you becoming a spinster. Fishwetter might seem a bit thick, but I am sure you would grow to love him."

"Our new friend, Master Spasm, said he is not a sorcerer, but actually an alchemist like myself," Olmsted interrupted.

"Of a sorts, but please call me Lorenzo."

"I have never heard of an alchemist besting a Ghennison viper mage," I replied skeptically.

"I'm afraid I can't take too much credit for the feat."

"You are much too humble."

"Not at all," he replied, ignoring my sarcasm. "It appears I naturally shed enchantments like an oil cloth repels water. Most spells rebound to their sources. The lack of magic is a common trait where I come from."

"Wonderful," breathed an elated Olmsted. "Imagine, no messy magic, but a place ruled only by metaphysical laws. A place where alchemists would be truly appreciated."

"It seems hard to believe," I couldn't help but mumble. "Olmsted, you believe in empirical proof. Why not cast some simple spell on our new traveling companion?"

"Jak, do not be such an ass," Jennair said, tired of my sulking.

"That's perfectly all right. I can see how such a statement would be hard to believe. Go ahead, Olmsted, but make it one you would not find too uncomfortable for yourself."

"Jak, I have told you many times I am not some bazaar conjurer," protested Olmsted. "I deal in science, not petty bewitchments."

"But this is science," I corrected him. "Think of Lorenzo as one of the experimental rodents you use in your search for truth. And I know you secretly dabble with magic when you think no one is around."

"I hardly think that you should compare our new friend to..."

"Yes, treat me as one of your laboratory rats," he laughed with much too good of humor. "I don't mind."

Olmsted furrowed his brow then flicked his hand at Lorenzo as he mouthed a few quickly spoken words. I recognized it as a simple spell often used by distraught nannies to cause drowsiness in their wards. Immediately my half brother began batting his eyes like a Verdian toad in a hailstorm, visibly fighting away languor. Since it was a simple spell, Olmsted managed to quickly shake it off.

I looked closer at our new traveling companion. I had not observed him making the slightest movement or sound to ward off the spell. If this Lorenzo was immune to magic, it made him one of the most remarkable men I have ever met.

Olmsted was also overwhelmed by the demonstration and began firing a battery of questions. "Where are you from? How many more have this talent? Where did you study?"

Jennair made a gesture for me to fall back to her side.

"What is the matter with you, Jak? I have never seen you behave so boorishly," she spoke in a low voice.

I didn't have an answer. I knew I was acting unreasonably, but there was something about this Lorenzo Spasm that provoked me.

"I know," she said when I didn't answer. "You are both too akin."

"Akin?" I almost shouted. "How can you say that?"

"I imagine he is what you will look and act like when you are older. Do you not notice the resemblance?"

I opened my mouth several times, but no words spilled out. Jennair was greatly amused by my speechlessness. I glanced again at Lorenzo, about to protest the silliness of her remark but fell silent as our new traveling companion turned to speak with Olmsted. His profile abruptly made me think of Genner, a half brother who works on a dairy farm. And also Hald, my brother in service to the Baron. Even Jennair, with her high cheekbones.

I do not know how I failed to notice this upon our first meeting, but there was at least one feature of his face that found itself in every one of my half-siblings on my father's side.

"Do you think...?" I began.

"No, I do not think he is our father," Jennair said as if reading my thoughts. "He does not act the gallant that my mother described. But maybe he is kin to our father."

The subject of my father always carried a mixture of emotions. It was a topic never discussed in my childhood home. Though my stepfather was kind enough to me, I knew he did not like dwelling upon my mother's past relationship, no matter how brief it was. I grew up uncomfortably knowing that I was a constant reminder to him of this other love. What I learned about my real father was only that of which I could glean from my siblings and what they had been told in turn by their own mothers.

I found myself suddenly at odds with a dozen conflicting feelings and thoughts. My father had always been a myth, a half-real figure from a child's fantasy. He was a man with no past or future. And here was someone who might be his kin, if not the actual person. I wanted to ride up and demand his story, but knew I would be too at odds with myself to speak. It was an unfamiliar state to find myself in.

Jennair recognized my distress and laid a comforting hand on my shoulder.

"Jak, me silly brother. It is all right for you to feel sorrow about our father. You can play the swaggerer with your tavern ruffians and harlots, but I have known you since you were a lad. You do not have to play the tough ferret with me."

"That is private inquisitor," I answered mechanically.

"I am saying that you do not have to beset this man because he reminds you of a pain, an injury that you will not admit to. You would do best to treat him as you would a puzzle set before you as a fer..., as a private inquisitor. I doubt he has anything to do with our father, but if he is kin, it does not mean he is similar to our fickle father. Think of how you and your brothers are disparate."

I acknowledged her words with a half nod and we rode forward in silence. She was right. I was forced to admit to myself that being a bastard child, no matter that I was in a great deal of similar company, had troubled my youth--and still did. I recalled the sniggers of playmates when they thought I could not hear, as well as the knowing looks of neighbors when they viewed my younger brother and I together. Fedward was a duplicate of my rugged, blond and blue-eyed stepfather, while I was slight, with brown hair and eyes--a description that better fit that mysterious subject of back yard prattle.

I shrugged my shoulders and decided to keep my eyes and ears open, as Jennair suggested, and treat Spasm as a puzzle to be unraveled. After all, wasn't I the greatest private inquisitor in Duburoake?

The caravan continued its slow crawl up the gorge. As the terrain became steeper, the mountain creek roared wildly below us over massive boulders, sending sprays of mist high enough to dampen both the road and our spirits. The swirling fog kept everyone chilled and uncomfortable. At night our train would pull into natural hollows that afforded some shelter and campfires were quickly lit to ward off the dampness.

On the third day we came to a widening of the highway and to the mouth of Masgarth's Throat. In ancient times, this trip to East Glavensdale would have taken an additional three days by way of a particularly nasty journey through high mountain passages instead of the half day through Masgarth's Throat. The long-dead King Masgarth ordered a tunnel laboriously cut through the mighty backbone of rock that now overshadowed our party. The reason behind the major endeavor, it is said, was so that the monarch could have fresh oysters from the coast. His gastronomical whimsy almost broke the royal treasury and cost the lives of hundreds of slaves and prisoners.

The tunnel was begun on both sides of the barrier. A grand ceremony was planned when the two wormholes were to finally connect. The king and a large retinue were on hand in the torch-lit tunnel as a court sorcerer prepared to blast away the final bit of rock dividing the new short cut. Dressed in the deep purple and black velvet robe of a master magician, the wizard waved his hands and grandly chanted in his best stage voice to the delight of the crowd.

The stone crumbled into gritty dust and was immediately swept out of sight. The engineers failed to consider the gales that constantly surge through the upper summits. The opening changed the flow of that river of air like a dike bursting along some waterway. The throng of sightseers clutched their tortured ears as a roaring tempest rushed about them then tried to grasp vainly for any secure hold as the wind snuffed out the torches and sent them tumbling and rolling into the dark.

Laborers at the other mouth of the tunnel were shoved back as if by some invisible giant's hand. The unlucky ones were swept off the road to their deaths in the river or onto the jagged rocks far below. Those remaining crawled to any handhold within reach. Several minutes later the king and retinue exited the burrow like beans from a child's blow tube and also disappeared into the dark depths of the gorge.

And now we were halted a safe distance from the shaft, waiting for the change of air tides that would send the winds surging through the tunnel in the opposite direction. For about two hours every day, the time it took a caravan to safely traverse the distance, the gale calmed to allow passage. An expert caravan master knew just when to enter the tunnel and battle the dying winds that would soon enough begin their reverse journey. A tardy departure meant being caught in the tunnel as the winds picked up--which wasn't a good thing. There were numerous tales dealing with such mishaps and the few hardy scavengers who would descend the perilous cliffs in search of spoils from the rotting and shattered corpses.

Olmsted was making small talk with Jennair as we waited for the caravan master's order to depart. There was tenseness in the air. Even Hazel shifted uneasily under me.

"I am looking forward to this part of the passage," Lorenzo said as he sat easily on his mount.

I stopped myself from commenting that only a fool would wish to tempt fate in such a way. I was keeping a secret truce with Master Spasm. It wasn't that difficult, since he proved to be an interesting conversationalist, though nothing he said was leading me closer to penetrating his mysterious background.

The truth is I was also looking forward to the infamous passage with an almost perverse glee. Though the round stage or traveling storytellers often make the adventures of a private inquisitor seem glamorous and bold, it is mostly made up of tiring questions and boring evenings shadowing philandering husbands. This trip would make an interesting tale to utter on a cold night at the King's Wart Inn.

The line shifted as the caravan master's call echoed off the canyon's walls over the constant drone of the river. The wagons in the front creaked as the horses strained to begin the march. One would have thought the numerous clusters of pilgrims and sightseers, many containing small children, would have been placed in the front. But caravan masters are notorious misers and prefer losing a few tattered travelers than the well-paying merchants and their valuable cargoes.

Wealthy enough to afford mounts, we followed the procession of wagons. Behind us were those on foot. Directly in front was the cheese monger and his goat cart. Ahead of him was the merchant's wagon carrying our baggage.

"The smell of the dealer's cheese invokes my hunger," Olmsted said, whose aberrant inclinations in vittles is well known.

"It makes me nauseous," I answered.

"Are you sure it is not just the dread of entering Masgarth's Throat that has your gut aquiver?" Jennair teased me.

"The cheese is an acquired taste," said Spasm. "I must admit, I would rather smell something less potent so early in the morning."

The winds were still rustling out of the cave's mouth as we entered, but not forceful enough to toss about us about as Masgarth and his court. For the first forty minutes the tempest would slowly abate, followed by another forty minutes of calm before the winds would begin to swell in the opposite direction. After that, the wind was much too fierce to battle and it would not be until the next day that passage could again be made from the opposite side. By tradition, traffic from West Glavendale had use of the tunnel on odd days of the calendar.

Without the wind, the passage through the mountain would have taken half the time, but battling the gale would have us moving at a crawl for much of the way. There was no more speech among us as our ears were punished by a roar of shrieks and howls that sounded more like tortured spirits of the damned than just the passage of air through rock. No torch could have withstood the assault and our way was lit by dim fairy lamps set in the walls.

I found myself blinking rapidly as my eyes watered from the constant wind and grit. Turning to see how my companions fared, I was startled to see a melee befalling the tail of our train. The silhouettes of panicking pilgrims could be seen in the tunnel's mouth. I knew at once it was no natural debacle. Brigands had set upon the defenseless travelers.

Though they carried little money, the tail of the train made safer targets to strike than those of the heavily guarded traders.

I motioned to my traveling companions to look to their rear, then urged Hazel into a trot and squeezed roughly by the wagons in front of me until I came to three of the caravan guards. I grabbed the tunic of the closest man and waved toward the fray. He turned, took in the scene, and shrugged. I grabbed his arm again and leaned away to avoid a backhanded blow. It was the surly guard I met at the onset of the trip, Fishwetter.

Guiding Hazel with heals and reins, I forced my way between the three guards. The first lout's refusal to aid members of our caravan had my blood roaring louder in my ears than the winds. The smaller mounts of the guards shied away when I slammed amidst them. I again motioned to the rear. It was immediately obvious that they did not care to intervene. Though they could not hear the curses I vainly shouted, there was no mistaking my meaning. One of the guards reached for his sword.

Hazel had not forgotten her training and the drawing of the weapon was all that was needed to send her into a battle mode. She stretched her large neck as if she was a goose snapping up a scuttling beetle and grabbed the fool by the shoulder, pulling him from his horse. I clung to her back and hoped she would not attempt to rear in the low-ceilinged tunnel as she danced into a more strategic stance. That was all that was needed to send the two remaining knaves fleeing to the head of the procession.

Seeing there was no help from that quarter, I rode swiftly back to my cohorts with the wind at my back. Lorenzo was at our wagon retrieving a scabbard from his possessions. I passed him by quickly and it was only as I neared the mouth of the tunnel that I questioned the wisdom of my actions. I had no idea how many thieves were involved or how they were armed.

It was too late for second thoughts. Hazel knew there was a fight and her battle reflexes took over. We burst into bright sunlight and she launched us directly into the midst of a half dozen highwaymen who were forcing a clutter of pilgrims to empty their bags and purses. They weren't an imposing lot, especially seen from the height of a war charger, but we were outnumbered. Down the road I could see several other small bands of brigands carrying out their thievery. Several of the pilgrims lay in grim puddles of red. The wails of frightened women and children could be heard now that there was no longer the shrieking winds.

I wasn't aware of drawing my own saber, but I found myself hacking downwards at the closest villain. I caught him in the shoulder and he collapsed after a short stagger to the ground. His companions were scattering and cursing. Hazel seemed to instinctively know who were our enemies, and she rode one bandit down, trampling him under her steel-shod hooves. I turned to seek a new target and was slammed back in my saddle, fell and hit the stone highway with such force that my breath was knocked from me. I hardly felt the torment in my shoulder over the pain of the fall.

I tried sitting, but my right side was numb and I fell back. A leering, dirty face filled my view. It was one of the highway men, a dagger in one hand and the leather straps of a slingshot in the other. I scrambled awkwardly backwards, but he easily followed me in a half crouch. The brigand was grinning as he raised his dagger for the downward thrust. He was a fool to not recognize a trained war steed and ignored the horse once I was downed. It was his last mistake. The side of his head shattered under the impact of her kick.

I rolled painfully to my side and staggered to my feet. Sparks flew as the horse's iron shoes pounded heavily on the stone. Hazel snorted and pawed the road as she circled me, making short, angry charges to keep the gathering bandits away from her master. I picked up the sword in my good hand and prepared to meet their charge. Hazel presented an intimidating opponent, but it was just a matter of time before one or more of the villains drew their own stone-loaded slings.

For once I was glad to see Lorenzo. His small mount skirted Hazel's defense perimeter and plowed through the thieves. I watched in near shock as his almost comically thin sword flashed and darted about. It was like no blade I have ever seen, seemingly too delicate for actual sword fighting. The bandits were taking it serious after the weapon felled three of their gang.

Olmsted and Jennair dismounted their horses and ran to my side. He clutched a long dirk and held it awkwardly. Jennair had drawn a wickedly sharp dagger of the Frajans.

"Are you injured, Jak?" the alchemist anxiously asked as he noted my pain and looked with worry for a wound.

"Just a bit battered. Stay behind me," I warned, "or Hazel might mistakenly tromp you."

I watched in anguish as a stone caught Lorenzo in the back. He bent over in pain, but did not fall. His confused mount, suddenly given a free head, wheeled sharply and galloped back toward us. Lorenzo managed to rein the horse in and slid from the saddle. At my urging, Olmsted ran to steady our comrade.

"I'm all right," Lorenzo gasped when he made it to my side. "Just a bit stunned. Give me a second and I'll skewer a few more of these assholes."

"Your sword, I have never seen one of its like before," I said, momentarily forgetting our dire straights in the wonder of the weapon. "Is it magic that keeps it from snapping?"

He laughed. "No, just good Damascus steel. It is called a rapier and is used more for lunging than slashing."

The thieves were regrouping and eying us more warily. Five of their men were already dead or dying for what had been considered an easy sacking of a few pilgrims, they now huddled in fear against the rock face of the mountain. Hazel was obviously the outlaws' greatest threat and several of the men were kneeling to gather stones.

"We must charge them before they pick us off with their slings," I warned my friends.

Olmsted paled and Lorenzo nodded in agreement, his stance still bent from the blow. I steeled myself and took a deep breath in preparation of the offense. I am a private inquisitor, not some sword happy oaf who enjoys blood and guts. Though I am fairly proficient with a saber, any campaign-tested soldier or mercenary could easily best me. I only wished that Jennair would not follow us, but I knew any protest would not deter her. Frajan women often joined their men in battle.

Before I could give the shout to attack, an arrow magically appeared in the chest of a bandit lustily windmilling a sling. The soft whisper of a second shaft passing over our heads was at odds with the arrow's brutal impact, taking another brigand in the throat. I spun to see the cheese monger kneeling to the side of the tunnel entrance. He released a third missile and I heard the scream before I could turn back to see a one of the knaves clutching an arrow protruding from his gut.

A grizzly giant dressed in a black horsehide cloak howled in rage and ordered his men to attack. They took heart as their leader charged forward and followed, showing more courage than the craven guards of the caravan. Hazel reared and pawed at the air. The robber chieftain passed dangerously close to flaying hooves as he skirted our group to lead his men in an encirclement. I was surprised by this bit of daring since most highway men shirk outright combat. The loss of his men must have driven him into a berserker rage.

I was even more shocked when the cheese monger leaped to his feet to receive the towering brigand head on. Their blades met with a resounding clash that echoed off the granite walls. The cheese monger let his opponent's blade slide to the side and he performed a graceful pirouette to bring his sword up into the giant's rib cage. The other thieves groaned in horror as their leader dropped to one knee and toppled onto his face. The loss of their chieftain was too much and they fled back to whatever crevices and fissures from which they'd erupted.

It was only after the brigands were completely out of sight that I turned again to our savior. I would have sooner believed Hazel taking up a sword than the unwashed monger in his rude burlap garb displaying such prowess. It was only after I recognized the sword scabbard that I realized who was within the disguise--the young man of the inn whom I took to be an Ayerian!

There was that brief moment of silence that often follows a

dramatic event, whether it be battle, storm, or bout of lovemaking. I stared dumbly at the young man before I found my tongue.

"We owe you our thanks, sir, whoever you are, though I am sure not that of a cheese monger."

He looked down at his bloody blade then up to meet my gaze. Thinking I could be amazed no more, I was again surprised when he turned without a word and ran back to the mouth of the tunnel. I looked at my party and saw that they were just as dazed by the turn of events. Even Lorenzo appeared unsettled and pale. I'm sure my resentment would have reappeared if he had remained unshaken.

"My brother, please sit and let me tend you."

I followed Jennair's command with no protest because I was just as shocked by her simple request as to that which had just transpired. Jennair never called me brother, nor was I used to anything but banter from her. She unbuttoned my tunic to expose a forming bruise.

"That was the lad of the inn," I said to Lorenzo as he approached. "The one who appeared shortly after your meeting with the viper mage."

I didn't even feel jealous as Jennair made Lorenzo also sit and examined his injury.

"There is no permanent damage, but you will both feel stiff and sore for the next week," she asserted as we buttoned our tunics.

"Our mysterious lad was disconcerted to have exposed his true identity," Lorenzo said as he tucked his tunic into his breeches.

"His secret will remain a while longer," I answered. "We will have to wait two days before we can again use the tunnel. It is too late for us to attempt passage. I only hope our mysterious friend is able to catch up with the caravan."

We were all treated as heroes once our fellow travelers came out of their shock. Even the villainous followers of Dorga offered thanks. Olmsted and Jennair helped with the administrations to the injured while Lorenzo and I rested under a rock overhang.

"I will catch up with those roguish guards," I vowed as we leaned with our backs to the rock, "and make them wish they were only facing a band of outlaws."

"That's the spirit," Lorenzo laughed. "There is nothing like vengeance to create tenacity while journeying. Just make sure you meet them one at a time."

That evening I walked the length of our company to stretch my legs. I was observed by the troupe of performers and they ardently begged me sit by their fire. The redheaded fortuneteller was even more appreciative and I found before the morning sun rose that I was not all that disabled.

Chapter Six

I sat uncomfortably in my saddle, shifting weight to ease the soreness where the bandit's stone had smacked my ribs. I was blurry eyed and my tongue felt as if it were coated with some unctuous fungi. Though all of our gear and provisions were a day's journey ahead of us in the merchant's wagon, the traveling troupe of actors were more than willing to share food and wine with one of their saviors. I would have still been entangled in the embrace of a thankful, green-eyed soothsayer if Lorenzo hadn't dragged me from her warm nest of perfumed quilts.

"Are you sure this is a good idea?" I asked for the third time. "Travelers take turns using this tunnel so as not to cause a blockage. If there is a caravan heading our way, they will be more than annoyed at meeting us halfway through. It is King's law and was proclaimed to prevent deadly blockages."

"The decree states it is illegal for a caravan to leave from this side on an even date, am I correct? Are we a caravan, or just three people on horse back?" Lorenzo attempted to assure me.

"The wording reflects the fact that only people traveling en masse brave this road," I corrected him with more patience in my voice than I felt. "Those bandits are minor irritants compared to what else is said to inhabit the wilder gorges and hollows. There is safety in numbers. Maybe we would be wise to wait the extra days with the others for the next caravan to pass through? The harpist tells me one from Landsend is slated to pass within three to five days."

I looked for support from Jennair and Olmsted, but they continued complacently waiting in silence for the gale to begin its ebb.

"We could do that, Master Jak, but by then the merchant may deem our gear as property belonging to dead men and sell it as his own."

I sighed in defeat and pushed back a lock of hair from my eyes. It was probably a good idea not to wait another day. Perhaps my reluctance was only a symptom of a hangover.

Our mounts jerked and took several steps back when an unexpected eruption of grit and pebbles belched from the mouth of the tunnel. More dust followed with small stones skipping across the road. We gaped at each other in surprise--the wind from the tunnel had suddenly ceased much sooner than it should have.

"What does this mean?" Jennair asked. The absence of the wind created a silence as overpowering as the roaring.

"I do not like it," I volunteered. "I have never heard of this happening."

Lorenzo flicked his reins and urged his horse to the mouth of the shaft. Several of our fellow travelers began nervously edging past our mounts. They were wringing their hands in consternation as they watched Lorenzo examining the tunnel.

"I believe this passage is no longer a viable option for our travels," he called over his shoulder. "It appears obstructed."

"What? What is my lord saying?" asked a ragged pilgrim.

"He says Masgarth's Throat is closed," I replied bitterly, still stunned by the sudden occurrence.

That set off a chorus of wails from the pilgrims, with laments of "What shall we do?" and "How will we get to the temple of...?"

I didn't really care how they were going to get to their heathenish ceremonies. They could take a short cut to their god by jumping off the cliff, as far as I cared. All I knew was that I had come a long way to turn around and go home. I sat motionless in my saddle and muttered curses at the mountains, the damned bandits that held us up, and those spineless guards. Even Jennair was scowling.

Lorenzo wheeled his horse around and trotted to my side.

"It appears our trip will be prolonged. I suggest we start now so that it is not even longer."

"What are you talking about?" I snapped. "The trip is over. You, yourself, said the tunnel is closed."

"There are other routes than the tunnel," he replied evenly, ignoring my ill temper.

"Right. Trails that have not been ventured upon for generations, plagued by who-knows-what beasts and possibly even washed out since they were last traveled."

"I am willing."

Jennair's voice caught me by surprise. I whirled in my saddle.

"Have you gone crazy, too? What pressing business do you have in Stagsford that calls for risking your life?"

"I am on my way to find our father, Master Jak," she huffed. "I am not your servant that I need answer to you. You can run back to Duburoake and your tavern cronies with your tail between your legs, but I will join Master Spasm."

Her outburst surprised me. She had never fully explained her desire to accompany us. I looked at her in bewilderment.

"What makes you think our father is in Stagsford? You have not spoken one word to me before about seeking our sire. You are on a fool's errand, Jennair, not one worth your life."

"Do not worry what I do," she snapped, obviously rankled by my speech. "I will say no more."

I opened my mouth, but no words came out. I looked to Olmsted, expecting to find him just as amazed as myself at this revelation. He just shrugged his shoulders.

I looked again at my half-sister, but her defiant look said it was best to breech this subject at a later time.

"Jak, I for one would be up for the roundabout. We will miss the opening days of ceremonies and workshops, but there are still several more weeks of activities," Olmsted volunteered.

I found my mouth still to be open and I clamped it shut. I had wanted to break the monotony of Duburoake, hadn't I? What better way than to get lost in the mountains and be eaten by savage creatures?

"And what about our traveling gear? Ours is ahead with the caravan." I asked then answered myself in the next breath. "Most of these pilgrims will be turning back. I am sure we can buy bedrolls and cooking ware from them."

Lorenzo grinned and gave me a hearty slap on the back. I winced, still sore from yesterday's battle.

The redheaded fortune teller tried convincing me to return with her troupe to Kaiserhelm. The offer was tempting, but I couldn't turn from danger when Olmsted and Jennair were continuing. Blood is thicker than water--I just hoped there would be no cause for me to find out just how much thicker.

Our fellow travelers chose to return to Kaiserhelm to join the relative safety of another caravan. I would have pointed out that the first caravan had not offered them much protection, but was glad most of them would not be traveling with us. Most of them were a loutish lot who presented more liabilities than assets.

The only four speaking in favor of continuing the trip were pilgrims bound for the temple of Dorga, the Fish-Headed God of Death. Their leader was a plump, pale man whose teeth appeared purposely sharpened to points. He resembled a dead shark, bloated and bleached by the sun--except I expected he remained as dangerous as any of those silent killers still circling vigorously in the dark depths.

His name was Olahn and he seemed quite taken with a private inquisitor riding a war steed, profusely thanking me several times for saving his and his fellow travelers' lives. He walked next to me and Hazel, his simpering gradually getting on my nerves.

"You must stop by the temple when we finally reach Stagsford," he said. "The priests will surely reward someone who has provided such service to followers of Dorga. I, myself, am a minor priest, and can assure you such a reception."

"Thanks, but sometimes just the simple pleasure of aiding a fellow human being is enough reward."

I'd rather roll naked in hog fat and jump into a pit of elephant maggots than take one step into the vile confines of Dorga's temple. Jennair, over her pique with me, watched on with a bemused smile that broadened whenever I glared back.

We retraced our steps several miles to an overgrown passage that was supposedly the original trail, or so said Olahn, who swore he'd overheard it described as such by a guard. There wasn't much else to do but give it a try. We were lucky that we had no wagons, as small aspens and firs were now growing sporadically on the path. Distant saplings half obscured by fog looked eerily like the forlorn spirits of cloaked travelers doomed to search vainly for a way out of these mountains.

The rest of the day was uneventful, spent threading our way through the brush and occasionally stopping to drink from the mini-falls flowing down the black stone walls. I wandered around a curve during one lull to empty my bladder and like a child, became enthralled with the sight of the liquid disappearing into the clouds below. I began tossing stones over the edge, watching as they also plummeted into the vaporous void.

I paused to gather in the many impressions--the smell of juniper, the feel of a damp breeze teasing my hair, and the bottomless cauldron of a valley and its seething stew of swirling fog and clouds. Within a month I would be back in Duburoake and all of this would seem but a dream. It's funny how the distant safety of a few weeks or months can turn the adversities and aches of travel into entertaining tavern tales.

I made up my mind that I would cease being such a complainer and enjoy the rest of the trip, even the travails. Those thoughts had barely left my head when a centipede as big as a mastiff dropped from an overhead ledge and slammed me to the ground. I didn't know it was a mastiff-size centipede at the time. I only knew that the world was suddenly a place of jarring pain and the taste of grit filled my bruised mouth.

The leather jerkin seemed to confuse the giant bug in its probing for a vital spot. I could feel the scurrying of a dozen legs rustling frantically over my back, tugging and pulling at the tunic. I forced myself to my knees in a panic and instinctively flipped onto my back, the thing taking its turn at being slammed into the ground. I would have screamed my throat raw if the monstrous bug had not already instilled a blind terror in me that squeezed my throat in a paralyzing grip.

I rolled again to my knees. The centipede lost its grip, its legs waving wildly as it struggled to regain its own feet. I scuttled rapidly away until I backed into a rock outcropping. My right hand fell upon a jagged piece of rock and my panic turned from flight to fight. I lurched forward and brought the shard down upon its belly with all my might. The blow appeared to have no effect on the beast. I lifted the rock and brought it crashing down upon the centipede's head--again and again.

Later, when my sobbing was over, I rose unsteadily to my feet. The creature was exceedingly dead, its front half pounded to a paste. I couldn't recall much after those first blows.

Voices called for me. Humans are strange creatures. Suddenly, my appearance seemed just as important as survival had but a few heartbeats ago. I quickly rubbed my eyes and slapped the dust from my clothes. I took several deep breathe sand forced what I hoped was a nonchalant look upon my face.

"There you are. We wondered where...what in Erhjard's gut is that?" sputtered Olmsted.

Lorenzo and Jennair were right at his heels, followed by the pilgrims. My half-sister gasped and threw her hands over her mouth.

"Dinner?" Lorenzo said simply as he approached and distastefully prodded the centipede with the toe of his boot. "You're cleaning it."

Jennair shuddered several times before taking a deep breath and straightening her back. "Are you hurt? Did it bite you? They are said to be poisonous."

"I am fine. It just caught me unaware. Be wary of what lies above your head."

My words made Olahn turn even paler. His shoulders bunched together and his eyes nervously scanned the bluff above him. Olahn's gaze returned to the dead centipede before resting upon me with amazement.

"To kill a demon hound with bare hands is unheard of. Many skilled swordsmen have died before their blade thrusts could find the evil hearts of the creatures."

"I, ah, knew that. That is why I used a stone."

My nausea slowly passed as the others continued eying the dead monster while making witless comments about its ugliness.

"I believe we should get back to our horses. Maybe it is not wise to leave our mounts unguarded," I finally said.

I was glad to be back on the comforting mass of Hazel. The mountain ponies bearing Jennair and Lorenzo rolled their eyes and whinnied nervously as we passed the carcass. Hazel snorted and I was forced to rein her in. The war steed was not satisfied with the apparent demise of the creature. She wanted to confirm the bug's death by turning the rest of its body into pulp under her iron-shod hooves.

We traveled the rest of the afternoon in silence, the members of both groups lost in their own thoughts or discreetly peering anxiously about. It was only as we made camp under another rock overhang that I realized that the smallest of the pilgrims was a young woman. A shrub ensnared her hood and pulled it back to release a cascade of lustrous golden hair.

I know my mouth dropped open. Her face was a perfect oval with eyes of such a deep blue that they appeared as portals to a dream sky. She looked about in panic and quickly covered herself. It appeared I was the only witness to the miracle.

What was this woman doing with such traveling companions? Why would she follow a god like Dorga, a deity I associated with cretins, losers, and assassins? I continued gathering fallen limbs for the campfire while observing the mysterious pilgrim helping in the preparation of supper. Several times her head lifted to catch my surveillance, though I could not see her shadowed face. I stared boldly back and she would furtively look away.

A small fire was built just far enough out that its smoke did not fill our shallow recess. It was decided that we would take turns standing guard through the night and I marked when the woman was to take her watch. I volunteered to be the first sentry and shifted into a comfortable position with my back against the rock wall and blade laid across my lap. I let the fire burn low so I would not be totally blinded as to what lay beyond the flames.

I found myself staring as often and intently at the reclining figure of the woman as I did scrutinizing the rugged trail running past our camp. Olmsted's snoring all but covered the relentless prattle of a nearby mountain creek. Insects sang in the wet ferns curtaining the cliffs and a faint haze of lightening bugs flickered in the mist.

I tensed when one of the pilgrims stood then sat back in disappointment when I saw it was not the woman. He disappeared for only a few minutes to answer a call of nature and soon the camp was as quiet as it could get with a chorus of insects, gurgling water, and a murmuring wind that intimately explored every leaf and rock hollow.

"I wondered how long it would take you to detect the woman."

I was well over my initial displeasure with Lorenzo, but his ability to silently appear at my elbow remained annoying.

"I'm sure you noticed she was the only pilgrim to keep continually covered, as well as having the gait of someone wearing much too large of boots that were meant to hide her small feet."

Silence--I wasn't playing his game.

"Then there was the fact that she seldom burped and was the only pilgrim without body odor. Most Dorga devotees, I have found in my brief exposure to them, are not so fastidious."

The chirping of a cricket was the only answer he received.

"You've seen her face," Lorenzo said as if he'd just guessed the answer to a storyteller's puzzle, "and you're smitten."

I maintained my silence for several more minutes before

surrendering. I turned to Lorenzo with every intention of confessing that, yes, I was a dunce. I'd seen but a glimpse of her face and was enthralled. Only he wasn't there. As silently as Lorenzo had deposited himself next to me, he had just a quietly returned to his sleeping mat.

Olmsted soon took his turn at the watch and I kicked off my boots to climb into my sleeping roll. I had planned to approach the mysterious pilgrim during her shift, but a long day of travel and the battering from the bug left me too exhausted to remain long awake. I woke to the smell of Lorenzo frying bacon and eggs.

Our progress was impeded by the pilgrims, who on foot and carrying their travel gear, traveled much slower than our steeds. Not that we would have been journeying much swifter alone. The trail was eroded in many spots and the utmost care was needed when crossing gullies or climbing landslides. We often had to dismount and slash our way through thickets.

There were also the remains of earlier travelers--bleached bones of draft animals, broken wagon wheels, worn-out boots, rusted pots, and other refuse sporadically littered the route. We paused to stare in silence at the smashed and scattered skeletons that had once definitely fitted inside human flesh. Olahn insisted on gathering the remains for a brief burial ceremony.

Try as I might, I could never weasel myself to the pilgrim's side when no one else was about. She knew I was on to her and maneuvered to keep a discreet distance between us. It was turning into a very frustrating game when we rounded a narrow bend in the road to find ourselves looking upon an uninhabited village.

The odd assortment of buildings nestled in the mouth of a narrow basin that widened like the flaring of a trumpet as it opened into the larger valley we were traveling along. There was a small, stone citadel with no roof that perched above our heads like a cliff swallow's nest. A perilously narrow path appeared the only route to the hold.

Just off our trail was an elongated log building. A faded sign hanging on a pole in front creaked in the wind and declared, "The Dupe

Drop Inn." A picture of a dunce being thrown over a cliff was painted beneath the name. Behind the inn were a half dozen rude huts.

"What is this?" asked Lorenzo as he nudged his horse next to me.

"They are called ghost hamlets," I answered.

"Oh? Because they are now deserted?"

"No," I replied, "because they are haunted. These settlements were once bustling repose stations before Masgarth's Throat was constructed. Abandoned, they were taken over by the unfortunate spirits of travelers lost to storms, misdeeds, and accidents. We must quickly skirt this place."

I nervously twisted the Cfxzyth ring on my right hand, a guard against such shades. Several vipers coiled about the band to enter behind a misshapen skull, there to leer out from empty eye sockets. Strange runes on the ring blurred and wavered when stared at too intently. Even so protected, I broke into a cold sweat just contemplating encountering spirits of the dead. I have always been discerning about such confrontations.

"Then those must be ghost horses," Lorenzo said.

I followed his gaze to a weathered lean-to. Inside were tied two horses and a mule.

"Look," one of the pilgrims exclaimed. He was pointing to the Dupe Drop Inn. A woman stepped from a side door and dumped a bucket of slop. Within seconds a dozen scrawny chickens raced from around back and began hungrily pecking at the mess. The woman paused as she reentered the building, giving us a sour look before disappearing.

"Great. I could do with some real food," Spasm said as he nudged his pony forward.

I opened my mouth to urge caution, but snapped it shut when the others immediately began to follow. There was a sinister air about the place I definitely did not like. It also made no sense that the settlement would still be inhabited. Only an infrequent smuggler might take this trail.

I didn't need to tie Hazel to one of the tethering stakes as were the other mounts. As a well-trained warhorse, she would not wander off. The rest of my party was already inside the inn.

I stopped and looked though the half-opened door. An odd assortment of mounted animal heads ringed the walls as if I were entering a hunting lodge. Running the length of the long, narrow room were stools and an oak counter. There were also a half dozen mismatched tables and chairs. A door behind the bar led to a kitchen and I could see part of a massive iron stove. The smell of cooking and wood smoke drifted into the main room. Behind the bar were several jars of pickled snacks, including wyvern eggs, pig hocks, peacock tongues, small fish, and greven eyeballs.

"In Zeythmea, god of the spear, we trust. All else must pay in coin," read a sign on the wall.

Most of the patrons were of a decidedly squalid and unsavory nature. At the counter were three grizzled men in dirty wool jerkins. They gnawed noisily on a pile of sheep ribs, sporadically running greasy paws through even oilier hair.

Further down the counter sat two men in faded infantry uniforms, their tunics missing the usual patches that would identify their nationality or rank. Both were lean and tall. I guessed them to be deserters. Not overly fond of any military, I wasn't about to judge them on their lack of patriotism, but I didn't like the way they were greedily eying Jennair.

I stepped through the door and saw two men at a table to my far left. They were a complete contrast to the riffraff at the counter, both garbed as noblemen on a hunt. Their clothing was made from rugged material, though it was of a fancy cut and dyed a deep green. They were immaculately groomed with waxed mustaches curling jauntily inwards.

All the parties had long bows leaning against the wall or counter.

The heavy odor of cooking fat filled the air. Great, I thought. I will be reeking of deep fat fried goat fritters for a week. Still, looking at some of the inn's clientele, I knew there were worse things to smell of.

Lorenzo had led everyone to the far end of the inn where we were taking over two of the tables. Seated nearby was an outlandishly clad individual about my age. His hat appeared to be of black felt with the widest rim I'd ever seen. He wore a red cloth tied around his neck.

Under a leather vest was a white tunic that buttoned all the way down the front and was tucked into faded blue breeches. The boots were also strange, with pointed toes and heels higher than those of any boot I'd seen worn by men. His mustache drooped almost past his chin.

I reached my traveling companions as the serving wench arrived with slate and chalk. She was young, but a ferocious scowl aged her in looks.

"Waddayahavin?" she asked as if the question were one long word.

"Waddayahgot?" Jennair replied.

The serving maid, chewing a wood splinter, scowled deeper at my half-sister, who retained an innocent, questioning look.

"Overdair," she said, pointing her thumb past her shoulder. On the wall was a yellowed sign listing a number of menu items, though several had been crossed out.

The followers of Dorga ordered gruel, a traditional sparse fare for pilgrimages. Lorenzo asked for a Jzhaft beef platter, while Olmsted and Jennair chose lamb dishes. I eyed the menu skeptically, wondering about the quality of fare in such a dilapidated lodging. The serving maid began impatiently tapping the chalk against the slate and I ordered chicken, figuring it would be a meal difficult to substitute with dog or rat meat.

"I wonder if the soup of the day," I wondered as the serving maid returned to the kitchen, "is made from the grease scrapped off the walls."

Lorenzo was intently surveying the inn and its inhabitants while the other patrons seemingly ignored us.

"It is strange that such a place exists in this isolated spot," he spoke, echoing my earlier thoughts.

The serving maid returned with a wine flask and mugs.

"Tell me, miss," Lorenzo said. "What brings patrons to such a lonely outpost?"

She sniffed and glared at Lorenzo. "Samethangasyah."

"We are only taking this way as a detour."

"Yahisnotgespehunters?"

"Gespe hunters?" I asked.

"Daswhatisaid," she snapped, now eying us with suspicion.

She slammed the vessel and mugs to the table and made a beeline back to the kitchen, pausing only long enough to bend and whisper into an ear of one of the uniformed men.

"What's a Gespe?" asked Olmsted, apparently not noticing the serving maid's strange behavior nor the vexatious looks now being cast our way.

"Damned if I know," I answered.

"I believe it is a large, woolly creature much like a bear. I saw a coat of incredible beauty made from such a beast at the royal bazaars of Kfhanistan," said Lorenzo. "Its cost would have drained the treasury of most lords. The trader said the beasts live high in the mountains."

That explained the hunting garb and the long bows.

The pilgrims were chatting in whispers at the other table. I looked at the woman, but she had seated herself with her back to me. She was a puzzle I was not going to let drop.

"Whatcha lookin' at?" snarled the man at our neighboring table, plainly irritated by Lorenzo's curiosity.

He had a thick accent that was curiously familiar, yet I could not place it. I tensed, wondering how the management would take to a brawl in the inn.

Lorenzo smiled oddly and spoke briefly in an unknown language. The man's eyes widened and he leaned eagerly forward to answer in the same strange tongue. I then realized that the stranger's accent was a much stronger version of Lorenzo's.

The conversation lasted several minutes until Lorenzo turned to the rest of us and said, "He is a countryman of mine, lost at that, and I am the first of our land that he has met since arriving in Glavendale."

I examined the stranger closely. His alien dress gave me no more clues to his origins than the mishmash of clothing Lorenzo wore. He did not look as I would have imagined a countryman of Lorenzo's would appear. The man was rough and with the weathered face of someone who spent most of his life under a harsh sun.

After several more minutes of talking with the excited stranger, Lorenzo spoke in Glavenish to the rest of the party.

"We will cease speaking in our own language since I told Eli Smith that it is bad table manners. He would like to travel with us since he has no other urgent engagements."

"Just let me ride up in the hills tomorrow to leave something off and I'll be ready to go. I will depart while it's still dark and be back as you're loadin' up."

"Leave something off, you say," Jennair asked, "...in the mountains?"

Eli shifted uncomfortably in his chair.

"Yeah, just a ..." he mumbled until his voice faded out.

"What?" Jennair persisted.

"I gotta let a Gespe youngin' go," he leaned forward and whispered, looking nervously about the inn. "There's people here who would slit my throat before they'd let a Gespe slip through their fingers."

"And why are you releasing a Gespe?" Olmsted asked. "Lorenzo tells us their pelts go for large amounts of money in the Kaiserhelm markets."

Eli's face wrinkled in disgust. "Are you all murdering devils here? Even the buffalo skinners or Apache I knew wouldn't be scalping no Gespe."

"I'm afraid none of us are familiar with Gespes," Lorenzo raised his hand and said. "I was under the impression that they were something like bears."

Eli calmed and took a long drink from his chalice. "They're not animals, even if they are covered with fur. They talk and scream too when they're being slaughtered."

He picked a spoon off the table and spun it nervously between his fingers. "I thought they were beasts when I first went on a hunt. Needed the money, but I didn't need it that bad. If there are any beasts in these mountains, they are here in this inn."

"And you have a young one?" asked Olmsted. "I would very much like to see it. I have never heard of these Gespes."

"She's not an it," growled Eli.

The man's eyes were red and he had the look of someone who'd been traveling for a great while with little sleep--or carried too heavy a burden.

"Oh, yes, I meant no harm," Olmsted apologized. "But I would like to see the child."

Lorenzo spoke to Eli in the mysterious language. Eli shrugged his shoulders.

"I guess there ain't no harm after supper. She's out in the cabin I've rented in back. Couldn't bring her in here without the others going nuts."

I looked up to see the woman pilgrim turned slightly in her chair as if she were listening. Her face continued to remain hidden within the shadows of her hood.

The food was actually not bad considering the appearance of the cook. He stepped to the doorway once to scan the room. His eyes stopped upon us. Balding and with the belly of a pregnant ox, he stood with crossed arms and a large cleaver in one hand. His once-white apron was brown with dried blood and grease.

We paid for the meals and inquired about rooms. The huts in back were for rent, with only two still vacant. They could fit six, though more than four would be uncomfortable. Eli had already rented a hut and invited us to sleep with him, still excited about finding a fellow countryman.

"That would be agreeable," Jennair interjected. "You men can rest together, leaving one of the huts for us ladies."

Jennair leaned back and placed her hand on the other woman's shoulder. "I am sure you do not want to crowd in with a mob of odious men. I know I do not."

The cowled figure tensed but for a moment before relaxing and nodding her head in agreement.

I glared at Jennair, wondering how long she had known one of the pilgrims was a woman. Olahn also seemed surprised at the turn of events, though he voiced no objections.

We walked our mounts to the crude stable. I rubbed Hazel down and led her to where she could eat from a hay manager. I paused to examine one of the horses. It was much smaller than Hazel but stood higher at the shoulders than our ponies or the horse and mule stabled in the lean-to.

"It's called a quarter horse. Must be Eli's," volunteered Lorenzo, noticing my curiosity. "It's considered an all-around work horse in my land."

"Just where is your land?" I asked, not expecting an answer and glad Jennair was not about to hear my bluntness. "I have listened to many travelers and have never heard of this place. Why are you here and what is your destination?"

"It is further than you can imagine, and yet near," he said and gazed up at the darkening sky. "And idle curiosity is my main motivation for travel."

"Vague words to hide behind."

"No, the truth. I will explain, though you may still not believe me," he said, dropping his usual bantering tone. "There are many worlds that exist side by side, divided by intangible curtains that can sometimes be parted with the right knowledge. I have slipped through such a gap."

"And Eli?"

"He apparently has also crossed between worlds, though in all honesty, I believe he is not from my homeland."

"But you speak the same language," I noted, still not understanding nor knowing whether to believe his story even if I did grasp all he was saying.

"Some of these worlds are very different and others amazingly similar. It appears Eli is from a land very much like my own was more than a hundred years ago."

"Parallel firmaments," gasped Olmsted from behind me. "Fjsten, a great metaphysicist, has hypothesized such manifestations."

"You believe him?" I turned to my half-brother.

"Jak, I know you pride yourself on being a skeptical ferret..."

"Private inquisitor," I corrected him.

"...but sometimes you are just a boor," he finished. "How else do you explain Lorenzo?"

He had me on that one. How else to explain the mysterious language, the death of the Ghennison viper mage, and Lorenzo in general?

"Jak, come you must see this," Jennair spoke breathlessly as she rushed into the stable and took my arm.

She pulled me outside and ignored my protests as she led me to one of the small huts in back of the inn. There is little use arguing with my half-sister and so knowing this, I only half-heartedly objected when she shoved me through the door. I opened my mouth to lodge another fruitless grievance when I saw the Gespe--and though young, she was no child.

The fey creature was only a bit shorter than Jennair and covered in a satiny white hair that looked as if it had the softness of milkweed silk. Only the palms of her hands were completely free of hair, though a shorter, soft down covered her face, stomach and breasts. It did little to hide the contours of a young woman's body. She looked up at me from Eli's side with large green eyes that froze me with their gentleness.

"Shut the door," Eli barked and I hastily slammed it behind me.

"Ah...good day," I stammered, completely entranced by her almost shimmering appearance. I felt embarrassed by an intense desire to run my fingers through her luxurious, satiny...coat, pelt?

"Quit standing there like a dumb ox, me half-wit brother. This is Chaatiguin--and this is Jak Barley, a bit dim at times, but good of heart."

I shook myself awake. "Thank you for the praise, I think. Good evening, Chaatiguin."

The Gespe girl nodded shyly.

"She speaks just a little of your tongue, but she is learning," Eli said. "Chaatiguin has also taught me a few of her own words."

I now noticed the pilgrim woman was also in the room. She sat on a crude stool in a corner and watched from the shadow of her cowl.

"And you, my lady," I said, taking advantage of the opportunity to finally question the pilgrim, as well as jostle myself loose from the Gespe's spell, "are you really a follower of Dorga? What is your story?"

"Jak," cried Jennair in a disapproving tone. "Why must you be so boorish in your manners? You know it is ill-mannered to ask of one's religion."

"It is all right. It is the nature of a ferret," a melodious voice escaped from the shadow of the hood.

"Private inquisitor," I corrected.

"Private inquisitor then. Why do you not tell me of myself? Is not that your profession?"

I smiled and gave a slight bow. "My lady is correct, though I am afraid she offers scant clues, hidden so."

"I would think those hints would be adequate for such a renowned private inquisitor."

"Jak," Jennair interrupted, "you might turn your supposed skills to helping Chaatiguin. I have told Eli that she must accompany us to Stagsford so that the King's ministers may be told of this evil trade."

"And how do we sneak her through these mountains when every blackguard we pass would want only to cut our throats for the treasure she wears, if not to keep their secret," Eli objected. "Chaatiguin has suffered enough. Her parents were murdered and she just barely escaped. I plan to take her to her tribe tomorrow."

"To be hunted again the next day?"

Jennair never lets go once she sinks her teeth into an idea. Eli shrugged in confusion.

"Can't we just tell them about this horrible crime--speak to these officials about the slaughter of a people? Surely, that will be enough," Eli half-heartedly asked.

"With gold involved, words are never enough. And there are those who would not willingly face the truth behind their precious furs, those of even the King's court. They must be forced to see the truth for themselves," Jennair countered.

"She right, I go to King. Must speak for my people."

Chaatiguin's outburst caught everyone by surprise, including Eli. He took her hands between his own.

"No, Chaatiguin. It is too dangerous."

"Always danger my people."

She gently pulled one of her hands free and ran a finger lightly across his cheek. You didn't need to be a private inquisitor to see that the two were in love, though Eli might not yet have reached that point of awareness. Then again, he might never. I have seen a lot of self-denials in my trade. No matter what, such a relationship would be encumbered with many difficulties. There are many who look upon love between humans and any fey people as blasphemes.

Eli sighed and looked into her eyes then remembered he was no longer alone with his Gespe maiden. He straightened his shoulders and looked defensively about. Jennair arose and took me by the arm.

"Please help Mahvan and me carry our luggage to our lodging, Jak."

Even I could see the real design behind my half-sister's request. The two needed some time together to sort out what they must do.

So her name was Mahvan. I nodded my goodbyes to the couple and opened the door for the women.

"You are of a highborn family from one of the mountainous provinces," I said as Mahvan passed me. "You are not a follower of Dorga, but using the garb of a pilgrim to keep your furtive traveling from the eyes of someone you fear. You are on an errand of vengeance and do not expect to survive."

She gasped and stopped as one running into a stone wall.

"You have been thinking of soliciting my help, but are not sure of my competency or trustworthiness. I can assure you, they are both unequaled, whether in East or West Glavendale. And now will you excuse me, ladies, while I check on my half-brother."

I walked away very pleased with myself. Her gasp said I had hit upon enough of the truth to warrant her surprise. This was the time to make a perfect exit and let Mahvan stew. The only dissatisfaction came from discovering her to be in peril.

I headed back to the lean-to in search of Lorenzo and Olmsted. This whole business of the Gespe was depraved and I felt guilty about being a member of a race that could do such an evil thing. Even the trolls, scorned by many humans, would never think to make a living at such a trade. It was good that Jennair was taking the lead in the problem. I am not comfortable playing the crusader, though many times I have been forced into such a role because of the inaction of others.

"Yooh, m'lord. We'd like a word with yah."

I turned to see the two men in faded infantry tunics exiting from the back door of the inn, walking with the exaggerated swagger of barroom bullies.

"So ifen yure not huntin' Gespe, just what ah yah doin' around here?"

I thought of Chaatiguin and what these two must do for a living. The enormity of the outrage had been just hitting me. There was no holding back the contempt in my voice.

"My business or that of my friends is of no concern to the likes of you."

The lead rowdy grinned, a wood splinter clenched between yellow teeth. "Perhaps wese make it our business. Whatya say to that?"

"Then you will soon find you have your hands very full of other people's business," said Lorenzo, who had quietly walked up behind them. Bringing up the rear was Olmsted with a dark scowl on his face.

The two suddenly didn't like the odds and sidestepped toward the inn.

"Maybes we will make youse business ours," said the second hooligan as he shut the door behind them.

I quickly described Eli's Gespe and the conversation. Olmsted rumbled from the bottom of his throat, a sure sign my alchemist half-brother was infuriated by the situation.

"There is no question that Chaatiguin must travel with us," Lorenzo said. "The proper authorities must be informed and these criminals brought to justice. I am tempted to follow my own means of justice, but this is probably just one of many such nests of such snakes."

"And just how are we to leave these parts with a Gespe in our party?" I asked Lorenzo.

"Easy, with a disguise."

"Hah," I chortled. "A change of expression and a new hat aren't going to work."

Lorenzo smiled easily and patted me on the shoulder. "But I'm sure you're up to it, as a trained private inquisitor."

Jennair and Mahvan had the windows open to their cabin, with Jennair wielding a broom and sending a storm of dust out the door.

"It be a pig sty," she complained. "I will use my own roll rather than sleep on those pestilent-ridden beddings and I advise you the same to do."

The sun was setting and the women lit a candle. Soon it would offer the only light.

"Maybe we should get to bed early so we can leave this place as soon as possible. There are more than bed bugs that I find abhorrent," I advised.

The door of Eli's hut opened and he stepped out, firmly pushing the door shut behind him.

"There's no arguing with her, Miss Jennair. She will be joining us."

Though he meant it as an approach, he didn't sound that indignant.

Jennair slowed in her sweeping then stopped altogether as she examined us men.

"Me thoughts are that Chaatiguin might be wanting to sleep with Mahvan and I tonight. She will be traveling away from her own kind and there is much for her to learn--from other women."

Eli was not pleased with Jennair's announcement, but he was learning that there isn't much a man can do when a Frajan maid is determined. Minutes later Jennair came out of Eli's cabin with her arm around a blanket-swathed Chaatiguin. The men and women then filed into their own cabins. I was closing the door when I saw the serving maid watching from a window.

Jennair was right about the bedding. We opened the door and flung the straw mattresses and their tiny inhabitants outside, spreading our own thinner travel bedding across the planking of the bunks.

We spoke a little while waiting for sleep. Olmsted told Eli of our traveling to Stagsford for the annual private inquisitors' convention and of his leading a symposium on "The Detection and Conviction of Brigands, Embezzlers, Highwaymen, Swindlers, and Assassins Through the Modern Science of Alchemy."

Eli, in turn, told of finding himself in this strange world after trailing stray cattle during a winter storm. The search took him through the narrow twists and turns of a strange rock formation; the walls were covered with the ancient paintings and symbols of a people who had lived there before his own. Herdsmen in Glavendale are usually a timid and unadventurous lot, but Lorenzo later explained that this is not so in his worlds.

Eli told of how he'd been forced to quickly adapt, learning a new language and eventually finding himself as a caravan guard. It was on one such trip that a merchant told Eli of the riches in Gespe hides. The lure of such wealth sent him eagerly in search of the Gespe. He almost killed one of the creatures before discovering just what the Gespe are.

On his way back out of the mountains, Eli came upon a pair of hunters who had just murdered Chaataguin's parents and were about to rape the young Gespe before also killing her. He was so enraged by the slaughter that he fell upon them in a rage and it was the hunters' turns to sprawl lifelessly on the mountainside. The two wandered aimlessly for several weeks until today when a shortage of supplies forced Eli to seek shelter for the night at the inn. This very day Chaatiguin had also seen traces of other Gespes and they had planned to go in search of them the next morning.

The conversation slowly died away and I was left thinking about Mahvan. Obviously Olahn had to know one of his traveling companions was not a real follower of Dorga. It would take a great deal of money to buy off even a minor priest traveling to Dorga's high temple, especially when his god is such a bloodthirsty deity. No shepherd's daughter would have that kind of fortune.

It was no leap of deduction to guess her of one of the mountainous provinces once she spoke, though an untrained ear might miss the subtle traces of accent that still clung to her tongue. Her crisp speech also pointed to being high born.

The slight swells and creases spoke of a number of deadly weapons carefully secreted beneath the bulky pilgrim garb, yet she paid scant attention to her meager luggage, which suggested she did not carry them to guard valuables. The disguise and small armory spoke of a fear of personal danger, though the slight outlines under the robe suggested weapons of an offensive nature, not defensive. I believe I detected a Jten blowgun with poisonous darts, a coil of silver wire used by Siwquo strangler priests, and even the serrated blade of a Hoonnish assassin. Strange companions for a young maiden.

The faint creak of a floorboard stopped my contemplations and sent my heart racing. The half moon offered only the feeblest of light shining through the one cracked window.

"Jak."

It was Lorenzo whispering my name.

I whispered in return. "What? Is something wrong?"

"There is someone or someones about and I believe they mean no good."

I strained to detect any unusual sound but could only hear the calliope of night insects and the never-quiet wind. I was about to tell Lorenzo that he was dreaming when a twig snapped. It would have normally gone unnoticed, but now it sounded like a barn beam splitting. Holding my breath, I carefully pulled away the covers and swung my bare feet to the dirt floor.

"What is it?" Eli echoed.

"There is mischief afoot," I whispered.

I was glad that Eli needed no prolonged explanations. He also climbed slowly from his bed. I could just barely make out his body in the gloom as he bent to pull something from a kit by his bunk. There was the sound of steel being drawn from a leather sheath.

Confused shouts and screams followed the startling crash of splintering wood. Someone had burst into a neighboring cabin. Lorenzo threw open our own door and was briefly silhouetted against a starry sky before disappearing into the night. I was close on his heels, followed just as closely by Eli.

"It's da wrong shack, yah simpletons," a dark figure was cursing from the blackness of the pilgrims' cabin.

Shadowy forms were also throwing themselves against Jennair's cabin door. I was only now realizing I'd rushed out without a weapon. A bloodcurdling shriek came from the pilgrims' hut. The night was complete confusion.

The door to Jennair's cabin gave way just as one of the attackers wailed and dropped to his knees after feeling Lorenzo's blade. I stooped and felt desperately around in the dark until I found the knave's dropped sword. Eli tripped over me in his rush to protect his Gespe maiden. A lantern was still burning in the women's hut and it at least offered enough light to tell friend from foe.

The lead rogue dropped to his knees with several blades of assorted sizes sticking from his chest. He'd fallen victim to Mahvan's armory. Jennair was parrying a short sword with a wooden stool when a loud explosion nearly deafened me. Jennair's attacker spun as if struck by a club and staggered a few steps before falling. A dark flower bloomed across the back of his vest.

Another thunderous blast caused me to flinch. Eli was pointing a hand at one of the men exiting the pilgrims' cabin. This villain also toppled after reeling a few steps. Only then did I notice Eli held a strange metal object with a shaft that extended several inches from the main body.

The unexpected vigor of the defense, the explosions, the loss of several of their cohorts--these all persuaded the rest of the scoundrels to take foot. I watched them disappear into the night to the ringing of my ears.

Eli jumped the fallen bodies and rushed into the cabin, there to take Chaatiguin into the shelter of his arms. I kneeled to study the face of the attacker Lorenzo had dispatched. I was squinting in the dim light cast from Jennair's hut when Lorenzo joined me. He flicked his thumb and a small flame leapt from a splinter.

"I thought you were magic bane."

"I am," he replied as we inspected the brigand. "It's all alchemy, just a chemical reaction."

"This was one of the prosperous hunters I saw eating earlier in the inn," I asserted.

"I would bet that the others are also our fellow patrons. Not a friendly lot, that's for sure."

The serving maid--she had been watching from the kitchen. Had she seen Chaatiguin? I told Lorenzo of my thoughts.

"Possibly, or maybe they are just suspicious of any strangers. One cannot be too careful when dealing in such trade," he said.

Mahvan was fastidiously wiping her blades on the tunic of her former assailant. Hood thrown back, her golden hair fell about her in waves that shimmered even in the dim candlelight. She looked up to see me watching her work. For just a second she looked chagrined then she straightened and turned her back as she returned the weapons to their hiding places.

"Jak, oh Jak, come quickly."

It was Jennair, standing in the doorway of the pilgrims' cabin and now sobbing quietly. I hurried to her side. The cabin was filled with the stench of death, of gore, of men's lives spilled from their bodies like a tipped wine pitcher.

"Lorenzo, come with your light."

His flickering flame only gave visual proof to what I already knew. The three pilgrims had been hacked to death before they could even rise from their bunks. Poor Olahn. He hadn't been a bad sort for a minor priest of Dorga. I remembered his overtures of friendship and now felt guilty of my rebuffs.

"We must depart immediately before the others regroup or come back with help," Lorenzo spoke. "What are the burial rituals for pilgrims such as these?"

"As with all followers of Dorga, cremation," I answered, still reeling from the suddenness of the attack.

Lorenzo nodded. "That will make it easier."

Olmsted, Eli and I went to ready the mounts while the women packed their gear. I returned to find that Lorenzo had plundered the kitchen of the inn and we packed the goods onto the horse and mule that must have belonged to the hunters. Chaatiguin was wearing the hooded garb of a pilgrim.

We silently set out on the road lit by the grim pyre light of the pilgrims' burning cabin, as well as by the flames rolling and crackling from the inn. That had been Eli's idea.

Chapter Seven

The slow ride through the night was depressing. The bone-chilling dampness made me draw my canvas cape tighter. I was tired, cold, and bruised. The disheartening slaughter weighed heavily upon me. The alluring memory of the redheaded fortuneteller's warm nest of quilts made the venture seem all the more wretched.

"How did you guess I seek vengeance?" Mahvan had pulled her horse up next to me.

"Guessing had nothing to do with it," I replied halfhearted and by rote. "A trained private inquisitor reads subtle signs and cues as easily as if they were inked script on a grand bishop's vellum."

"Vague words to hide behind," she snapped.

I laughed at the words, the same I'd spoken to Lorenzo only hours before.

Mahvan must have thought I laughed at her, for her retort was laden with ire. "You find me humorous, Master Barley?"

I remembered her hidden weapons and the proficiency in which she dispatched an attacker. "No, my lady. Just an errant thought."

This time I would not relent to a beautiful face. Why the gods toy with me so, I do not know. Too many times I have lain out my well-crafted deductions, only to find I had reached the right revelation but by a wrong path.

"As with a stage illusionist, a private inquisitor seldom reveals his methods. Let us just say that I observe obvious signs an untrained eye will miss. Once explained, I'm afraid my deductions would suddenly plunge from the realm of wonder to a more mundane plane."

She remained silent and I wished I could view her face. Our discussion was lightening my heart, as it is often when speaking to a beautiful woman.

"You are of high birth," I explained, keeping to safe ground. "You have rid yourself only recently of jewelry, so speaks the light rings of skin about your fingers. Your speech also gives you away, as well as your obvious unease at the informality of being addressed by your bestowed name. Would you rather I call you mistress or lady?"

"You find me prissy?" she snapped.

I was relieved to have sidestepped her queries.

"I hardly think that word would describe a maiden who travels as a boyish follower of Dorga, carries a battery of hidden weapons, and uses those same arms with the skill of a Hoonnish assassin."

"Are you for hire?"

I grimaced. The last thing I wanted to do was reduce my status from fellow traveler to that of a common hireling.

She mistook my hesitancy. "I can pay you. I am not without resources, despite my current appearance."

"It is not that my lady..."

"Mahvan," she corrected.

"I, ah, have many commitments when we arrive at Stagsford. I had not thought to work. To take on a case now..."

"I see, please excuse me if I trouble you with my problems," she interrupted again, this time more coolly. "I should have realized you take not just any task."

"Why, no, er, yes. It is not..."

"And I am sure you have more important things to do than aid some helpless maiden in distress. I have heard private inquisitors are a reticent sort, made reserved by their unpleasant tasks."

"Well, that is not wholly true," I sputtered, wanting to defend my trade. "We private inquisitors are not without feelings..."

"You will help me as a friend then, Master... Jak?" she said with a voice groping for hope.

"Ah..."

"Thank you. We will talk more of this tomorrow." She nudged her mount and dropped back with Eli and Chaatiguin.

Soft laughter drifted from Jennair's muffled form silhouetted against the stars. She rode not far ahead and obviously had overheard my conversation with Mahvan.

"She played you like a master harpist," Jennair spoke softly in a mirthful tone, "and you sang beautifully at every pluck of the strings. I just hope your gallantry does not lead you into a nest of hornets."

I would have snapped back with a witty retort if I hadn't realized my half-sister was right. Mahvan danced, sprang in, and skewered me like a dim-witted rabbit bred for the spit.

"Helpless," I remember her describing herself and snorted. That right there should have warned me. She was about as helpless as a craggy marsh boar, armed with blades and wiles sharper than any tusks. My silence must have spoken volumes to Jennair, as she refrained from any further taunting.

"Now what is this about searching for our father?" I decided to change the subject. "I have never heard you speak of such a yearning."

"That is because you are not of Frajan blood," she replied. "It is important to a maiden, come the wedlock ceremony, to be able to list her heritage. I would be disgraced if I could not do this. My mother, through the network of Frajan refugees scattered about Glavensdale and beyond, followed dropped hints left by our father."

"You know his name?" I asked in amazement. That Jennair carried this secret so far into the trip amazed me.

"I have a possible person in mind. He lives outside of Stagsford and I will seek him out to ascertain his responsibility."

"What is his name?"

She shook her head and laughed. "Nay, me half-brother, this is my task. I will show you that there be more than one ferret in our ample family."

I chewed on her words for a great time. I could not decide how to feel about this revelation. I sighed and let the problem pass until it actually reared its head. There was always the possibility that Jennair was following a false lead.

Hours later as the horizon took on a rosy tinge, Lorenzo suggested we make camp in an unusual grove of ancient oaks. Gnarled and stunted by the rocky soil and thin air, they resembled the miniature trees nurture by Lormian monks. The upper branches scarcely topped my head and were covered with thin vines bearing colorful trumpet flowers. I felt as if I were a giant walking through a strange forest. It was all the more a fairy woods when a bevy of tiny ruby larks burst from the canopy of one tree and swarmed about us unafraid. One tried landing upon Hazel's head and she shook her mane in annoyance.

We unrolled our sleeping gear to the back of the grove and gratefully lay down as Lorenzo took the first guard shift. I squirmed a bit, tying to shape myself to where several hard lumps were not pressing into my back. I hate adventures.

Chapter Eight

A hand pressing against my shoulder woke me. I opened my eyes to see Lorenzo bending closely over me.

"Quiet," he whispered. "We have guests and I don't like their looks."

I groaned silently. Would I ever get rest? Lorenzo crawled away to wake the others while I rubbed my eyes and ran my fingers through a thatch of unkempt hair.

It took but a minute to crawl to where I could see into the roadside clearing. Seven men had dismounted, several of them now kneeling about a cooking fire. I could hear the hot grease sizzling in the cast iron skillet as the smell of wood smoke and frying sausage reached me.

The four soldiers were not academy types. They had the look of shabby, second-rate mercenaries who would kill their own parents for a bit of silver-- except for the fact that their mothers were more likely to be better with a blade. Their virtue appeared also of a dubious nature. Lacking in such essential job skills, they probably resorted regularly to petty larceny. I knew their kind well, since many of my beer-drinking associates at the King's Wart Inn were of that ilk.

The fifth man was an obese lord sitting on a pack. Maybe even a duke by the look of his well-cut though faded clothes.

Standing rigidly to the side was the sixth member of the group, a man so nondescript and ordinary that it had to be a studied facade. He was not thin, nor fat. Not tall, nor short. Not overly wealthy appearing, nor poverty stricken. He dressed in drab browns and grays and I doubted I would be able to remember his face within ten minutes.

But those six I ignored and groaned silently to myself. The seventh traveler pacing angrily back and forth could have been the twin of the Ghennison viper mage I saw enkindled outside Lorenzo's room at the inn. He bore the same ill-colored complexion, skeletal frame and long fingers as gnarled at the limbs of the dwarf oaks I now hid among. I clamped my eyelids shut least the odious sorcerer feel my stare upon him. It was all very well and good that Lorenzo appeared immune to the sorcerer, but that wouldn't help me if the mage turned his poison my way.

I could hear the faint rustling as several of the others came to join me. I carefully curled around and motioned them to retreat. Olmsted and Mahvan looked at me in puzzlement. I began mouthing the words, "Ghennison viper mage." Olmsted's eyes widened and even in the shadows I could see his face lose color.

What if one of the visitors decided to void his bladder and wandered back to where we laid? I motioned again for them to retreat and if it hadn't been for the dire situation we were in, I would have laughed at Olmsted's clumsy, backward slithering.

"Who do you think they are?"

I fought against the yelp, clamping my teeth together and burying my face in the crook of my arm. How did Lorenzo manage to surprise me every time? Why did he do it? I swear I came close to swallowing my tongue in surprise and shock.

"I will kill you," I hissed.

"What?" he whispered back in puzzlement.

"Nothing, nothing," I answered. "What are we going to do?"

"Do?"

"Yes, do. I would rather deal with them now with an element of surprise than have our roles reversed in Stagsford. You will have to go explain the recent happenings to the mage."

"That's your idea of a plan?"

"They are after us," I defended my stance. "By accident or

calculation, we have become ensnared in some kind of tangled plot and for the life of me, I cannot yet unravel it. But we must convince the mage that we have nothing to do with their quest."

Lorenzo remained silent.

"Look at the trail. They have not been following us, but are coming from Stagsford, which means we must be near the halfway point of the detour. They will have already interrogated the caravan members, including the two soldiers who saw you kill the Ghennison viper mage. I am sure they gave this group our descriptions. A Frajan maid, hunchback and a strange foreigner would not be hard to describe."

"Then let them pass and they will search vainly for us."

"No," I continued. "The soldiers will see our tracks as soon as they break camp, which lead straight back to our hiding place. I believe they seek that young man disguised as the cheese monger. It appears he has slipped through their fingers undetected at the other side of the tunnel. But even our slightest of contact with him make us of interest."

"And to become of interest to a Ghennison viper mage," I turned to Lorenzo and added, "is not a good thing. Only you can speak safely to him, otherwise he will never stop until he has killed us all."

"It strikes me as rude just to leap out and begin arguing with strangers."

"Rude?"

"Yes. I admit I was a bit gruff with that last mage, but he woke me from a sound sleep."

I looked at my new traveling companion with amazement. "Do you know what a Ghennison viper mage is? To even become an apprentice one must perform abominable rituals involving a dozen newborns. They can only progress in their studies by perpetrating even more perverse acts. It is said they have depopulated surrounding provinces seeking young sacrificial maidens..."

"When is Lorenzo going to confront the wizard?" Eli had crawled up to my side. Right behind him was Mahvan.

"What?"

"Lorenzo said he would have to face the wizard now or have him on our butt for the rest of the trip to Stagsford."

I examined Lorenzo through half-closed eyes. He smiled innocently.

"It was just a thought. And now your powers of reasoning have convinced me that this is the right path to follow."

"And just what reasoning will you use to persuade the mage to cease in his pursuit of us?" I asked.

"If I take out the sorcerer, I'm sure the rest of the group will be shocked enough to cause no problems. People around here appear overly intimidated by these wizards."

I eyed the mage, who stood with his back to us while voiding his bladder over the edge of the cliff. "What do you mean by 'take out?'"

"This," Lorenzo said and climbed to his feet, though remaining in a crouched stance.

I watched in alarm as Lorenzo silently glided out of the trees and across the clearing. A mercenary looked up just as Lorenzo reached the mage and he opened his mouth as if to shout a warning. It would have come too late. Lorenzo slammed into the wizard's back with his shoulder and sent the sorcerer hurtling over the edge, his arms windmilling wildly. Lucky for us, he saved his last few remaining seconds of life to yell lustily in dismay, rather than hurl some evil curse.

The event caused some consternation in the camp. The mercenaries frantically drew their swords as the fat official jumped to his feet with an agility not guessed of in one so blubberous. Ghennison viper mages are reputed to be invulnerable to armed or unarmed attacks. Their wards not only turn aside steel, the protective spells will also painfully dissolve the bowels of anyone who touches a mage. That Lorenzo still stood unfazed after his brief brush with the wizard confounded the men in front of us.

I unhappily climbed to my feet, not relishing a battle with the four brigands.

"I would return your blades to their sheathes," Lorenzo advised in

98

an all too calm of voice.

The men eyed the stranger warily, unsure what they should do--or what they could do. He obviously had to be a powerful (and therefore dangerous) wizard to destroy a Ghennison viper mage. The leader licked his lips nervously and looked to the fat lord, who appeared even more distraught.

"Ah, you seem to have an intense dislike of Ghennison viper mages for one who supposedly knows little about them--unless you habitually toss strangers off mountains," I muttered as I gained Lorenzo's side.

"Of course not," laughed my new traveling companion, "I'm seldom in mountains."

"Captain, arrest these men for the murder of a King's servant."

I turned and was surprised to see that it was not the corpulent lord who had issued the command, but the other civilian. Taking a serious look at him for the first time, the man's blatant blandness now seemed to shriek at me. A nagging fear grew and I began a quick assessment. My stomach knotted. There could be no doubt.

Though most of his garb could be purchased at any modestly priced tailor, the unpretentious shoes were still definitely first rate leather and masterful stitching. As part of my private inquisitor apprenticeship, I learned to identify footwear by the prints left behind at crime scenes. The pair of boots in front of me were definitely made by Narmvian Shoe Elves--the preferred footwear of the King's Clandestine Information Authority.

This was no pissed-off Baron after his wife's lover nor member of the royal court seeking to collect an outstanding gambling debt. First the mages, now a C.I.A. agent. This could only signify that the dung was falling from the very top, and that meant it would be traveling very fast by the time it landed on us.

"Ah, maybe we ought to..." I began to say. Lorenzo didn't wait to hear me through.

"Yes, Captain, I would find that attempt very amusing," Lorenzo said in an exaggerated, melodramatic voice of some third-rate street Thespian.

"And you, who I take to be a representative of some repressive state organ, would do well to hold your tongue," he told the agent.

"Ah, Lorenzo..." I wasn't sure what I was going to tell him, but the C.I.A. is nothing to play the fool with. They have informers in every corner of the kingdom and are rumored to be behind most mysterious disappearances, as well as many seemingly natural deaths. To vanish into their interrogation chambers is to disappear forever, or at the least return a person destroyed in both mind and body.

"Why are you after that young man?" Lorenzo abruptly asked, receiving a momentary look of surprise from the agent, who quickly returned to his professional, permanent sneer.

"Do you know who you are talking to?" asked the outraged King's human pit bull. "I have personally crushed a hundred men better than you. I ask the questions, not some foreign buffoon. Where is this person of whom you just inquired?"

"Listen, toady, I'm giving you two minutes to answer me or you're joining the wizard."

"Ah, Lorenzo," I tried again, feeling the sweat begin to gather on my forehead. "I do not think threatening this man will bring us gain. If we tell him what we know, I am sure he will see that we are just innocent bystanders."

"Except for the small incident dealing with their wizard," he reminded me.

There was that. Most everyone intensely loathed Ghennison viper mages, I desperately reasoned. Maybe the agent would forgive us that one small infraction.

"No, I think our best course is to toss this villainous wretch over the side if he doesn't cooperate."

I could now see what Lorenzo was up to. He was playing good constable, bad constable with the agent. I was the good constable, though I was afraid the bluff wouldn't work with Lorenzo's theatrical performance too much of a parody.

"You would not dare. Cease this mockery and turn your weapons over to the captain. I would never answer filth such as yourselves," the agent snarled.

It was my turn and my role would be to blunt my partner's threats.

"If you..." I began.

Lorenzo cut me off again, this time with a firm jab of his index finger to a spot right above the bridge of the agent's nose. The man tried grabbing at Lorenzo, but wound up mimicking the windmilling of the Ghennison viper mage as he too disappeared over the edge.

"Isn't it funny how if you find someone's center of balance, it only takes one finger to push them over?"

"By the gods of Fywquy," I barely chocked out. "What have you done? You killed a C.I.A. agent."

"His two minutes were up."

The death of both a Ghennison viper mage and a C.I.A. agent left the rest of the group stunned. Two of the most feared classes of humans in Glavendale had just been unceremoniously chucked off the road and into a foggy void as easily as pulling the head off a midget.

"You," Lorenzo now addressed the leader of the ruffians, "take your men and leave us."

The man was braver than I guessed, if not underwhelmingly enthused. He pointed his blade at Lorenzo with all the zeal of a small house cat about to give birth to kittens sired by a Habrin tiger.

"We canna go back without he we seek," he said in a strained voice about to crack. "It would be our necks."

"Then I suggest you go somewhere else."

The mercenary looked as if he were seriously considering Lorenzo's recommendation when the sharp explosion of Eli's strange weapon burst from the hollow and echoed across the valley. I jumped in surprise and I had heard the report before. The eyes of the thugs were popped wide open in shock and the leader leaped into the air, wildly waving one hand about after he dropped his sword. The impact of the projectile upon the blade must have been quite painful for the mercenary.

The three other roughnecks awkwardly back pedaled to their steeds, mounted, and were riding away before their former leader was aware they had saddled. When the situation became clear to the lone mercenary, he was soon hot on the heals of his companions.

That left the corpulent nobleman standing alone with his sword still drawn. Sweat was beading on his face and he exhibited a queasy half smile.

"I believe my entourage has left," he said in a surprisingly pleasing voice that seemed to come deep within, as if there were another body hidden beneath the fat. "It would be best if I made haste after them."

"No, I think not," Lorenzo disagreed. "We need some answers from you."

"What could I..." he began in a nervous voice, then in a whirlwind of motion that surprised even Lorenzo, dipped to the side and spun like a top to abruptly be holding the tip of his blade against my throat.

"One foolish move from either of you and the shorter one will be speaking with a new mouth."

"Harm my friend and you join your fellow travelers in a quick trip to the bottom of this valley," threatened Lorenzo.

"Ah, Lorenzo, maybe this isn't the time for such insensitive prattle," I squeaked. I could feel my Adam's apple moving uncomfortably against the edge of the sword as I spoke. "Our friend looks like a reasonable man."

"Oh, but I am," he replied, yet still kept the steel pressed against my throat. "I would be prone to bargain if I did not feel that your friend is just a mite too hasty in carrying out his threats. I like to believe in the best of people, but I am remorseful to say that one must judge others by their past actions."

"It is all right," Lorenzo assured the man. "I only tapped the one who Jak calls a C.I.A. agent with enough force to propel him onto a bramble-covered ledge not 15 feet down the cliff. I am not normally a violent man. You must agree that I did not have the same option with the wizard."

"Oh?" said my possible assassin with a cheerful smile of one playing an enjoyable game of chess. "And why have we not heard from our most honorable King's officer if he loiters just out of sight?"

Lorenzo smiled back, which was easy for him to do since he was not the one with a saber at his wind pipe. "I believe he thinks himself clever and undetected."

Reaching out with a fist the size of a ham, the immense lord took me by the collar and pulled me toward the ravine, sword still at my throat.

"I believe you have another companion hidden in the shrubs from where the explosion erupted. Please advise him not to use whatever spell or weapon he applied earlier. I doubt he could kill me before I deplorably punctured your friend's neck."

I walked on tiptoes to keep the point from piercing the underside of my chin as he lumbered to the edge of the precipice. I cocked my head and strained to look down without touching the point.

There was a narrow ledge a dozen feet or more down the rock face and it was covered with thorny brush. The C.I.A. agent was not on it. He had climbed the rock face and was clinging just beneath our feet. He snarled at me with a face crisscrossed with briar scratches.

"You are correct," my obese warden observed. "It pleases me greatly to know you are not a capricious executioner."

"Haul me up, you oaf," ordered the King's special agent as he struggled to pull himself over the ledge.

"But it is unfortunate that your mercy was wasted on such a contemptible person," the lord said with a sigh as he stomped the agent's fingers that were searching for a handhold over the ledge.

The King's man roared and snatched his hand away. The fat noble shook his head and nudged a stone with his foot, sending the rock downward. It caught the agent square in the face. This time the lower ledge didn't stop his fall.

The nobleman lowered his sword and I immediately took several steps away in case he decided I should join his former traveling companions. He turned to Lorenzo and bowed, whipping off his floppy-brimmed hat and sweeping it down and up in one practiced motion.

"Let me introduced myself," he declared. "I am Baron Garsten Stee Hragen. I must thank you for ridding me of those two very disagreeable individuals. Can you imagine? Traveling with an officer in the King's Clandestine Information Authority and a Ghennison viper mage? It was a nightmare."

Lorenzo walked over to the edge of the precipice and looked down. "I was hoping the first fall would have loosened his tongue."

"Never," said the duke in a soft voice as he returned to sit on a pack near the fire. "They are a hardened lot, trained against the most grim tortures."

He looked up and smiled. "There is no use letting this food go to waste, is there? Why not call to the rest of your party for breakfast?"

Eli came sauntering out from the trees keeping a wary eye on the newcomer. Mahvan was also cautious. She moved as if she were ready to whip out one of her fancy blades. Jennair appeared arm-and-arm with the cloaked figure of Chaatiguin, now also garbed as a pilgrim.

Our group remained strangely silent, still weary from traveling through the night. We watched as Garsten removed cheeses and bread from a sack, proficiently stirred the soup, and flipped the meat simmering over the fire. We retrieved our own traveling supware and made a circle.

The food was good and we were quickly halfway through the meal when the Baron spoke. Until then we had eyed the newcomer with a great deal of curiosity.

"I was not originally part of that appalling party," he volunteered, as if knowing what questions we would first ask. "What errand they were on, I cannot say with certainty. They said initially they had been looking for just one man. Then after questioning members of a caravan, I believe they widen their pursuit to include more. I presume those 'more' are you."

"And why were you with them?" I asked.

He smiled and swallowed the last of his meal with the savoring of someone trying their very first bite.

"I'm afraid I offended our King's agent. Through no fault of my honorable forefathers and me, our estate has fallen upon severe times. The Stee Hragen family was once a prosperous and illustrious lineage, with connections to the throne. But when that scourge of Masgarth's Throat was constructed, our family's honest efforts in commerce were destroyed and we fell upon hard times. Our beautiful estate has fallen into ruin and disrepair.

"When traffic began once again traveling through my domicile, I only endeavored to requisition what I was owed. It was unfortunate that I only spied those ragged ruffians at first and not the mage and agent."

How droll, I thought then said, "In other words, your ancestors were robber barons who extorted money from the caravans. You tried shaking down this bunch and the C.I.A. agent arrested you. Is that how it is?"

"Please, my good fellow, you put it in such harsh terms--though pithily. I believe your statement is too simplistic and ignores the historical context in which my ancestors lived. Too judge them by today's standards..."

"But since your deed is current, can we judge your extortion by today's standards?" I asked, amused by this frayed lord in spite of myself.

He smiled back. "Ah, the brashness of youth. You remind me of myself before I became what you now see before you; a shadow, a hollow husk of my once audacious youth."

Not such a shadow, I thought as I eyed his girth. A suspicion suddenly crossed my mind. What a lucky twist of fate for the Baron that Masgarth's Throat was out of commission. It meant the return of paying travelers through his land.

I was about to place that puzzle before him when he spoke, "You all appear the worst for road wear, in need of hot water and a soft bed. My estate is just a half-day ride from here. You are welcomed to stay with me as my exalted guests. It is the least I can do for the services you have performed for me today."

Despite my weariness, the thought of a real bed and bath was enough to lure me to continue traveling through the day. The others agreed and soon we were once again riding single file along the rubble-strewn road. Baron Garsten Stee Hragen had quickly assumed ownership of the two orphaned horses. He was riding the largest of the mounts, but it still appeared as if the mare might buckle any time under the strain.

We stopped several times for brief rests. Twice I found myself almost slipping into sleep and off the saddle. I would shake myself and take a deep breath, fighting to keep my aching eyes open.

The Baron's estate surprised me. I expected a half-ruins crumbling among a tangle of thorny weeds and twisted shrubs. The Stee Hragens of the past must have conducted a lucrative shake down of merchants before the tunnel opening. The robber baron's holdings remained impressive, a mansion of good repair made with the black granite of the surrounding cliffs so that it seemed to be an extension of the mountain. Massive urns larger than small cottages were planted with flowering trees and lined the drive to the Baron's family home.

To our right was a yard of well-groomed grass covered with a number of heroic statues battling demons and dragons. To our left was a grain field. It was the greatest open area I'd seen in days.

We were met at the wide steps by a row of servants. They seemed happy to see the early return of their lord. He waved them inside with orders to prepare quarters for his guests.

Eli hovered protectively about Chaatiguin. He dropped his arm from her shoulder when several servants raised their brows at a man appearing so intimate with a pilgrim. Though Chaatiguin and Mahvan were cloaked as humble religious travelers, something in their bearing drew the Baron's staff to compete in carrying the visitors' meager luggage.

I normally feel uncomfortable having others wait on me, refusing even boot shines because it seems to demean the person kneeling at my feet--though they usually have more coins clinking in their pockets than I. I was preparing to refuse help with my own bags when the lot of them disappeared in a chatting flurry.

I watched as the massive snailnut doors slammed in my face.

Having missed sleep for the past two days, the immediate situation seemed unremarkable in its strangeness. I felt dazed and confused, as bad as the morning after a long drunk. Hazel's snorting turned me around to see several grooms taking away the horses. The other tired nags were eager to be fed and brushed, but my own mount wasn't about to let strangers lead her off without my say. I smiled at this one's consistency.

"Go on, Hazel, it's all right," I urged her.

One of the stable hands appeared surprise as the giant horse suddenly ended her stubborn refusal to be led away. He looked at me and said, "She obeys ya as if ya were her master."

"I am."

"How can a servant own such a fine steed?" he asked in disbelief.

"Servant? What?" I asked, trying to shake off the fog about my mind. "I am no servant."

"But ya wear the beige of a scrvant."

For the first time I noticed all the servants, men and women alike, wore tan clothing in much the same shade as my own.

Laughing, I said, "Be that as the case, I am my own man and will appreciate the good care you give my horse."

I flipped the boy a copper coin and watched as they disappeared around the corner. I turned to follow my friends, but stopped when I considered the freedom of the grounds that my status as servant gave me. Tired as I was, I decided to check out the estate first and began circling the residence.

A small herd of milk goats, only ants in the far distance, foraged along a steep side of the mountain. Closer to the mansion was a checkerboard of grain and vegetable gardens fitted like a colorful quilt over a lumpy bed. Old women bobbed for weeds like herons spearing fish.

"Hey there, boy, what mischief are you about?"

I turned to encounter an Elf. It was a surprise. Elves seldom stray far from their enchanted woods and even more rare is it to see one as a servant to humans, yet he was dressed in the tan of a hireling.

"I'm in anguish," I replied to the creature who stood only half my height, "that you would think I be about mischief. For an illustrious dweller of the cool and deep shade to even suggest in banter such admonition strikes a shaft of cruel ice through my heart."

A number of seconds passed as the Elf eyed me. He finally shook his head and said, "You be not very good at Elf speech. I suggest we conduct this conversation in the insipid speech patterns more common to you humans so that we do not overtax your wee brain."

It was my turn to examine him. I have only briefly met Elves in the past--and they had all been exceedingly polite in a poetic gentleness. I maintained a strained smile as I sorted through a number of possible responses. I finally decided upon, "You're are just about the right size to drop kick over the milk house. Give me any more excrement and I will see how well you bounce. That is if your pointed little head does not make you stick in the dirt like some warped arrow."

The Elf grinned. "I find it extremely amusing that someone with such obvious cranial deformities should make those comments."

There was no doubt about it. Before me stood one of the mythical Lost Elves, a member of a tribe that disappeared across the Flgehtian Sea generations ago and was believed to have been forever lost. Recent odd tales and seemingly contrived sagas tell of some of these Elves returning. But instead of the overly decorous and gracious Little People we are familiar with, these lost tribal members are said to be insolent to an extreme.

I held out my hand, "Jak Barley, private inquisitor."

"You mean weasel."

"No, I mean ferret, ah, no I mean private inquisitor, you pygmy of meager graces."

We again continued eying each other as if neither knew what to say now that the introductions were over.

"Ah, what are you doing here as a mere servant to humans," I broke the ice, deciding to forbear from the poetic cant of Elf speech.

"Such directness. Not a polite way to broach such a sensitive subject in a civilized conversation."

"Who but me in this conversation is civilized?" I asked.

"There you are, Jak. I thought we had lost you," Mahvan said after cornering the mansion. "Oh, good day to you sir. I did not know Jak had company."

"I do not have company, just this baneful dwarf of doubtful heritage," I said, still caught up in the Lost Elf banter.

Mahvan's eyes widened and her mouth formed an O.

"Jak, how can you be so rude?" she scolded. "I am sorry he should speak to you, most honored guest from the cool and deep shade."

"Forget it, Mahvan. It does not work with him. He is one of those lost obnoxious Elves."

"I thank you, fair maiden. Your kindness exceeds all but your beauty. I forgive your friend his coarse manners. I see you are one of a demure and sensitive nature. May I walk you back to the hall? I hear the master of the estate is preparing a repast for his honored guests."

She smiled and took his hand. I watched their retreat in stunned silence. The Elf had cut me off and absconded with the maid neater than a fox snatching a chicken from the watering jaws of a wolf. He even looked over his shoulder as they disappeared around the corner, smirking at me.

But I was tired, too weary to verbally battle an impudent Elf half the size of the woman with whom I was enamored. Sighing, I followed them back to the front of the Baron's stronghold, up the steps, and through the open doorway.

A number of torches had been lit and I walked down the smoky hall into a large chamber bustling with servants. My traveling companions were already seated, with the Baron installed at the end of a long, massive table. Lorenzo moved over and motioned for me to sit.

"Are servants allowed to sup with gentlepersons?" I asked, not thinking that he would catch my quip.

"We will make an exception," he laughed, "even though you are dressed in more of an acorn than beige.

"You are too kind," I muttered and scowled at Mahvan, who was leaning over so that the Elf could whisper in her ear. She had thrown back her hood and her golden hair spilled about her shoulders.

"I must thank you again, my esteemed guests, for freeing me from that boorish company in which I found myself," announced Baron Garsten Stee Hragen as he waved a large drumstick about.

"The Baron wants to join us on our trip to Stagsford," Jennair said from across the table.

"At least we should eat well for the rest of the trip," I observed, noting his plate filled with salmon, stuffed lake squirrel, and a colorful assortment of mushrooms.

"And the Elf will also be journeying with us," she continued. "Imagine, us traveling with a real Elf."

"You are gushing," I replied as I reached for a plate of garlic sheep tongue.

Jennair scrutinized me with her all too familiar of look, the kind she gave me when we were both children then turned to gaze at Mahvan and the Elf. She smiled and said, "Jak, me addled brother, you can not be jealous of a Little People? Everyone loves the Elves."

"He is a troll in Elf clothing," I grumbled.

She shook her head in mock censure. I directed my attention to the food, knowing future fare on our journey might be meager. I ignored the swirl of servants and light banter. The wine and food did nothing to keep me wakeful. I welcomed the servant who was to see us to our rooms and I followed him as one in a daze, taking little note of my room and collapsing into the high postered bed without shedding my garments.

I don't know how long I slept when a soft rapping woke me. Lifting my head, at first confused to my surroundings, I gazed about the room now lit only by the soft glow from the fireplace. I was about to answer the knocking when the door slid slowly open. It was a servant girl, peeking shyly at me as I fumbled my way out of bed.

"It is time to rise, master," she spoke. "The Baron says he wants to leave with the dawn. I have come to draw your bath."

I rubbed my suffering eyes and looked out a window to see that it was still dark. Before I could protest the rude hour, she stepped into the room, bent under the weight of two heavy buckets brimming with steaming water. She carried them across the room to an ornate bathing tub in the shape of a swan.

I had to admit, weary as I still was, that a hot bath had its allure. I felt the layers of dust upon me like the rings of a tree, a coating of grime for each of the past days spent upon the road. I recovered with more speed when she filled the tub and motioned me over, gripping a wash rag. I had just noticed she was attired in a flimsy shift. I knew that the genteel of Duburoakians back home often were bathed by comely servants, but it was an experience a lowly private inquisitor never enjoyed.

I tried to maintain a rakish air as I sauntered to the tub, but she noticed my hesitation as I stood over the enticingly hot water.

"Ah, as a simple private inquisitor, I am not accustomed to being undressed in the presence of a maid," I finally admitted.

I was about to add that there was first time for everything, when she coyly slipped the straps of her shift off her shoulders and the gown dropped to the floor. Her milky body glowed a radiant pink from the coals of the fire. She reached out and pushed away my fumbling fingers, her own deft hands quickly unbuttoning my tunic then going to the ties of my trousers. I placed my hands on her shoulders and felt the firm smoothness of her body.

There was something to aristocracy, I admitted an hour later as she disappeared out the door and I collapsed back into a very wet bed.

I found the rest of my party eating breakfast with the Baron. Lorenzo appeared well rested and I wondered if he had also been awakened as I.

"You're looking more chipper than yesterday," he noted.

I nodded my agreement. The sleep and following bath had done much to clear my mind. I looked over to see the Elf and Mahvan again in deep conversation. The Elf looked up to catch my gaze and a mocking smirk crossed his lips for just a second. I kept myself busy contemplating twisting the pygmy into a number of anatomically impossible contortions until my plate of food arrived.

"If looks could kill," Lorenzo said as I scooped up a spoonful of garlic and sage-glazed peacock tongues over eggs. "I take it you are not as enchanted with Master Ebert as the rest of our troupe?"

"Ebert? Is that the wretched bantam's name?"

Lorenzo raised an eyebrow.

"He's one of the Lost Elves," I explained as I vigorously stabbed my knife into a piece of roc liver grilled in basil and wine. "He may play the part of a cordial fellow, but he has the tongue of a civet toad."

Lorenzo smiled. "Do I detect a bit of jealousy?"

"Me, jealous of a runtling?" I scowled and engaged my meal with greater tenacity.

Later, I sighed and loosened my belt. The meal did much to soften my mood. I hoped the Baron packed accordingly for the rest of the journey.

Olmsted passed behind my chair and I turned and grabbed his tunic. "What gives with the Baron? Why has he decided to travel to Stagsford?"

My half-brother looked very content, filled with a fine breakfast and looking cleaner than usual. I cocked my head but didn't enquire about his wakeup call. A thought suddenly entered my head and I turned to look suspiciously at Jennair then Mahvan.

"It appears the Baron wants to promote this alternative trade route as being a safer passage through the mountains," the alchemist broke into my speculations.

I snorted. At least I could understand Baron Garsten Stee Hragen's motives. He hoped to regain the once-lucrative thievery of his ancestors.

Everyone stood and pushed back their chairs. It appeared the Baron was ready to depart. A gentle tap on the shoulder drew me around. It was the servant girl who had so kindly awoken me. She was holding my canvas kit.

"I washed your garments," she said demurely.

"You are a very immaculate maiden."

She dimpled. "I am here to serve."

A rough jerk pulled me away before I could answer.

"Come on, you spotless gallant," Jennair said in an exasperated voice. "The day begins."

The ruby undersides of clouds were lit by a morning sun still a couple hours from rising above the peaks. I smiled. The air was sweet and clean and I took a deep breathe in appreciation.

Servants were leading our mounts to the gate, all except Hazel. I quickly made my way to the stables to find a frightened servant lad backed against the wall.

"Come on Hazel, quit fooling around," I said. "The others are waiting for us."

The boy quickly ducked and scooted out of the stall.

I hurriedly saddled up, partly amazed at the ease in which I now performed the task. The trip was turning me into an accomplished horseman.

The others were impatiently waiting for me at the gate. I looked over my shoulder and saw the maid waving from the steps. I self-consciously returned the farewell, knowing Jennair would be smirking.

The road was well maintained since this section was used frequently by the Baron's estate to Stagsford. Our pace was now much faster. I was able to relax without being knocked from my saddle by saplings or landslides.

We stopped for a midday lunch, with the servant dishing out another fine meal. Besides the scrawny aide-de-camp, Baron Garsten Stee Hragen was accompanied by several pack horses, one which had a colt at its side. It appeared we were to also be treated to fresh mare's milk. Eli and Chaatiguin ate off to the edge of the group. Lorenzo and Olmsted were in animated conversation with the Baron, who roared loudly with laughter between spoonfuls of soup. Jennair and Mahvan sat with the Elf.

For some reason I felt disinclined to join any of the small gatherings. Eli enjoyed his private conversations with Chaatiguin. I didn't feel jocular enough to join the Baron and I wasn't about to eat with the obnoxious Elf.

I took a piece of smoked beef and bread and wandered to the edge of the chasm. It appeared to be not as deep as earlier in the trip and I knew we would be soon leaving the mountains. Deep in thought, I walked down the road barely aware of chewing on the spicy meat and course bread. My attention was only momentarily regained by a sharp pain to the head before my vision turned black.

Chapter Nine

I regained my senses to find my body a mass of aches--some old, some very new. My head throbbed agonizingly to the beat of my pulse. Voices sounded not far from me and I remained motionless, slowly opening one eye. About 30 feet away were several ruffians sitting about a small fire.

I cautiously flexed my muscles, which set off a number of sharp protests throughout my body. My hands and feet were bound and I lay on my stomach like a hog tied for the market.

"Me thinks our guest is finally joining us," one rough voice crowed from the rabble.

A lean silhouette moved from the campfire and advanced toward me, stopping when a pair of very worn boots halted inches from my face.

"Awake?"

I feigned unconsciousness.

"I asked if yah awake." The question was followed by a nasty kick to the ribs.

I gasped and rolled to my side, involuntarily curling into a ball.

"Yes," I managed to spit out before he had to ask again.

"Good, I hate tah kill a sleepin' man."

The rest of the thugs roared with laughter.

"What do you want? I have no silver nor am I worth ransoming."

"Yah looked as much and yah pockets proved it. But yah was there and so were we. And being creatures of habit, we could not as let yah alone as a fat cat canna stop itself from stalking a mouse. It be the nature of the beast."

Again the others laughed at the wit of their compatriot.

"Now what?" I asked, though I wasn't overly anxious to discover their plans.

"Oh, we must have our fun where we can find it, the lot of brigands in these poor parts being a lamentable one."

I didn't want to imagine what turns their notion of entertainment took. My eyes were slowly becoming accustomed to the dim light and I examined my captor.

"You're from Grifif, a second son, and were once a kennel helper before your wife died. You..."

"He's a wizard," screamed an ignorant lout near the fire.

My attempt at diverting them to a less injurious sport was obviously a failure. The foot pulled back for another kick and I closed my eyes.

Bright sunlight met my sight when I next opened my eyes and I grimaced from the brightness. I forced my lids open a second time and wished I hadn't. The floor of the valley was gently rotating beneath my head. I was hanging over the chasm, upside down, bound and gagged. And from the light breeze playing about my aching body, I could tell I was naked.

It would be safe to say that I have never found myself in a more troubling dilemma. I couldn't even yell for help, though it was unlikely there would be assistance close at hand on this remote highway. My slow spinning now brought me around to face the rock wall. Clutching to the stone face with large sucker toes were a number of tiny, green lizards. They nervously scampered back and forth while never taking their bright red eyes off me, like anxious puppies scared to make the jump to their master's wagon.

One finally gained the courage and leaped, landing and clutching onto the ropes that bound my arms to my side. It forthwith tried a tasting of the large feast before it and I jerked from the needle-sharp nip. The lizard did not have a secure grip and my spasm sent it toppling into the void. Its mates paused in their pacing long enough to watch their unlucky hatchmate dwindle into nothingness then resumed their hungry scurrying.

My revolution continued and I again faced out over the gorge. I felt the mad scrambling of another lizard as it slid down my back to finally catch in my hair. I vigorously shook my head and dislodged the second attacker at the expense of violently exasperating my headache.

I tried not imagining myself covered with scavenging reptiles, the tiny creatures swiftly reducing my body to a few meatless bones dangling in the breeze like some frightful wind chime. My private inquisitor instructors said cool heads prevail, but I doubted any of them had found themselves in similar circumstances. If they did, the solution to such a conundrum was never imparted during class.

I was given another view of the lizards, still excitedly scampering about. A shadow crossing the rock abruptly sent them scrambling for the safety of cracks and fissures. Now what, I wondered bleakly, though believing the situation could not get much worse. I was wrong.

The slow rotation brought me face-to-face with a harpy. She was straining to hover in one spot as she examined me.

Some harpies, such as this one, can be quite beautiful from the waist up, though they all have sullen, loathsome dispositions. They are known to eat men who will not have sex with them, which must be quite often since their feathered bodies reek of nest droppings and are infested with a number of ravenous, parasitical creatures.

Of course, they also usually eat the men who will have sex with them. I think the harpy word for men also translates as lunch.

Harpies are magical creatures, depending upon enchantment for a number of things. Olmsted says a harpy would fall like a stone if it were not for her magic, since their wings and muscles are not large enough to carry their weight. He added that after so many generations of crossing with men, harpies should have begun to take on more human attributes. They do not, said my half-brother, also because of their enchantment.

The harpy made up her mind about me just as she was spinning from my field of vision. I felt the rough texture of her feathers about my feet as she worked at the bindings with her talons. Suddenly I was dizzily falling into the void. She fought hard to counter my weight and our plummet slowed. The gag held in a scream that had been building since I awoke. I vainly tried thinking of a god to beseech, any deity that I hadn't offended at least once in the past, even Gep, the god of good dental health. Trust me on this one--there is no more helpless feeling than to be naked, upside down, bound and gagged, and in the clutches of a harpy over a deep canyon.

The descent continued until I was roughly dumped onto the rim of the creature's nest, there to roll unceremoniously to the floor of the abode. She eyed me as if to make sure I would not be leaving soon then leaped into the air and disappeared from sight.

It was a relief not to be hanging head over heels. I twisted to view my newest surroundings. The harpy's domain was a woven bowl of saplings lined with smaller branches. Staring directly at me was a rotting skull, no longer attached to its equally decaying body further away. That at least partially explained the vile stench permeating the air.

My attention was drawn to a sword still attached at the corpse's waist. I gritted my teeth and began inching toward the blade, trying to disregard the sharp sticks biting into my flesh. Any moment I feared the return of the harpy and whatever repulsive plans she had for me. I was breathing heavily through my nose when I finally managed to maneuver my fingers to the hilt then draw the sword by slithering away from the dead man.

I was relieved when I finally felt the cords fall away from my wrists, which was quickly followed by searing pain as the blood rushed back into my swollen hands. They were nearly useless, numb pieces of meat. I clumsily held the sword and worked at the cords about my chest then freed my ankles.

Foraging about the nest, I found a cache that all harpies keep. These hoards contain the possessions of their victims. There was an odd assortment of clothing and footwear along with some coins and meager jewelry. The only garb that had not rotted to pieces was the simple attire of a milk maid. I hesitated for just a moment before pulling on the dress then tried several boots until finding a pair that fit my swollen feet.

Being garbed, even in a gown, added much to my spirits. I stuffed the coins and jewelry into a pocket and climbed to look over the rim of the nest. The harpy's eyrie was constructed on a broad ledge. There appeared no way down or up except by wing.

A snapping sound rattled behind me and I spun in panic, almost tumbling into the void. The latest shock sent my body into uncontrollable shakes. I waited until the tremors subsided before climbing down to investigate. I stooped and pushed away some leaves that partially obscured a blue oval object spotted with black specks. It was larger than the rotting skull and a crack ran lengthwise across its smooth surface. Another crack splintered from off the main branch with a sharp pop.

I fell backwards to sit and watch in amazement as the egg burst apart to reveal a wet, tiny harpy. It staggered about on unsteady legs for several seconds before spotting me then screeched and tottered toward me. My battered muscles refused to respond and it fumbled to my side where it fluttered about my leg. Instead of the expected gnawing, it began mewing pitifully like a lost kitten.

I eyed it with suspicion. My recent encounters had left me wary. The mewings continued and I cautiously reached down for the harpling. It immediately scrambled for my outstretched hands and I found myself holding the puppy-sized creature to my chest where it vainly searched for a teat. I patted it helplessly and stiffly climbed to my feet just in time for the return of the mother.

She squawked in rage when she saw her chick and swooped low to tear it from my grasp, only to have her offspring struggle free. It dropped to the floor of the nest, from there to lurch back to me where it again clung to my leg. Like a duckling that attaches to the first creature it sees from the egg, the harpling had bonded to me.

The harpy was little amused and threw herself at me. We rolled around in a tangle of wings and legs. It was all I could do to keep her talons from gutting me or her snapping teeth from taking off my nose. I wrestled free and desperately climbed to higher ground, closely followed by the infuriated mother and her crying offspring. I reached the top and stopped helplessly at the ridge. There was no place for me to go. She again threw herself at me and the three of us plunged over the edge.

This time no gag stopped my screams and I wailed bleakly as we fell. I threw my arms around the creature's waist and pushed my face against what would have been a pleasant bosom had it been on a human female. She beat her wings furiously as we plummeted. I struggled to maintain my hold as she fought to dislodge me.

The battle continued until we roughly struck the ground. At that moment I was on top and her body softened the impact. I lay too fearful to move until realizing my foe was stunned by the landing.

My body strongly complained against having to move, but I forced myself to my knees then to my feet. We had crashed onto a roadway. I turned to make my escape while the getting was good. Something grabbed my ankle after only taking a few steps. I yelped and looked down to see the harpling again attached to my leg. Frantic to get as quickly from the harpy as possible, I didn't try to fight off the little beast, but scooped it up and continued my painful plodding.

I maintained the march as long as possible before collapsing against a small tree. I was in danger of fainting and strove to catch my breath. The sparks finally stopped their dancing before my eyes. I was just feeling safe when another damned shadow loomed upon me.

"There you are," Jennair's voice said accusingly. "We have been worried sick and here you are napping in the middle of the road wearing a woman's garb. The Baron was leading us to a forester's post for help."

"I am delighted to see you also," I replied, it coming out raspy from my parched throat.

Jennair, now seeing my pitiful state, jumped from her horse and kneeled at my side. The others quickly joined her.

"What has befallen you?"

"I was kidnapped by highwaymen, beaten, left dangling naked

over the gorge, attacked by flesh-eating lizards, snatched by a harpy, and just recently fell thousands of feet to this road."

Jennair snorted. "Jak, me brother. Canna you ever talk straight without some wild tale coming from your mouth?"

She reached to tenderly touch a scrape on my chin when a little whirlwind of feathers angrily fought her hand away. Jennair fell back and her mouth dropped in surprise. The baby harpy stood guard on my chest, squawking angrily at the others.

"You were saying?" I asked before slipping into blackness.

I awoke this time to find Mahvan gently shaking me. She held a bowl of steaming soup.

"Lorenzo said you have slept long enough and need food," she spoke as she lifted my head and brought a spoon to my mouth. I hungrily slurped it down.

"We have been quite worried about you, Jak. You have been dozing for much of the day. We tried to make you as comfortable as possible with that harpling about. Olmsted and Lorenzo finally lured it away with mare's milk and it now sleeps on one of your tunics."

I turned my head to see the little creature curled into a ball not far away. It had the face and torso of a miniature one-year-old girl grafted onto the legs and wings of a hawk.

"You have other sentinels," she added as Hazel's giant head bent to gently nudge me. "For a hardened private inquisitor, you seem to easily gain the affection of many folk and creatures. Your half-siblings were beside themselves. This horse was almost impossible to move from the spot where you disappeared."

"It is only a front," I admitted, gazing into Mahvan's blue eyes. "In truth, we private inquisitors are a sensitive sort who only need the tender hand of a caring maiden to lure us from our shells."

"Such poignancy he speaks. He is verily a tender soul."

It was the Missing Elf, Ebert. Mahvan smiled at his words, though I knew the mockery behind them.

"Thank you, kind Elf. I assure you my feelings are mutual," I replied.

"Mind him while I tell Jennair her brother awakens," Mahvan told Ebert.

He watched her depart then turned to me.

"Well, my wayward lad. It appears you had a love match with a harpy and she had the better of you. Tell me, how was the hen in heat?" he asked then nudged me with his elbow.

I was simmering at his aspersions, but was too bruised to cuff the vulgar little pygmy. He moved to nudge me again, but was bowled over by a madly chirping harpling. The chick's foray forced the Elf to his feet and backed him away. When it was satisfied Ebert had retreated far enough, the harpling returned to land on my chest. It had taken to flying while I slept.

"You are a quick lad to have so soon fathered a daughter," Ebert bantered. "I believe she has your eyes."

"I am told they grow very quickly," I countered, "and soon she may be large enough to have yours."

The taunt gave the Elf a thought to ponder and he walked away. I slowly sat up and the chick tumbled to my lap, there to look up at me in adoration. I patted it gently on the back and it mewed in pleasure.

"You seem to have found yourself a new friend."

It was Lorenzo who now kneeled at my side. The harpling seemed content with his presence, probably because Lorenzo had fed it.

"I am told these chicks have as evil tempers as their mothers, but this one seems amiable enough," I observed.

"Probably due to a lack of affection on the part of their parents. Be a good big brother by raising it well and the creature may remain that way."

"What?" I sputtered. "I have no time to wet nurse a harpy chick. We must let it go free."

"It's too young for that," he observed. "I'm afraid you must nurture this little creature or abandon it to its death."

I looked down at the chick, who returned my look with as sweet a smile as any human child. What was I to do with a harpling? I'd be the laughing stock of the King's Wart Inn. Why me?

"This will be a most interesting experiment. I have never heard of a harpy chick reared by a human." Olmsted had joined us. "I have read about captured harplings and they retained a disagreeable nature, but none were ever snared at this young of age."

"If you want an experiment," I said irritably, "you take it."

"I would find it most interesting, but I am afraid she has already linked to you. Most interesting."

They had made camp at the spot where I was found. Chaatiguin stopped to visit and seemed enthralled with the tiny creature. The chick appeared not to mind the Gespe maiden and even allowed Chaatiguin to stroke its hair.

"Would name Osyani?" Chaatiguin shyly asked.

"Osyani?"

"Name of small sister. She dead."

"Yes, that is a pretty name. Her name is now Osyani," I answered, saddened again by another brief glimpse of her life. The naming of the chick suddenly made the harpling a she instead of an it.

Baron Garsten Stee Hragen dropped by later and stared at the chick asleep on my lap.

"I will give ten silver marks for the creature."

"What?"

"Ten marks, though I doubt I can get more than fifteen for it at the market. Still, it is an oddity that may pique some collector's interest."

"She is not an animal to sell like some beast," I replied indignantly, unconsciously cradling Osyani closer to my chest.

The Baron was startled and looked at me as if examining a fever victim babbling nonsense. He shook his head and returned to the tent his servant had erected.

It was pure torture climbing back onto Hazel and each following jolt of the journey echoed through my bones. The chick grew stronger as the sun climbed higher and she would flit from my shoulder to the top of

Hazel's head then to the mounts of everyone else in the band except that of the Elf. She even seemed to take a liking to the Baron's old servant, whose name was Vorin.

At one point Mahvan again pressed me about my assistance.

"Just what is it you require of me?" I finally asked.

"It cannot be spoken of at this point."

I frowned.

"It is nothing dishonorable, I assure you," she quickly spoke when noticing my look. "But I do not feel free to reveal it at this part of the journey."

"What about illegal?" I asked, having experience with some people's concept of what is honorable.

She gave me a haughty look. "Do you so worry about government constraints, even if they be unjust?"

"Unjust or just, both can get you into prison. Constables look upon private inquisitors with little regard as it is and need only the flimsiest of excuses to invite us into their cells."

"But," I said as I saw the disappointment on her beautiful face, "I have now and then tweaked the King's agents if it helped a client."

She smiled, though I silently cursed myself for the slip. I did not want this winsome maiden, no matter what instruments of destruction and slaughter she hid beneath her pilgrim's cloak, to think of me as a hireling.

I was at her mercy, doomed now that she rode with her hood thrown back. I had been keeping purposely to the back where I would not constantly see Mahvan's comely face. Her smile, the dimples under high cheek bones, impish eyes, and supple figure--all calling to me.

Mahvan smiled and patted my arm before urging her horse ahead to chat with Lorenzo. I let out a deep sigh of relief.

"Ah, you make a fine harp." It was Jennair again. "You sing at every pluck of her fingers."

I chose to ignore my half-sister by playing with Osyani, who was becoming more nimble as the day progressed. It was hard to imagine the newhatch growing up to become an evil harpy. The small creature had large brown eyes and black hair that now only covered her ears. The hair would grow shoulder-length like the wild mane of her mother's.

Chapter Ten

Lorenzo gave me a strange, burning elixir for my pain. He called it whiskey. I rode the rest of the day in a stupor and barely remember stumbling from Hazel to sleep for the night.

The next day's ride was uneventful. Not that I was complaining. I'd had enough adventure and enough batterings to last me for a long time. But there was one bit of excitement.

"Come to Jako," I jokingly said to the harpling when we stopped for a rest and I was gathering wood for the cook fire. Osyani landed on my shoulder, nuzzled my hair, and then chirped, "Jako."

I stumbled in surprise and dropped the kindling. The startled chick took to the air and circled me several times before being coaxed down.

"Jako," I repeated.

The little oval face looked at me solemnly, sensing my excitement. I was holding my breath and just as I was about to let it go, Osyani jumped to my shoulder and again chirped the name.

Lorenzo was passing by and I excitedly grabbed his arm. "This harpling just called me Jako,"

"Congratulations. They grow so fast. It won't be long and she'll be going on her first date and molting. It seems like only yesterday she was learning to fly."

"It was only yesterday," I said in exasperation. "You do not understand. Harpies do not speak. They are only shrill, shrieking monsters."

"Careful what you say around the children," he admonished me.

"Are you sure they are only s-h-r-i-l-l, s-h-r-i-e-k-i-n-g, m-o-n-s-t-e-r-s?" he spelled out.

I turned my head to examine Osyani, who seemed to be intently following our conversation. She smiled and leaned over to nuzzle my nose.

"Ah.., I...ah..."

"It could be that the creatures we are talking about," Lorenzo interrupted my floundering, "are more than just dumb entities led solely by instinct. They may need socialization as do many immature beings to reach their full potential, which they do not receive due to severely dysfunctional families."

"What?"

"I'm saying if you exhibit the proper nurturing skills, she may grow up to be a fine, civilized harpy any parent would be proud of. Just keep her away from bad influences like black magic and ghoul gangs."

"What? Proper nurturing skills? Me? Lorenzo, I cannot even cottage train a cat."

"Hm-m-m," he mumbled thoughtfully. "Then she may just grow up to c-l-a-w your eyes out."

Lorenzo took pity on me when he saw my stricken expression and slapped me on the back. "Just kidding. I'm sure you'll do fine."

We arrived in Stagsford by late afternoon and picked a modest, but respectable inn on the outskirts of the city. I would have been happy to let a room in a cheaper and less reputable section of the city, but the Baron, who for some reason insisted on staying with our troupe, persisted in maintaining appearances.

I threw my pack in the room I was sharing with Olmsted then staggered down to a rathskeller and demanded a pint of the best ale for my head. The basement tavern could have been painted the color of an infected dragon's spleen and populated by naked naiads slithering in butterfly oil and I wouldn't have noticed. My head was pounding more and more and I was having a difficult time focusing my eyes.

"You don't look so good," Lorenzo said as he sat down next to me. "I think you need to see a doctor. You took quite a beating and could have a mild concussion."

"I hate leeches. Doctors are mostly quacks and charlatans."

"Come on, you big baby. I'll go with you."

He led me out of the tavern and into the city streets. I was in a daze and followed meekly behind him. We were soon climbing the narrow and steep steps of a three-story brick and pushing our way into a waiting room.

I hate waiting rooms. It is bad enough to be infirm, but to sit among a crowd of hackers and moaners, with vile secretions oozing from an assortment of ruptures, makes me worry that I will return home with more scourges than with which I arrived. And the way some of the others shuffled nervously out of my path, I knew they worried that I must suffer a contagious affliction.

Lorenzo checked me in at the window staffed by a midwife and we took our seats. He picked up a scroll dealing with chariot racing while I just cradled my head in my hands.

"Aay, vot's that? Aay, Em talken ta ya."

I grimaced and rubbed my temples. The oaf in the next chair had a very annoying voice.

"Aay, Em talken ta ya, Kant ya hear? Ah said, vot's tat?"

I turned to look at someone too immense to be of pure human blood, or else prone to monstrous glandular problems. He sat on a large oak stump brought in as a stool since no bench could survive his weighty onslaught. His face was puffed out like bread dough left too long to raise, his beady eyes just slits in the blubber.

"Are you talking to me?" I asked with more civility than I felt at the moment--there is something intimidating about such a sheer mass of fat, bone, and meat that is all in one hunk and still breathing.

"Vot's tat?"

His rumbling voice was the hammer pounding a wedge into my rent skull. What in the name of the hairy serpent gods of Jreyl was this leviathan lump of lard babbling about? He was pointing at my shoulder. I looked over to see Osyani had gone to sleep, head tucked under a wing, her talons firmly gripping my tunic.

There are a lot of people who hate harpies. In defense of these people, it is true harpies have a nasty reputation for devouring infants, pets, and virile young men.

"Ah, a cyst," I answered cautiously.

"A cyst?"

"Ah, yes, I have come to have it removed."

"Ton't look like no cyst, look like bird."

Osyani lifted her head at just that moment. She blinked several times and turned to examine the bloated blockhead.

"Ackh," he screeched. "Tat no cyst."

"You're totally correct. It is a sensitive subject for my friend," Lorenzo interjected. "It is his sister. They were born joined at the shoulder. She has finally won a court order to have themselves surgically separated. Unfortunately, my friend depends upon her for his liver functions. You can see why he doesn't want to talk about it."

"Master Jak Barley?"

"Here," Lorenzo answered for me, taking Osyani and turning me over to the midwife. She, in turn, took me down a long hall and deposited me in a small room. It was furnished only with a cot, two chairs and a table covered with an assortment of medical instruments.

I hate these chambers almost as much as the crowded waiting room. There are no scrolls to read nor people to talk to, just the silence that nourishes fears until you start believing your bellyache is caused by a malignancy eating away at your guts, spreading putrefaction...

I shook myself to fend off such thoughts. On the wall were several certificates and I began scanning them. "Royal ACME Academy of Family Healers," one read. Another purported my diagnostician to be a graduate of a curative academy on The Isle of Jimica.

I leaned over and picked up an odd scope that's appearance suggested it was used to probe some orifice or another. I grimaced at the jar of large leeches, the creatures sullenly curled into green balls.

Next to the bloodsuckers was a thick, red tome entitled, "The Healer's Desk Reference." I turned the pages and marveled at the voluminous amount of small print detailing an array of potions and elixirs.

"Crushed snail, wartbane sap, eye of newt, and bat blood," read a title. "For the cure of dropsy, fits, and bowel purgings. Warning; As a consequence of its purification properties of the bowels, some individuals may experience renal failure, nausea, dyspepsia, increased salivation, rash, hearing loss, insomnia, vertigo, vision disturbances, convulsions, extreme sweating, sensitivity to alcohol, bloody discharges, cramps, hair loss, impotency, and/or death."

I shook my head. Who would want to take an elixir that threatened a sensitivity to beer? The entire book was filled with such warnings, which made me wonder how anyone survived their trip to a healer.

"And how are we today?" The bone-sawer had arrived and I sheepishly closed the book and replaced it on the table.

"We are fine," I answered, skeptically eying the man. He was dressed in a white laboratory tunic stained with bloodstains and had a round mirror over his forehead held by a leather band. The bloodstains did not seem to augur well his medical procedures.

"Oh, than why is we here?"

"Ah, we have experienced a miraculous recovery. Sorry to waste your time."

He pushed me back into the chair. "Let we be the judge of that."

Taking my wrist, the healer watched a small sand clock he'd just flipped. He pried back my eyelids then examined my tongue.

"Ah, have you been oozing a vitreous liquid from the nostrils?"

"What? No, I am here because I have had several unfortunate knocks and batterings. My head aches severely."

"Hum," he answered while waving a finger back in forth in front of my nose. "Yes, I see. It appears we shall need to bleed you."

"Bleed me. What are you prattling about?"

"We must remove the sour serum poisoning your body."

"Sour serum. I have no sour serum. I told you, I am a victim of pummelings."

Remaining silent, the doctor just crossed his arms and looked at me with a patronizing smile that said I was a dull as wyvern dung.

"And besides, how does that leech know only to suck off the bad blood? What if it starts sucking my good blood?"

"We will also have to put you on a strict regimen of crushed snail, wartbane sap, eye of newt, and bat blood."

Hades, I thought, I will have to give up ale.

"What health warranty provision are you covered under?" he asked while pulling several phials from a cupboard.

"Health warranty provisions?"

He spun and looked at me. "You are covered by a health warranty provision, are you not?"

"A what?"

"I see." He continued peering at me with a frown then said, "Well, I believe you are correct. You have experienced a miraculous recovery."

The healer pushed me out the door and yelled to the midwife, "Next invalid."

"But..."

I found myself alone in the hall. A midwife passed me leading a troll on crutches.

"Keep away from the leeches," I warned him as he went by.

Lorenzo stood as I returned to the waiting room. "So, how goes it?"

"I have had a miraculous recovery."

Lorenzo examined me skeptically. "You don't look any better."

"But I am not oozing a vitreous liquid from the nostrils and my blood is not sour."

"One can always be thankful for that," Lorenzo agreed as we entered the street.

As a matter of fact, I was feeling a bit better. Though my body still complained with numerous small aches, my head was clearing. Osyani had returned to my shoulder and we made our way through the crowded streets back to our inn.

I took note of my surroundings for the first time. In the distance were the immense temples and government buildings that dominated the skyline. I could see the famous towers of the Temple of Dorga, the fish-headed god of death. The dark Castle Raven of King Kenton loomed above them all, squatting across the river upon the largest hill like a monstrous bird on its nest.

"I should register at the private inquisitor convention," I said as we wove through the throng of merchants, soldiers, pilgrims, and townspeople. "Tonight is a social feast sponsored by the guild. Olmsted is to give his paper tomorrow before a gathering of forensic alchemists."

"It sounds interesting. I think I will attend as an observer," replied Lorenzo. "I've always been fascinated by such matters."

Once again I looked questioningly at my companion. Was it true that he was from a different world? "You seem to be intrigued by many things."

"I guess that's why I travel a lot," he smiled. "It broadens one's horizons."

"Have you been to this world before?" I asked, trying to sound as if I was only making idle conversation.

"Yes, Jak. I have, but I am not your father."

The unexpectedness of the rejoinder took me back. I fished for a reply, but none came.

"Jennair told me of your relationship to her and Olmsted--and of your wanting to meet him. Your father sounds like a remarkable man, but be cautious of what you wish for."

"I have never said I wished to meet..." My retort was cut short as we rounded a corner to see a group of guardsmen gathered about the entrance to our inn. They had our group against a garden wall.

I hurried forward and confronted the captain of the squad.

"What is this about?" I asked heatedly. "Since when are honest

Glavendalians treated so?"

The captain turned to me and slowly examined me from head to toe.

"Your identification papers, please?" he asked in a bored voice.

"They are in my pack," I answered.

"Which one is yours?"

I looked to where he pointed and saw that our gear was strewn in front of the inn, much of it opened as if it had been rifled through.

"This is an outrage. What right have you to accost us as criminals?"

He continued ignoring my questions and waved over a guardsman who held a fist full of papers.

"Let us see, you would be the ferret, Jak Barley? Your party seems to travel lightly. And is that a harplet on your shoulder?"

"That be private inquisitor," I snapped. "I am sure the others have told you of our trouble at the pass. And yes, it is a harpy."

As with many military men, he showed a remarkable lack of imagination when it came to matters not dealing with his duty. He appeared not at all surprised that a harpling would be sitting on my shoulder.

"Well, at least you all cohere to the same tale. And you would be...?" the captain asked Lorenzo, who handed over a packet of papers.

The guardsman examined the different sheets marked with a variety of stamps.

"You seem to be a great traveler, Master Spasm. I see you have been to a number of mountain provinces."

"I become jaded easily."

"Why is our group being harassed like this?" I again asked. "This is unheard of."

"These are strange times, which means dubious strangers are of interest for security reasons."

"But I am a citizen of Duburoake, unless the King has allowed us to become a sovereign city-state."

"Careful with your tongue, ferret. Talk like that is seditious. And not all of you are citizens of Glavendale."

"And have we closed our borders? I have heard of no wars."

"The borders are always closed to those with no legal papers."

I looked nervously at Chaatiguin and Mahvan. "But pilgrims need no papers. They are holy and the gods know no human borders."

"And what about him," the captain said, pointing to Eli, who leaned sullenly against the wall. "He has refused to speak to us and has no papers."

"I believe I can satisfy that problem," Lorenzo replied while withdrawing another sheaf of papers. "He gave them to me for safekeeping."

The captain irritably snatched the packet and rummaged through it. "Your Master Hempcache would have made it easier on himself if he would have informed us of this at the beginning."

"He's often shy."

"He does not look like an Abyserian scribe," the captain noted, looking warily from the papers to Eli and back to Lorenzo. The guardsman motioned one of his men to bring Eli over to us.

"Here are your papers, Master Ran Hempcache. You would be wiser to explain such things to the king's representatives on the outset."

The captain was distracted by a clamor as Baron Garsten Stee Hragen plowed through the crowd to our side.

"This is outrageous. I will have all of your heads. King Kenton is my cousin and he will hear of this. Since when do lackeys such as you bedevil those of royal blood?"

"I am not a lackey," the captain drew himself up in indignation. "I am..."

"You are beetle dung," the Baron cut the captain off and pressed his nose to the soldier's face, or at least as close as his monumental belly would allow. "You are scum, born of some tête-à-tête in a barn loft or back alley. I trace my lineage to Gobor the Great on my father's side. My mother is your king's aunt. My ancestors have ruled you peasant stock since time began."

Taken aback by the verbal onslaught, the officer's mouth opened and closed silently while he grasped for a retort. Baron Garsten Stee Hragen took advantage of his bewilderment and pressed on.

"I will give your men five minutes to finish their business and be gone or you will answer personally to the King."

Drawing what little tattered dignity he had left, the captain clicked his heals and began barking orders to his men. They scurried about and were gone. I could hardly believe my eyes.

"Sometimes it just takes a firm hand to handle their sort," the Baron huffed.

"I didn't know you were on such good terms with the King," Lorenzo noted as we walked back to the others.

"I am not. My father's branch of the family has been out of favor with the court for generations. My mother fled Stagsford when King Kenton's father intrigued for the throne, but I doubted a common guard captain would be knowledgeable on such court trivia. Still, I should be able to get an audience with Kenton to speak of again using the Stee Hragen mountain passage."

"And of the Gespe," Eli reminded him, having gotten a promise earlier from the Baron to speak on behalf of Chaatiguin's people.

"Do you always carry spare identification papers with you?" I turned to Lorenzo.

He smiled and answered, "It's become a habit. You never know when they might come in handy. And from now on Eli, you are Ran Hempcache, an Abyserian scribe."

"A scribe? I can't even read the scribbles on these papers."

Jennair was gathering up her meager belongings to return to her room.

"What was this all about?" I asked.

"They would not tell us, but I believe they are searching all inns."

"Probably looking for that young lad we met in Kaiserhelm. He certainly has stirred up a hornet nest," I guessed.

"Ah, another pilgrim. I will be pleased to escort you to the Temple of Dorga."

More trouble. A tall, gaunt priest dressed in a black shroud had appeared from nowhere and was now towering over Mahvan. Chaatiguin, luckily, had already gone back into the inn with Eli.

I did not like the looks of the cleric. Many priests of Dorga are said to be black sorcerers. He radiated a sinister presence. I could see Mahvan tensing under her robe. She had waited too long to discard her disguise and it was a very serious offense to masquerade as a pilgrim.

"Come, we will be late for evening services," the priest snapped when she did not immediately react.

There was nothing we could do with so many witnesses about. I could tell Mahvan debated the advisability of turning the priest into a pincushion, but finally thought the better of it. She meekly picked up her pack and followed the Dorga cleric. I helplessly watched her walk away.

"Don't worry," Lorenzo said as he laid a hand on my shoulder. "We'll go for a visit later tonight and see that she's all right."

"Are you mad? Are you aware what they would do to an impostor entering their temple? It is no guest lodge that allows visitors in for wine and bread. Have you seen the structure? It is more of a fortress than a temple. Not even the King would dare send in soldiers uninvited."

"No sweat, I've had experience with this sect before. For now we should settle in and get you and Olmsted registered for the convention. Eyes are watching us and it wouldn't be wise to act out of character."

Chapter Eleven

"I hate these lizard suits," I grumbled as the hotel servant led us to our table while I covertly tried unbunching the crotch of my hose. "That is the trouble with having conventions in Stagsford, they always think they have to be pompous toads. If we were in Duburoake, we could relax instead of parading around like peacocks in heat. And these shoes are killing me."

I don't like formal dress, especially what Stagsford high society considers fashionable wear. Something has to be novel each year to be in vogue, with more subdued variations filtering to the coast a year or two later. This year some rakish knave decided silk hose, the more garish the better, and knee-length embroidered tunics with ruffled collars and cuffs were to be in fashion for men.

To top it off, we were made to wear ridiculous identity badges. Below our names were in bold the letters "GAPI," for Glavendale Association of Private Inquisitors. Beneath that was an eyeball looking through a keyhole, our professional fraternity's symbol.

I was most certain I did not look as much the lunatic as Olmsted, who had gone to the extreme. His tunic had to be the work of some demented tailor driven mad over the years by his foppish, moronic clients and from staring too long and intently at his oscillating needle and thread.

My half-brother's attire consisted of a lavender pair of silken tights and a tunic that appeared as if it had been made from a quilt blanket--with the burnished cloth remnants from the wardrobe of an addict of a hallucinogenic Frevbt Mountain fungus known for its wit-altering properties.

I believe he looked better in the tunic proclaiming, "Me Brother Acquired A Sacred Relic And All I Got Was This Tunic--Kaiserhelm."

My own apparel was a subdued green tunic and gray hose, though I had to stand my ground at the rental stall. The proprietor had been determined to see me decked out in mauve and teal.

Lorenzo was eye-catching, dressed in an alien garb that made heads turn. He wore a black outer coat that hung split and low in the back, along with black loose pantaloons. Beneath the opened-front jacket was a white tunic and a black strip of material about his neck tied in a bow. He called the attire a tuxedo.

"Desist in your grimacing, me Jak. You appear as if you be approaching the hangman," Jennair laughed in her best Frajan accent.

It was hard to frown when looking at Jennair. She wore a simple black gown that clung to her in a way that made me once again wish she were not my half-sister. It placed in contrast even more her milky skin and white-gold hair.

We were led into a cavernous room of ice. The candles and sphinx oil lamps rebounded and blazed a thousand times among the crystal chandeliers. I fought hard not to gawk, feeling for the first time the country bumpkin. It was a fairyland inhabited by foolish-looking poppycocks and their wondrous female partners dressed in revealing strips of gauze, silk, and satin. Maybe not all Stagsford fashions are that grievous.

"Close your mouth before some gnats flit in," Jennair spoke as one lithesome naiad drifted by in a cloud of pink.

We were led to four empty seats at a long table. I slid a chair out for Jennair and groaned as I took my own. We were being placed directly opposite Ferred Kloppenhorsh, the bane of my student days at the private inquisitor academy.

Ferred was the son of a rich merchant who never failed to point out his high standing compared to that of a West Glavendale bastard townie from Duburoake. While I worked in the dormitory kitchen and cleaned rooms at night to pay my way through school, Ferred went on revelries with his moneyed compatriots.

"Jak. I wondered if you would make the convention. I know how awkward it is for the provincials to travel this far," Ferred greeted me with an oily smile.

"That is true," I replied as I unrolled a napkin and placed it on my lap. "We are a guileless and simple lot, unused to the subtleties employed by the pimps, miscreants, thieves, and incestuous dullards you call residents here in our royal capitol."

Jennair kicked me under the table.

"Ah, the same Master Barley I knew in school. Always the jester."

She kicked me again before I could note that he had put on a goodly number of pounds since I'd last seen his chinless, pocked-mark countenance.

"And who are your delightful guests?"

I grudgingly introduced Jennair, Olmsted, and Lorenzo.

"I am charmed. And is this your mistress?"

"You know full well Olmsted and Jennair are my half-siblings. And unlike Stagsfordians, we do not go to kin gatherings looking for mates."

Ferred ignored my gibe and turned to Lorenzo, undoubtedly to make some impudent remark on his peculiar garb before taking aim on my hunchbacked brother.

Before Ferred could speak, Lorenzo said in a nonchalant voice while pouring himself a glass of wine, "Don't fuck with me or I'll kill you."

Used to affronts couched in pretty words, a disconcerted Ferred appeared speechless. I think I saw an almost indiscernible jerk from Lorenzo after his curt words, guessing Jennair had aimed a kick his way. I was beginning to like my traveling companion.

"Excuse my friend, he is from a far land and not familiar with the ways of Stagsford, so often he speaks what he thinks. A fault I am sure you do not possess."

"Can I not take you two anywhere?" Jennair grumbled under her breathe at the two of us when Ferred was distracted by a serving wench bearing a plate of smoked carp. "I have not the many chances to dine in such grand surroundings. Do not ruin it for me with your childish declarations."

"Jak, so you did manage to make it."

I sighed. The convention was becoming a class reunion, an occasion I'd striven hard to miss in the past.

"Vil, you are looking well," I said before even turning to the familiar voice.

Vil Hemloch was the prodigy of our class, an unusually quiet student from an affluent family with distant blood ties to the throne. Unlike Ferred, he didn't wave his high standings among his classmates. Vil was well liked, but his studious ways kept him from having close friends.

"I take it you have traveled this far for the King's summons? You showed talent at the trade and I am sure you will be one of the inquisitors to receive a commission."

"Hah, I'm sure the Royal Office of Public Safety will be looking for agents who can travel easily amongst court society, those with refined decorum," Ferred interrupted, obviously sending the barb in my direction.

"I am considering such a proposal. Though after the heavy case loads at home, I tend to view this trip as a respite from such work," I answered, not having the slightest idea what Vil was talking about. "Are you applying?"

Ferred laughed sarcastically and again interrupted. "I hardly think so, with our Vil being an agent for the King's Clandestine Information Authority."

Holy carp tripe! I should have guessed. Taking in his colorful garb, I failed to notice he wore the CIA trademark footwear made by Narmvian Shoe Elves. It was difficult imagining the amiable Vil working with such snakes.

"And you, Ferred, how do you like working as an indemnity agent, spending your days uncovering fraudulent thefts, bogus damage claims, and house burnings. It must be quite the exciting life, though one which probably has not prepared you for real private inquiry work."

"It suits me, as well as having acquainted me with many ranking citizens of Stagsford," he huffed back.

I was right. The faded ink stains on his right hand, the squint wrinkles about his eyes, and the closely cropped hair were the trademarks of an insurance investigator. He probably had made many friends in high finance, getting a kickback for looking the other way at a number of shams.

"Enough talk about business, our meals await us," Vil said when the servants began bringing the initial courses. "Come to room 709 after the banquet if you are interested in such a game."

I was already on edge, knowing Lorenzo had some half-crazed scheme to free Mahvan from Dorga's temple in the middle of the night. Now I had an invitation to meet with a CIA agent about some mysterious call from the king.

Since when did King Kenton need private inquisitors when his own army of rogues virtually slinked in every crack and cranny? I was beginning to think this was an ill chosen time to visit the Capital.

The meal was without incident, Ferred leaving us alone to focus his charm on the girlfriend of a bail bondsmen/inquisitor named Dun Leberman. I kept hoping in vain that Dun, a short and broad-shouldered man, would lean past his lady and break Ferred's nose.

I finally leaned back in my seat, patted my stomach, and sighed. "I think I could now sleep for a month."

"Make that several hours, we have a mission to complete tonight," Lorenzo rudely interrupted my tranquility. "But first you must visit with your old friend, Vil Hemloch. I think that meeting may answer many of the strange happenings we have been plagued with lately."

I groaned, "I do not wish to put my head in the noose after so narrowly escaping it on the road. The CIA are not the workmates I would freely choose to associate with."

"I hear that Ferred chap bragging to the lady that he will be chosen for the assignment because of his breeding and wit," Lorenzo noted. "It is just as well. The qualifications for such a commission would be stringent."

I shook my head. "Such talk will not work. I see your words trying to goad me. I will not go to room 709 for passion or coin."

"Whoa, the real reason me half-brother will not go is that he is afraid of lifts," Jennair laughed as she clapped her hands.

I studied her with a cold fish eye. "That is not the reason. Yes, I do not care for small boxes being hoisted up and down a tiny shaft, propelled by some hapless ponies living a bleak life in a sunless basement. I find these hostels very pretentious that they cannot use ordinary stairs. But I am here for a respite from work."

"What work, me brother? You have not had a task since finding Squinty Doog's missing daughter, and you spent most of that relentless search in the King's Wart Inn."

"It matters not; I am definitely not going to that gathering."

I was sweating like a stuck pig. There were seven other people crowded into the lift and the unseen ropes groaned under the load as we traveled upwards in jerks. I also hate lift melodies. Echoing faintly up the shaft could be heard the leaden tunes of a three-piece band also exiled to the basement with the ponies. The music grated on my nerves, probably because it was always dreary versions of popular standards at least a decade old.

A faint voice from the basement was heard momentarily over the music, "Come on, Berdda, put yah shoulders into it, we ain't got all night."

I was silently cursing Lorenzo for convincing me to go on this lunatic errand while he escorted Jennair back to the inn. Yes, I do detest lifts. I feel trapped whenever in one and I just know bad things are going to happen.

Some noxious perfume, probably from Ferred, was churning my

stomach and I pledged to myself that if I were going to disgorge, it would be down his back. Also in the lift were Dun and several other private inquisitors.

The box finally came to a halt and the doors begrudgingly opened--upon a scene from some mad house. The hallway was chaos, filled with battling Dorga priests, hillmen in Ayerian militia uniforms, CIA agents, and royal guards. An arrow zipped over my head to strike with a thud into the oak wall.

The few passengers at the front of the elevator who had automatically begun to exit the lift were now scrambling backwards. Vil, who was wrestling over a sword with one of the hillmen, saw us in the open lift and shouted for help. Pressed back against the wall, I could only watch as a Revian Ascetic fried the eyeballs of a Dorgian priest who screamed and clutched his face before being impaled by a guardsman.

One of the passengers at the door of the lift dropped from an arrow. The lift doors began to shut, but his body blocked the opening. Another missile thudded above my head. I felt like a carp in a barrel shoot and forced my may to the front of the lift, there to begin shoving the corpse into the hallway. The bondsman, the only other passenger not now cowering with arms above head, came to my aid.

A CIA agent pushed his way past me and joined the other lift occupants, shoving a moaning Ferred to the front as a shield.

The shattering of glass signaled the exit en masse of the hillmen, who were leaping out the windows to ropes apparently dangling from the roof. As one of the last hillman dropped from sight, we locked eyes for just a second--it was the young man from the Kaiserhelm inn and the caravan. He was wearing a smart, scarlet uniform unlike the green and grey garb of the other Ayerians.

The mayhem was subsiding, the Dorga priests now fleeing down the hall and vanishing around the turn. I was still in a bit of shock when Vil slapped me on the shoulder.

"Quite the after-dinner entertainment, do not you think?" he asked.

"I prefer a floor show of semi-clothed dancing Harspin maidens,"

I replied as I turned back to the elevator. "Ferred was correct; an ignorant country lad like me would be of no use in your quest."

"No so hastily, Jak. The king has need of your services."

"I am sure Ferred will be most helpful with his deep knowledge of Stagsford." I was now desperate to get out of the hotel and return to my companions. "And I must get back to a twelve o'clock feeding. You know how tykes are."

Vil took my arm and forced me to stop. "I noticed how dauntless Ferrin was when the lift opened. Only you and the bondsman kept clear heads. But Jak, my files do not show you to be a father."

"So, you have files on me?" I asked. "Then you know what an undependable fellow I am. Not the sort to be doing the king's errands."

Vil laughed remarkably easily for someone just minutes past a pitched battle. "I am sure many of my associates would agree, but I remember your cleverness from school and I see where your past cases, however so removed from the problem now facing us, were completed with imagination and skill."

"You know, coming from you, that means a lot. I mean it, but I believe my schedule here in Stagsford is full."

"It will have to be unfilled," Vil said in a sympathetic voice, as a leach announcing an incurable ailment. "The king's orders are not to be ignored. I hereby conscript you and the bondsman until further notice."

I vainly argued for several more minutes, but my former schoolmate could not be swayed.

"At least tell me was this is all about," I said as I waved my hand at the rushing of guardsmen about us as hotel stewards began scrubbing blood from the carpets.

"I would normally have to swear you to secrecy upon your life, but this matter has already escaped the palace and it will be but a matter of time until it is on the streets," Vil said, now leading me away from the others. "It appears our King Kenton has placed himself in a hot stew. His financial follies forced him to seek a loan from the priests of Dorga. In return, he was to aid in their yearly ceremony of offering a beautiful maiden to the fish-headed god of death. Not just any damsel, but one reputed to be the most fair of all women--the maiden Queen Elay of the mountain kingdom of Ayers."

We stopped at the end of the hall. I was becoming impatient with Vil's grip on my arm.

"Before King Kenton sent a force to abduct the queen, a seer predicted the venture would result in the king's demise. The Ayers royal guardsmen were skilled in a number of combat arts and notorious for their loyalty. King Kenton reasoned, therefore, that they were the most likely assassins. He had the soothsayer burned and ordered that the members of the queen's personal force be dispatched to the very last man.

"Obviously, the mission was not completely successful. The queen was taken in an ambush and her guards slain, but one escaped. Other conjurers have ascertained this, and tonight's mischief supports this. The Ayrian militia was here tonight seeking the whereabouts of their queen. You will have noticed that one of the Ayerians wore the ruby uniform of the Queen's Guard.

"We suspect he was a cadet, maybe home on leave when the raid occurred. Youngster or not, the King takes such premonitions seriously and a lengthy search has been waged for this young Ayerian."

"Is not the CIA capable of hunting for this lad?" I asked. "It would seem you have enough forces for such a simple task."

"True, but our energies are also being directed in other areas. It seems the king has become quite enamored with Queen Elay and now refuses to surrender the intended Dorga sacrifice. The priests are understandably upset and have been making some rather loathsome threats. All the king's agents and wizards have been called in to safeguard him and the Ayers queen."

"So this ravisher of child-queens needs the help of common ferrets," I sneered.

"Careful, Jak," Vil warned as he tightened his grip. "We are schoolmates and perhaps carry like opinions, but such talk in the company of those now about us can be dangerous.

"Yes, we are calling in auxiliary forces in this search for the Queen's Guardsman. We are surprised how cleverly he has eluded us. We even lost two Ghennison viper mages--a most puzzling and alarming occurrence."

"What a lamentable thing to befall such sweet creatures as the viper mages," I replied, trying not to show my unease. "I wish I could give their widows my condolences, but I must be back to the inn. It was a long and tiring trip and I need my rest."

"Certainly, Jak," Vil said as he finally let go of my arm. "I will be by your quarters at midmorning. Be ready."

I paused to look longingly out the window at a dangling rope before forcing myself to return to the lift. I was almost to the door when I spun and said to Vil, "I have a favor to ask in return."

"You mean besides the generous coins to be paid by the King?"

"Yes, it concerns the Gespe."

"Strange, Master Barley, but I do not take you for one who would sport such a coat," he answered in slight bafflement.

"I am not, and there lies the trouble."

He looked even more puzzled as the lift doors slid shut between us.

~ * ~

"I am telling you, we are in the middle of an ant's nest and the gods are poking at it with a big stick," I repeated to Lorenzo. "With all the King's men about, as well as those crazy priests on the rampage, there is no way we can enter the Temple of Dorga."

Lorenzo, Eli, and I sat by the fireplace in my room. Olmsted snored loudly from the bed.

"But this is the time to act, when confusion reigns," Lorenzo said and patted me on the back as if I were a fearful child.

Osyani was nestled against my neck and watched on with eyes much too solemn for such a young chick. I nuzzled her under the chin and she chirped in pleasure.

"I'm coming," Eli said in a tone that asserted no debate. "A man doesn't let his partners down."

"Eli, Chaatiguin needs you by her side," I tried to reason. "She is in a strange place and requires your comforting."

"She'll be okay for the night with Jennair. I've heard a bit about these Dorga dudes and it sounds like they need a comin' down. I wanna be in the posse."

"What?" I asked, perplexed by his strange idioms.

"He says he's coming along," Lorenzo translated as he opened one of his pouches.

I watched in disbelief as he pulled out the garb of the dead Dorgian priest, Olahn. He followed up with the hooded robes of two of the slain pilgrims.

"Are you mad?" I demanded, already knowing the answer. "Are you aware of how the followers of Dorga answer such sacrilege?"

"Probably as they will do to Mahvan before the next day is done. Don't worry about it; I do this all the time."

I caught myself just before I slapped the side of my head, which would have clipped Osyani. The harplet had already grown more three inches and was now able to nibble on sausage and cheese.

I was bruised, tired, and at my wits end. I silently cursed whatever god was making such sport of me--probably Manalow. At the age of twelve, I had pocketed a devotional plate of small coins from a neighborhood Manalow temple. Who would have ever guessed a minor deity in charge of lift melodies would have such a long arm or memory?

"What is the matter?" Lorenzo asked at my pained expression.

"Nothing, I just realized why lifts make me so nervous."

"Why?"

"It is the music."

"That's perfectly understandable," he answered then threw one of the pilgrim robes to me.

"Will not they wonder about the blood?" I asked as I distastefully held it up to the light.

"They'll just think you're a messy eater."

"And the knife rents?"

"Relax, we're not going to no fancy ball. We're tired and dirty pilgrims."

Lorenzo ignored my grumbling as I folded the robe and put it under my arm, it's association with the fish-headed god of death more offensive than the filth. We were to don the disguises once away from the inn and in deep shadows.

"Be careful, Master Jak," Jennair said from her parted door as I handed over Osyani. "I have not so many half-brothers that I can still stand to lose one."

The harpling struggled a bit in Jennair's hold when she realized I was about to leave, but my half-sister quickly calmed her with gentle words and soft strokes.

"Do not worry about me," I said in my best swaggering tone. "Worry about those poor Dorgian priests."

"Oh, you must always play the tavern dolt," Jennair sadly shook her head, but I could see the trace of a smile.

Chapter Twelve

It was two hours before dawn, but there were still people about. A vendor sold roasted sea serpent meat on a stick, it's fishy odor clashing with the stink of rat fritters being grilled over another monger's hot coals. They nervously paused in their hawking as we walked by in our garb. Outright war had not yet been declared between the Temple of Dorga and King Kenton, but all knew a tense state of rancor now existed.

We wove our way through murky streets and alleys, only occasional intersections lit by street lamps and small bonfires. At these islands of light would be late night revelers, most of them tourists floundering about in drunken or drugged stupors to the simple tunes of street corner musicians. Some haggled prices with painted women trying to turn one last trick before daylight. Others were already passed out in doorways.

Looking over them all would be at least two guardsmen in bored silence, paid by the city fathers to keep a minimum amount of peace through the night. Too many dead or robbed tourists would be bad for business.

The carousers were safe enough if they stayed to the well-lit sanctuaries--but wolves of a two-footed kind hunted in the shadows, ready to bring down any sheep foolish enough to wander from their shepherds.

If Stagsford does not live up to its nickname of "The City That Never Sleeps," it at least is one that has only fitful naps.

We walked both the lit and unlit streets in peace, no one risking the wrath of the priests of Dorga.

All too soon we came to the temple of Dorga. A towering statue of the god crouched at the domed top. Dorga had the lower body of a man, the drooping breasts of a very corpulent woman, and the head of a carp. Lorenzo led us in a wide circle to the back of the massive stone structure, it more a fortress than a dwelling for a god.

"Ah, there is where we want to go," he said.

"Where?"

"There."

He said no more, but set off with a purposeful stride. It wasn't until we got closer that I could make out a narrow door set within the giant stone blocks. The black walls of the temple now loomed menacingly above us. I nervously licked my lips.

"How do we get in the door? It looks well braced and no doubt guards are positioned nearby," I whispered.

Lorenzo enthusiastically hammered on the thick wooden planks before turning to me and saying, "Take it."

"Take it?"

"Take it."

"Take what?"

"The lead."

"The lead?"

"Yes, the lead. Take it."

"No."

"Yes."

"Are you a lunatic?" I managed to croak. "What kind of plan is this? What am I to do?"

"You'll think of something."

A sour, narrow face peered forth from the barred window.

"Yah? What do you want? This is the kitchen door. You gotta go around to the front."

Lorenzo shoved me forward. I fought back an overpowering

impulse to run.

"Ah, we cannot." I stammered.

"Are you as dim-witted as you look? I said this door be only for kitchen supplies and help. Be gone or I will dispatch Dorga's Hounds upon you."

The man was obviously a feeble-minded buffoon who, given the least amount of authority, wielded it like a blunt sword.

"It is you who are the dolt," I snapped back. "Do you know who you are speaking to?"

"No, pray tell, who?" he snidely asked while looking with contempt at my soiled pilgrim's garb.

That stumped me. I took a deep breath. They can only burn you at the stake once, I thought to myself, but tried not to dwell upon the tortures that can be inflicted before the pyre.

"This is His Exalted Patriarch High Advocate of Dorga, the Arch Priest Comft," I announced with as much pomp as I could muster while pointing to Lorenzo.

The little weasel's beady eyes snapped wide and his mouth mirrored the pursed lips of his carp-headed god. He took several steps back before finally regaining control.

"Hey, what is the Arch Priest Comft doing at the kitchen door?" the man asked warily.

"We are on a secret mission. You know the plight we now face with King Kenton. Why has not someone been placed here to see to our safe entry?" I snapped.

"No one has told me about this. Wait while I get one of Dorga's Hounds."

"Stop," I ordered. "Get the guards and you will die a very painful and slow death. This mission is very secret and there are reasons to believe we have spies among us. They must have detained the one who was to be at this door and perhaps even now send assassins to murder Arch Priest Comft."

The man pushed his face to the bars to view the two behind me.

He was looking very distressed.

"Blood of Dorga, I do not know. No one is to pass through these doors but those of the kitchen. How do I know you speak the truth? No offense, Arch Priest Comft, if that be really you."

"Take several paces back," I ordered.

The visibly trembling follower of Dorga took several hesitant steps backwards under the light of a flickering torch. I put my face to the bars and examined the man. He wore a simple, stained tunic and worn linen hose. Over the garb was a discolored apron that might once have been white. I hoped what I read of this knave was correct.

"You are in charge of discarding the fat and grease, though instead of always taking it to the temple soapmakers, you occasionally sneak some to an outside merchant. Before becoming a lard servant, you worked in the stables. Your mother was a whore and you spend most of your ill-gained grease money upon those who follow the profession of your mother."

The knave gasped at the all-seeing eyes of Dorga and hid his face behind his hands.

"Oh, spare me," he wailed. "Spare me and I will never again steal fat from Dorga. I am but a poor servant who has sinned but has now seen the error of his ways."

It was obvious that Dorga dispersed some very harsh punishment, even for petty crimes. The kitchen knave was literally shaking in his sandals.

"Open this door straightaway and your sins will be forgiven, but make haste," I mercilessly prodded the bewildered man.

He began fumbling with the locks and latches and soon the door swung outwards. I motioned Lorenzo and Eli in first, then pulled the door shut behind me.

"Lock it and never let the happenings of this night pass your lips," I ordered.

It was easy to see the knave would gladly want to forget this night.

Lorenzo brushed past me and I turned to follow. We passed a

large archway leading into the kitchen. Giant kettles of evil-smelling mush boiled away, obviously meant as breakfast for the pilgrims and other lesser visitors. I let my questmate lead us down several twisting hallways before clutching his cloak and turning him to me, though I could not see his face hidden by the shadow of the hood.

"What was the meaning of that?" I hissed, anxiously looking down both lengths of the hall.

"Meaning of what?"

"Do not sport with me. You know well what I mean. Why bring us to the very gate of Dorga's temple, dressed in the garb of his followers, and say, 'Take it?'"

"This venture will require the sharpened wits of us all, and I was afraid yours were dulling from weariness. You needed to whet them a bit."

"What if they had called those Dorga's Hounds upon us?" I retorted.

"I could have plugged 'em between the eyes, but I'm afraid these Colts are a bit noisy," volunteered Eli.

"I knew you could do it," Lorenzo said as he slapped me on the back. "Now what?"

My look must have been grim because Lorenzo quickly held up his hands and said, "Just kidding. This way."

"Tell me you have a plan," I almost begged as I rushed to keep up with his fast pace.

"I have a plan."

"Truth?"

"Do you think I would lead us into the hellish bowls of a demonic sanctuary of pure terror, evil, and horror without a plan?"

"That was my query."

"Yes, I have a plan."

"And could you please tell us?" I asked. "I would very much like to hear it."

"We will find Mahvan's cell, release her, and go back to the inn."

"Oh, yes. Why did not I think of that scheme? It is all so simple."

"That's the beauty of it," admitted Lorenzo. "The simpler the plan, the less to go wrong."

"And what do you think of this plan, Eli?" I looked over my shoulder and asked.

"Sounds simple."

I waited for elaboration, but none came. We slowed down at the turn of a corner when several apprentices appeared. They looked at us in curiosity. They appeared surprised to see a village priest and two pilgrims roaming the inner sanctums of the temple.

"Novices, we have become separated from our guide and cannot find our way back to the visitors' quarters. We need one of you to lead our return," Lorenzo ordered.

They hesitated, but even a humble village priest ranks above a novitiate.

"I will direct you, priest," one reluctantly volunteered and set off without looking back to see if we followed.

We marched silently through numerous halls for what seemed like hours, descending several long stairs until the air became dank. The stone walls gleamed with an oily sweat under the light of a torch taken by the apprentice at the last flight of steps.

I was becoming impatient. "Are we almost there?"

The novice ignored me. Everyone outranked a pilgrim. I was thinking of smacking the back of his head when a far off disturbance could be heard. It echoed faintly at first. The four of us stopped to listen. The sound grew. It was the angry shouting of a number of men.

The apprentice priest paled, pointed toward the clamor, and said, "It be that way." He then turned and bolted.

We were too slow to react. With his disappearance also went the light.

"What now?" I asked in the pitch darkness. "And remember, keep it simple."

A narrow, white ray of light winked on, making a circle on the stone floor in front of Lorenzo.

"I thought you were magic bane." I said.

"It's not magic, just a penlight," Lorenzo replied, as if that were an answer. He began leading us toward the pandemonium.

"Is this wise?" I wanted to know. "That does not appear to be the sound of mirth."

"No. I'm guessing Mahvan lost her patience."

"Mahvan? Well there goes your simple plan."

"Yes, I admit this does rather complicate things."

The hallway opened into gallery of sorts that overlooked a large chamber. Door after door lined the walls of the large room below us. Several were open and anxious pilgrims looked out from their cramped warrens. A number of armed priests in black robes were roughly questioning a group of pilgrims, one whose motionless form reflected the severity of the interrogations. I guessed the soldier priests to be the Hounds of Dorga.

I then noticed a second lifeless body. It was that of a regular priest in a brown robe similar to Lorenzo's in more ways than one--it too had blood stains, only much more recent.

As we watched, one of the hounds jerked open another door to drag a protesting pilgrim from his cubicle. His screams and protests of ignorance did nothing to stop a merciless beating. The priest warriors were ready to kill or maim all the pilgrims in their search for the slayer of a fellow priest of Dorga.

"How are we going to tell which one is Mahvan?" I whispered to Lorenzo.

Another door was opened and a pilgrim rudely grabbed by the cowl, only this time it was a Hound of Dorga's turn to howl. He staggered back, holding a bloody stump where once had been a hand.

"I'm guessing that's her," said Lorenzo.

Mahvan threw back her hood and the priests were momentarily astounded by the spilling free of her long, golden hair. She used the brief seconds to her advantage, darting between two of the warrior priests with her hands a blur of motion. Both hounds clutched their sides in agony.

She was attempting to fight her way to the stairs leading up to the gallery. There were too many priests and they now had their swords drawn. I tightly gripped the banister in helplessness. There was no way Mahvan could make it.

I almost fell over the railing in fright. The quick string of explosions echoed within the chamber like the thundering duels of lightening gods. My ears were ringing.

Eli was again holding the strange iron weapon and a wisp of smoke drifted from its mouth. Down below, several priests who had been preventing Mahvan's escape were now sprawled on the floor.

"Up here." I yelled and waved my arms.

Mahvan looked up in surprise. She frowned and paused at the stairs, as if deciding whether to look for another escape route.

I realized what was amiss and flung back my hood. "Mahvan, it is we. Hurry."

She looked even more startled but quickly climbed the stairs. The Hounds of Dorga were looking in stunned amazement at their fallen comrades--powerful spells that permeated every stone of the temple should have prevented such deadly magic.

"What are you doing here?" Mahvan gasped as she reached our sides.

"We are taking a tour and were just about to visit the priests' lounge for a quick ale when we thought of inviting you," I answered. "But I think we used up our welcome."

The black-robed priests were coming out of their dazes. One yelled orders and they began following the leader to the stairway.

"Drop a few more, would you, Eli?" I asked.

"Better not, got only a few shots left. I think we better hoof it out of here, pronto."

I believed I was beginning to fathom Eli's gibberish, but one did not need to be a wizard to know it was time to take wing. We turned en masse and began running. Lorenzo was in the vanguard and he led us through side hallways and up a number of stairways, some straight and others twisting madly like ireful serpents. We slowed whenever we traversed unlit halls, depending upon Lorenzo's small beam of light for guidance.

"Where are we going," I huffed as we paused at the top of one flight of steps.

"I'm not sure."

"Why am I not surprised?"

"But if we don't know where we are going, neither do our pursuers," Lorenzo tried to mollify me with his strange logic. "Still, soon the temple will be waking and word of an errant village priest and several pilgrims will be spreading."

We continued down the endless hallways until Lorenzo paused before a particularly massive and ornate door, "Let's see what is behind one of these doors."

I was prepared to force the door but the handle turned after only a few tugs and it swung inwards. Lorenzo's beam was not strong enough to penetrate very far into the interior. He shined it about until spotting a torch. Though he claimed no magic was involved, he flicked a small device and a flame appeared. A bit more searching found us all torches and we set off to investigate the seemingly endless chamber. Even with our torches, the ceiling was lost in blackness.

"What are you doing here?" Mahvan again asked when the two of us were by ourselves.

"What else? We came to find you?"

"Why? What would compel you to brave the Temple of Dorga for me?" she asked in disbelief. It almost sounded like mistrust. "Do not give me some fantasy that you came because you are smitten with me."

"We came because you were one of our travel mates and were in need of help," I protested. "What other possible reason could there be?"

We paused and searched each other's face. A faint breeze flickered our torches and played with her hair. She brushed a wayward strand from her face. I felt as if we were in an empty field at night rather than in the bowels of an abominable temple.

She turned and continued the exploration and soon we reached the opposite side of the room. We found another empty expanse of wall. We had seen nothing but bare stone floor during the crossing.

Mahvan appeared to consider my speech. "True, I am nearly certain you are just the ferret..."

"Private inquisitor," I automatically corrected.

"...you claim to be," she continued. "Therefore, I thank you and the others for such unexpected bravery."

A distant whoosh was followed by an eruption of light across the distant floor. The towering flames easily illuminated the vast hall and I saw we were in a vast chamber with only two articles of furniture--if they could be called that. A stone platform, almost to one end of the hall, which supported a large pedestal--one long enough for a person to recline upon. Behind it loomed the bronze, leviathan likeness of the fish-headed god of death.

There was no doubt about it. We were in the sacrificial hall of Dorga, where no eyes have gazed but those belonging to the most devout of the carp-faced god's followers.

"Deity dung," I croaked. "We have done it now."

Even Mahvan seemed impressed.

"Lorenzo, put out that blaze," I shouted.

Lorenzo and the others were hastily backing away from the fire that appeared to be consuming a number of massive tree trunks. The logs had to have been impregnated with some volatile oil to have taken flame so quickly. Greasy black smoke twisted and swirled wildly until it disappeared through a large hole in the ceiling.

"I think it has to burn itself out," Lorenzo yelled back. He and Eli quickly ran to join us.

"Come on, let us keep moving," I urged. "Someone is going to be very distraught over this and I do not want to be about when they discover it."

"Which will be soon," Lorenzo added. "It's almost sunrise and that smoke will be seen across all of Stagsford. No doubt that is one of the traditions of Dorga's yearly sacrifice."

I groaned as we tried a number of doors. They were all locked and too massive for us to knock or kick down with just shoulders and feet. Where was the door we had entered by?

Lorenzo snapped his fingers. "Why didn't I think of this before? Quick, follow me."

He took off in a trot and we were soon at the crossed legs of Dorga. An object that looked more like a sickly snake than a god's limp penis dangled over an ankle.

My mouth actually dropped open when Lorenzo did not halt at the god's feet but leaped to scramble up into Dorga's lap.

"Are you crazy?" I railed, becoming very tired of asking that question.

Lorenzo continued climbing, crawling between the ponderous breasts and up to the head. None of the twisted insanity so far on this trip prepared me for his next course of action. Lorenzo hoisted himself up and disappeared between Dorga's fish lips. A head popped out an instant later to yell, "Hurry. They will be here soon."

There didn't appear to be any choice. Lorenzo had already accomplished the feat without being struck down by a bolt of lightening.

Mahvan distastefully used Dorga's penis for a handhold and managed to clamber into the lap. I went next, followed by Eli. I tried not to notice the occasional flash of a comely leg from the pilgrim's robe above me. I knew that though Mahvan would never believe the truth, part of the reason I came on this rescue was because I was smitten by the maiden.

The mouth was about thirty-five feet above the floor and I felt my right leg nervously quiver as I strained with one hand to reach the bottom lip. Lorenzo grabbed my wrist and help me the rest of the way. He motioned for me to crawl past him.

"But be careful," he warned. "Dorga's gullet soon takes a downward turn and it's a slippery throat."

We were soon all hunched at the back of Dorga's mouth.

"How did you know of this place and what are we to do now?" I was so overwhelmed from recent experiences and lack of sleep that I felt completely numb, removed from my surroundings as if they were but a story being recited to me.

"A friend once told of a similar experience in another Dorga temple," Lorenzo answered. "He said the body was hollow and a trap door in the floor led to a secret passage."

"Where did the secret passage go?" asked Mahvan.

Lorenzo smiled crookedly. "That's a good question. My friend never had to use it."

This would have normally been my cue to moan. Instead I said, "Well, let us do it," and pushed myself feet first into the dark cavity of Dorga's throat.

The sudden fall into blackness caused my stomach to do a flip and finally snapped me from the lethargy that had been building. I panicked and clawed vainly for a hold. My fall came abruptly to an end when I hit a mound of bagged sheep wool. I rolled a bit and came to a final stop on a decidedly more solid stone floor.

"Are you crazy?" Lorenzo's voice echoed down to me. I could but only smile at the turnabout.

"Come, follow my lead. A soft landing awaits you."

Their whispered conversations reached me as only meaningless mumbling, but soon I heard the faint rasp of clothing against the metal of Dorga's throat. I climbed my way to the top of the padding and felt around in the dark until I grasped an arm.

"Quick, before the next one comes," I urged and we rolled to the bottom.

I did not need a light to tell it was Mahvan. I could feel the soft swell of her body as we came to a stop, as well as the numerous hard-edge weapons she carried under her cloak.

"Are you going to get off me, Master Jak?"

I scrambled to my feet as another of our party landed among the bags of wool. We called him down and soon the last of our party was safely at the bottom. Lorenzo had lit his small talisman and he ran its beam across the inside of Dorga's brass belly.

We all froze at the same time. We could hear voices, very upset voices.

Lorenzo approached an odd tube and placed one eye against it.

"It's a periscope, a device that utilizes mirrors to view around corners," he informed us. "Take a look."

I peered into the tube and saw a flood of Dorga's Hounds flowing into the giant sacrificial hall. They spread out to search the chamber. With there being only a few places to hide, they quickly began checking the numerous doors.

I moved to the side to let Mahvan and Eli take their turns peering through the tube.

"Let us look for that escape door," I prompted Lorenzo. "I am in great need of a beer."

We circled the interior, but could not detect a trap door. The group sat to rest and take stock of our options. I again looked through the optical tube and watched the scurrying priests. They appeared in a panic, having no idea what madness not of their own making had invaded their most sacred sanctuary.

"It doesn't make much sense to have these big pillows to catch someone's fall," Lorenzo speculated out loud. "Why use such an awkward entrance? And once in, how would a priest get out?"

I kicked at a bag while pondering similar thoughts and I stepped where the sack had been. My heel came down with an odd thunk. There was the edge of the trap door.

We quickly cleared away the wool and examined the possible exit by Lorenzo's light. The door was made of stout oak and appeared locked from beneath. Mahvan produced a wicked, thick blade and began vainly digging into the stout wood. She gave up minutes later.

"Hum, this is a problem," mused Lorenzo. He wandered to the periscope and peered through the tube.

We each pondered our own thoughts in the dark silence of Dorga's belly. Eli was the first to detect the faint sliding of latches and he drew his weapon in one fluid motion. I winced at the thought of it discharging in this closed space.

The door swung up and over to land on couple bags of wool. Lorenzo turned off his light and Mahvan landed like a cat next to the opening as a head and hand emerged with a lantern. She stomped the wrist as I leaped to catch the lantern.

A surprised curse ended in mid-sentence as Lorenzo flipped the door closed, it landing solidly on the priest's head. He quickly reopened the trap door and aimed his light down at the crumpled form.

"Quick, we need to move before the reinforcements arrive," I told the others.

Eli took the lead with the lantern, weapon drawn. Lorenzo was the last one down and he paused to examine the priest.

"There is the possibility the secret of this passage is only passed down from one single priest to another. By having just killed this one, the Dorgians are no longer aware of its existence," he said while turning the body over with one foot.

I could not help but gasp. The scarlet stitching and gold trim could only mean it was His Exalted Patriarch High Advocate of Dorga, the Arch Priest Comft!

"Lorenzo, you have just killed the high priest of Dorga."

Mahvan kneeled to feel the priest's throat. "You are correct. Comft is dead and may his soul rot in whatever hell his spirit travels to."

"Now what are you doing?" I asked as he began tugging at the high priest's clothing.

"What's it look like? I'm borrowing Comft's attire. He won't be needing it again."

"Lorenzo, you cannot disguise yourself as the high priest of Dorga."

"Why not?" he replied. "You have already passed me off once as His Exalted Patriarch High Advocate of Dorga, the Arch Priest Comft.

And that time I was only wearing a village priest's robe."

"But that was to an ignorant kitchen wretch," I argued.

He ignored my protests and soon was dressed as the high priest of Dorga. I shuddered to stand next to the cowled figure, even while knowing it was Lorenzo beneath the cowl.

Eli continued leading the way, though the tunnel quickly changed into a crawl space. We stopped at several small doors, somehow disguised or blended into the exterior decor. We cracked them one at a time, gazing into a various bedrooms, a large courtroom, and several storage rooms.

"Ah hah," Lorenzo declared after about an hour.

My knees were killing me and I felt in bad humor. "Ah hah, what?"

"Smell that?"

"Why would the vile smell of mush make you so happy?"

"Because, Master Jak. Once more we are near the kitchen and our way of escape."

We cautiously crawled out the small door and stiffly stood. Was I ever going to know a day free of pain again?

After several false starts, we found the passage leading to the kitchen and slipped past it to the door we originally entered.

A pitiful wail met us as we turned a corner. It was the lard lad. He had spied Lorenzo and was prostrating himself on the floor.

"I have done as you ordered. I told no one. Please, your Arch Priest Comft. I am just a humble servant," he pleaded.

Lorenzo motioned him to his feet and said, "We leave for another secret ploy. Tell no one and your soul will remain with your body. Lock the door behind us."

I took a deep breath of the fresh air once we were outside. We pressed ourselves against the side of the temple, noticing that a sliver of morning sky was turning pink. We quickly shed our robes and for the first time I saw Mahvan wearing something other than a Pilgrim's garb. It was the rough attire of a caravan guard. She drew a cloth cap from her vest and began hiding her beautiful locks beneath it.

"I had been hoping you were wearing a dress," I sighed.

Chapter Thirteen

I burrowed deeper, hoping the villainous ogres torturing me would soon lose their interest. But the badgering and torment continued until I believed I could no longer survive the suffering.

"Come, Master Jak, it's rise and shine," Lorenzo's loathsome voice beleaguered me. He pulled away the blankets and I curled like an unborn child wanting only to remain in the warm haven of its mother's womb.

"By the gods," I protested weakly, "how can you be as cruel to bedevil me like this? Cannot you see I am near death?"

"Nonsense, you've had four hours of sleep. You just need some breakfast before your friend, Vil, arrives."

I stumbled from my cot to the washbasin where I doused my face. Looking up into a bewitched mirror, I flinched to see the image of someone recently dead. The specter looked just as shocked to see me. It was a ghostly white, with dark circles crouching beneath bloodshot eyes and hair that stood like the spikes on a morning star.

"Hm-m-m, maybe you could have used a little more sleep," admitted Lorenzo as he came to stand behind me and gaze at my grim reflection. "Still, a little food in your belly will perk you up."

"I do not wish to be 'perked up,' whatever that means. I just want to sleep a couple days."

"Don't whine, time's a wasting,' he urged me on.

The breakfast did help, but only a little. I was downing several cups of a hot liquid known for its rousting abilities. It was made from the leaves of a tree that only grew upon the sides of active volcanoes.

Our entire troupe, excepting Chaatiguin and Eli, circled the several tables pulled together near the hearth of the inn. The garb of a pilgrim was no longer a safe disguise and we could think of no other that would adequately hide the Gespe maiden.

Osyani was on a chair next to me, excitedly pacing back and forth in anticipation of the next scrap from my plate. She had grown even more over the night. Across the table was Baron Garsten Stee Hragen, sampling a variety of breakfast dishes in such numbers that the serving wench was kept busy running back and forth to the kitchen.

The obnoxious Lost Elf, Ebert, was far enough down the table to avoid conversation.

Mahvan was to my right, but she seemed more restrained than usual. She was still in the clothing of a caravan guard and kept the cloak pulled closely about her. Even Jennair seemed withdrawn.

Olmsted and Lorenzo were to my right, and my half-brother was noisily decimating a plate of boiled ham hocks.

"Jako?"

"Yes," I answered, still not used to having the harplet learning to speak.

"What be that?"

"It be a chair," I replied with more patience that I felt. Osyani had been chattering nonstop with her questions. Twice I made to rebuke her, but each time I turned my head and saw those trusting brown eyes looking back at me.

"Master Jak, I am pleased to see you are up."

It was Vil and he was escorted by several city guardsmen.

"Would you excuse your friend for just a moment and I will have him back before the sausage is cold."

I groaned to myself and pushed away from the table, the movement awakening several complaints in my back and knees. I followed Vil outside and the bright daylight sent needles into my eyeballs.

"You do not look well, Master Jak. Too much of the ale last night?"

"Yes, that is my misfortune," I agreed, and wished my pain was just from a bottle.

"Well, I have just the assignment you need."

I eyed Vil with suspicion. "Just what kind of task fits a man with a hangover?"

"One that calls for hair of the dog," he laughed. "I would that you loiter in some of the more unsavory drinking establishments and garner overheard conversations and bits of gossip that might be of interest.

"I know it be a vague mission, but our established sources are as dry as the Hvelt Steppes. Most our agents do not fit in those surroundings as well as you. Here is something to only exhibit if you are having serious trouble with royal authorities. It identifies you as under liege to me."

Vil handed me a small golden coin. One side was blank, the other only reading "CIA."

"This looks easy enough to counterfeit," I noted, rubbing the written side with my thumb.

"There is more to it than meets the eye," replied Vil.

"Magic?"

"Yes."

I placed it in my pocket and looked at Vil warily, trying to judge his character. He had always seemed honorable and on occasions in school, even seemed to pick me out for friendship. Several times he sprang for a supper when my own pockets were bare.

"Remember that favor I asked about last night?"

"Certainly, but I did not take you for the sort who would want such wear."

"There is someone I would like you to meet. But only you, not your storm troopers," I spoke in a low voice.

He cocked his head and returned the probing stare. He had been good in class. Was he detecting anything about last night? I was a fool for arousing his curiosity.

"I do have one question?"

"Yes?" I replied cautiously.

"Just what are you doing with a baby harpy on your shoulder?"

~ * ~

I knocked gently on the door and spoke softly, "Eli, Chaatiguin? It is Jak. I bring a friend who can help."

We slid through the partly opened door. I could tell I had piqued Vil's curiosity. I recognized the probing look of a trained private inquisitor as he looked about the room before his eyes settled upon Eli. I knew the alien garb was puzzling Vil as much as it had me.

"Chaatiguin," I spoke, "will you come out and meet Vil? He can help us."

She moved shyly into the room from a small storage area. Chaatiguin merged with the light streaming in from the window and she seemed to blaze like a golden mirror. Vil gasped but quickly regained his composure.

"Greeting, Vil," the Gept maiden's musical voice chimed.

"Good morning, Chaatiguin," he replied softly.

His gaze went back and forth between Eli and Chaatiguin.

"You do have a puzzle for me, Jak. And some still remains. But I take it this maiden is a Gespe?"

"Yes," I answered. "Eli saved her from being killed by hunters, though they murdered her family."

"Revolting. Such hunting must be stopped," Vil said as a frown clouded his face. "It is difficult to believe this trade has remained a secret for so long. There must be payoffs in high places. I will certainly investigate this once the king's matter is cleared.

"For now I advise you to keep her well hidden. There is a tempest swirling through the Temple of Dorga," he spoke as he headed for the door. "Rumors have it that Arch Priest Comft has disappeared and they blame it on agents of King Kenton. Now, without a high priest as well as

168

a sacrificial victim, they flounder about like headless harpies.

"Oh, sorry," he apologized to Osyani as he shook his head. "You keep odd company, Jak. But what I say is that the followers of Dorga are restless and there are rumors they will soon scour the city for a sacrificial replacement and no maiden will be safe. Someone like Chaatiguin would make for a rare offering."

There was plenty of food for thought while I leisurely walked the streets, seeking an interesting tavern. I had made sure Hazel was well stabled and was now in no hurry to do the King's work, though I was thirsty.

A sign reading "The Boar's Ninth Teat" drew my attention to a tavern. If the eight teats on a boar are useless, I surmised, then a ninth would be even of less value. I walked into a small establishment slightly smoky from the fireplace. A large kettle of soup simmered over the coals, creating a wonderful aroma. The establishment had a homey feeling I liked.

"I will have a pint," I told the elderly woman who came to my table.

"Oh, Kaasta, come here quick. Look what this gentleman has," she shouted over her shoulder.

I had brought Osyani. There was not much of a chance that I could blend in with the crowd accompanied by a harpling, but I really didn't care, having been drafted unwillingly into royal service.

A small girl about eight or nine appeared and her eyes lit up at the sight of Osyani. Kaasta ran across the room clapping her hands and shouting. I thought the ruckus would set the harpling's feathers a ruffle, but she also danced excitedly upon my shoulder.

Osyani had never seen a little girl and it appeared the harpling had been waiting for just such a playmate. The harpy chick took to the air and fluttered about the child before landing at her feet.

I drank my ale and watched the two dash about the room. The old lady obviously doted on the little girl, whom I took to be a grandchild.

"Eye, nose, ear, mouth," Kaasta chanted as she taught Osyani the words. She clapped with glee each time the harpling successfully repeated her.

I was not going to be finding information in a neighborhood tavern such as the Boar's Ninth Teat. Needed was a more sinister establishment that catered to thieves, brigands, highwaymen, and assassins--the kind of taverns I normally frequented in Duburoake.

The child pleaded with me to allow Osyani to stay and play. Since the harpling was enjoying herself, I agreed to return for her in several hours.

I let my instincts guide me as I wandered though the streets. The mood of the neighborhood began to change. Within minutes I knew I was in an area I dared not brave after dark.

A shadowed doorway caught my attention. I wore the drab uniform of most travelers--plain canvas tunic and leggings, a nondescript cape, and sturdy walking boots. Yet all eyes followed me across the room as if I had ridden Hazel into the tavern. There was an edgy air about the place I did not like.

I ordered my pint and went to sit at a corner table. There was no chance of striking up a careless conversation in this tavern.

One sullen lump of lard looked over at me and muttered, "Yer not a Dorgian, are you?"

It is the height of bad taste to ask strangers their religion, but I wasn't feeling up to teaching the knave his manners.

"Do I look so?" I curtly asked. Followers of Dorga do not let their hair grow as long as mine.

He grunted and went back to a glass of some rank concoction that I could smell from even my table. I had the feeling it was a good thing not to be a follower of Dorga in this dark den.

"They be stealing women for their awful rites," he restarted the conversation.

"Ah, the bastards. They are devils."

"Yer telling me," he agreed. "Things are going crazy, what with the Dorgians, our king, and the Ayerians running all about the city."

I tried not to show my concern. There was little chance that I would stumble so quickly onto my quarry. I knew the king was flooding the city with agents, both professionals and idiots like my old classmate, Ferred Kloppenhorsh. Word was out about the search and any stranger was suspect. Was this a trap?

I tried not to be obvious as I examined my surroundings, taking in the clientele with what I hoped look like a bored glance. They all seemed what they appeared to be, hopeless dunces and simpletons leading meaningless lives while bent on annihilating their livers with rotgut liquor.

My neighbor seemed surprised I wasn't taking the bait.

"Yah know, I have some information that could be very valuable. For the right coin, I be willing to talk about it," he offered.

I let out my breath. It was just a pathetically bad con artist looking to pull a swindle. I'd been recognized as a private inquisitor or a king's agent. The others must be throwing money all over the place. I would find nothing out in this tavern. Nodding my head, I quickly exited and continued my walk.

An hour passed and five or six times I spied what appeared to be Ayerians but in Glavendale garb. This was not all that singular since many people take on the clothing of their adopted country.

I stopped and scratched my chin. Was it a coincidence that each of those men were walking west? Not one had been heading in a different direction. I continued my stroll and began following another young man I believed to be a hillman. He was dressed as a farmer, but had the gait and complexion of someone from the East Mountains. He also had a suspicious bulge beneath his cape. What would a tiller of grain be doing with a sword?

The shadowing took me into an old section of the city with narrow, winding streets and tumbled down fountains. He led me to a walled courtyard. Within was a decaying mansion surrounded by a wilderness of weeds and old, misshapen trees. The young man looked cautiously about and opened the iron gate enough to squeeze through the gap. I waited a dozen heartbeats before following and reached the gateway to watch him running up a buckling brick path to the manor house.

I followed through the entry and made my trek not by the walkway, but by way of the courtyard's wild vegetation, using every bit of hedge, bush, and clump of weeds for cover.

It wasn't until I had almost reached the mansion that I paused to take stock of the situation. Did I really want to risk my life for a depraved old monarch who would have been hanged long ago if it were not for him being royalty? Didn't I hope in my heart that these hillman were successful? But if they were, would Vil still help Chaatiguin?

I hugged the ground even closer. Several more Ayerians trotted by to what could only be the hillmen's headquarters.

I now knew what all of the other king's agents did not--where the assassins' den was. That was enough exertion for one day, I decided, and was turning to work my way back to the gate when I spotted another visitor. I hid behind the stump of what once had been a giant of a tree, the hollow trunk big enough to hold a table and a half dozen card players.

I wasn't overly shocked by the identity of the latest guest. There were just too many strange things going on to continue being too amazed by any one incident. It could have been the king himself and I would have just shrugged my shoulders. Still, I have to admit I was just a bit surprised to see the Lost Elf. He wasn't skulking, but strolled by as if he were a welcomed guest on the way to a ball. He was met at the corner of the manor house.

"The King leaves soon with Queen Elay. He fears an upcoming battle with the followers of Dorga," I heard the Lost Elf tell a young hillman.

My retreat quickly took me back to the Boar's Ninth Teat where I picked up Osyani. The harpling was tired enough that she didn't complain about being separated from her new friend. She was fast asleep on my shoulder before I had walked but two blocks. She was becoming almost too heavy to comfortably carry in such a manner.

Just what did all this mean? There were more than enough curious occurrences during the past week to dwell upon. I ran several puzzles through my mind while traversing a farmers' market. An old lady shoved a plucked chicken under my nose and a servant girl smiled shyly at me as she made her way home with a basket of liver beans and salted fish.

Mahvan was somehow connected to it all. She was obviously from the East Mountains, no matter how she tried to disguise her birth. I was willing to wager she was also an Ayerian and bent upon the destruction of King Kenton as much as any of her male kinsmen. Was she a cousin to Queen Elay, a former lady in waiting, a sister, or wife of a slain guardsman? But who of them would be trained as an assassin? Where did the Lost Elf come in?

These chafing notions engaged me to where I hardly noticed the crowd thinning or the street narrowing into a crudely cobble-stoned alley. A flicker from the corner of my eye barely nudged my awareness, but the following shadow speeding over the irregular stones caused me to drop to my knees just as quickly as would a boot to the head.

Greedy talons grazed one shoulder and I heard the frustrated shriek of a very disappointed harpy. It was Osyani's mother, bent on revenge. The harpling had taken to the air and was defiantly spitting and hissing above my head.

I quickly struggled to my feet and ran toward the open door of a small eatery. The swoosh of air from the harpy's wings sent me diving through the entrance and rolling across the floor. I lay, gasping for breath, heart pounding, while little Osyani landed in the doorway, chirping loudly with wings spread as if to block her mother's entrance.

"And to think I thought I had problems at home."

I lifted my head to see Dun Leaberman drinking ale and snacking on a plate of spiced fish heads.

"Aye, she is a real harpy," I replied as I stiffly rose and slapped the dust from my tunic.

"I believe she takes after her mother," Dun observed of the harpling while peeling the last bit of flesh from a fish head with his teeth.

He tossed it over his shoulder and two miniature wyverns scrambled to beat each other to the booty. The crunching sound of bone followed.

"But she has my eyes." I wearily pulled a chair out from Dun's table and sat. Just how many more of these batterings could I take?

"How is the luck? Any revelations?" I asked.

"Not much," the bondsman replied with a detectable guardedness. "And you?"

I shrugged my shoulders. Dun threw another head over his shoulder, but before it hit the floor, Osyani snatched it in midair. The two wyverns, their wings clipped, squealed with indignation as they followed beneath her across the floor.

Osyani dropped the morsel after discovering it stripped of all meat and the two wyverns fell to fighting over the scrap. Before I could open my mouth to scold the harpling, she flickered over Dun's plate, snagged a fresh fish head, and was across the room.

"Osyani!" I rebuked. "Bring that back."

Dun laughed and shook his head. "She can have it. This be the first time I have had a harpy share a meal with me."

I nervously looked to the door. I was more or less certain Osyani's mother would not dare enter the inn. Harpies are said to fear human abodes, but then they are also said to shun cities and yet I could see a ruffled one perched menacingly across the street on a giant wooden tooth proclaiming the services of a barber and dentist.

"I have scoured the rathskellers favored by many of my clients, yet no one seems to know of these hillmen," Dun finally said as he picked his teeth with a carp rib.

"No doubt they shy from public places least their identities be discovered."

"This would be true," he admitted. "But I also have my people checking on resident Ayerians hosting strange visitors, and this too has produced no results."

"It is a puzzle."

Dun stared at me as if weighing me in balance then leaned

forward to softly say, "There are some who care not if this puzzle be answered. You are of Duburoake. I know you westerners hold no high esteem for the king."

It was my turn to weigh Dun. Was he a plant by the CIA, wanting to test my loyalty? But Vil already knew my feelings.

"There are some who think King Kenton goes too far with his vile amusements," I answered. "I find his doings with the Ayerians as unkingly."

"Master Leaberman," called a young boy from the doorway.

The pager's unexpected appearance made me jerk in my chair. I could see over his shoulder that the harpy still perched across the street.

"You have someone in need of bail," continue the boy. "His wife be waiting at your office."

"Damn, I cannot even eat without my pager interrupting me," Dun muttered. "Tell the kind woman I will be right there."

He looked at me as he was rising from his seat. "We have strange times now in Stagsford. It must be even more the quandary for those not familiar with the royal city. Take care, Master Barley, not to become entangled in the many webs that are now being woven."

I watched the private inquisitor/bail bondsmen stop at the door and look hesitantly at the harpy across the street.

"I believe she has a quarrel with only me," I said. "It appears she takes an affront to any prey that escapes her feminine charms."

"Strange days," Leaberman muttered as he went out the door.

Once he was gone, Osyani came fluttering back to the table and landed by the plate of fish heads. I gave her a stern look and she gazed back with the innocent eyes of a child.

"You must not take from others plates without first asking," I chided her.

"No?"

"No."

"I sorry, Jako."

"Just that you remember this. You are getting too big to act like a baby. Proper dining etiquette is very important in polite company."

"Et-t-t...etiquette?"

"How you act correctly with other people."

"I will, Jako."

I forced myself not to roll my eyes. If the patrons of the King's Wart Inn could hear me giving lessons in decorous supping to anyone, let alone a harpling, I would never be able to show my face there again.

I sighed and motioned for her to eat from the plate. She picked up a fish head in one small bird foot and began daintily chewing. At least there was no need to teach her how to correctly use tableware since she had no hands.

I looked up to see the innkeeper frowning from behind the counter. Not everyone is amused at the sight of a harpling dining on fish heads.

"You best be off when it has finished those fish heads," he growled. "I do not want me regular patrons appetites to be repulsed by such freaks as you be."

I eyed the cretin. He stood not much taller than me, but he was stout of shoulder and had a face that looked to be no stranger to knuckles and boots. I especially did not like his piggish little eyes.

Osyani was too enraptured with her feast to have heard the villain's prattle. I still wasn't sure how much she understood.

I shut my eyes for a second and began to count to ten, not needing any more bruises or scrapes. He interrupted me at four.

"And make sure it does not foul the table."

I stood slowly from my chair as not to draw the harpling's attention from her repast and walked to the bar.

I eyed the oaf again and didn't like what I saw. Closer up, my inspection led me to believe I was facing a veteran of back-street brawls and outright pillaging and rape. I believed I could take the brute, but not in a fair fight, and it was unfortunate that this wretch looked too well versed in such vile engagements to be taken by surprise.

I leaned over the counter and almost whispered, "Listen, you who should not find a half-chick, half child, so amiss when it is obvious you are the fruit of a union between a swine and a woman, a woman already condemned enough by the pig rape without having to give birth to a feeble-minded and vexatious monstrosity like yourself. Does your wife know of your wee redheaded miss? Do the king's taxmen know of your felonious behavior in purchasing wine that has not been tariff paid? And are the king's men aware you are a deserter from the militia, most likely caused by a cowardly attribute inherited from your tusked father?"

Ha! I struck a nerve with most or all of my deductions. He was swiftly turning pale. I would not have to batter his lumpy head with his own benches after all. My pricks had deflated him like a fish bladder.

I will admit that though I have a talent of unveiling a man's past, I am not always as sufficient in predicting their future actions--such as in this instance. The knave reached under the counter, pulled out a short cudgel studded with bits of jagged glass, and took a vicious swipe at my head.

He missed, barely. I back-pedaled into a table and was almost shredded by a second swing after he jumped the bar. I ducked under the table and rolled to the other side. This tactic was good but for a fleeting moment. The villain kicked the sturdy table out of his way as if it were a child's furnishings.

"You will never live to voice your croakings, you misbegotten sneak, I vow that," he roared.

"I do not presume there is anyway we could discuss this matter like civilized men?"

Another vicious swing of the cudgel was answer enough. I continue to sidestep between tables and he continued to kick them out of his way.

"I must warn you that I am a private inquisitor on King's business," I shouted while holding up both thumbs at chin level. "And that I also am versed in Kim Chi, such a deadly form of unarmed combat that I must register my thumbs as weapons."

He was not intimidated and prepared for another swing.

"No, Osyani," I yelled.

The harpling brushed past the rogue's face, leaving small talon marks across his cheeks. It was enough of a distraction for me to dart in and aim a robust kick between his legs. It might not be looked upon as sporting among the king's knights, but it sufficed for me.

The innkeeper bent in pain and I broke a chair over his back. He disappointed me again by not falling. He straightened up, his face now a fire-red and wearing a ferocious scowl.

There was but one thing to do--run. It was only after I was out in the streets that I remembered the harpy. She launched herself with a gleeful shriek. I braked and pivoted, only to face the enraged innkeeper chasing with raised cudgel.

I dropped and rolled to the side just as the harpy thunderbolted over me, crashing into the pursuing oaf. I leaped up and took off running with just one brief glance over my shoulder to see the two careening about the street like drunken lovers in some frenzied dance.

I stopped several blocks away in a small park and took a deep drink of water from the fountain. Osyani landed beside me and bobbed to take a few sips. She then wet the feathers of her wings and fluttered about to dry them.

"Etiquette?" she chirped.

"What?"

"That etiquette with man?"

I looked at her with what I hoped was a deadpan face.

"No."

"No?"

"No."

I mopped sweat from my forehead with the cuff of my tunic. She continued looking up at me as if for an answer. I resorted to what my stepfather continually advised.

"Just do as I say, not as I do," I said and quickly stood to continue our trip back to our inn before she could ask more questions. The harpling landed on my shoulder and we walked the rest of the way in silence.

"There you are," Olmsted greeted us as we entered the inn. He was seated at a table eating turtle fritters. I turned to eye Osyani who was hungrily eying the fritters.

"Etiquette?" she asked.

"Yes."

She looked disappointed, having not had time to finish Leberman's meal.

"How be it with you, brother?" I asked as I took a seat.

"Disappointing," he sighed. "I am afraid this year's convention has been ruined by the uproar. The hall was almost empty when I gave my presentation on 'The Detection and Conviction of Brigands, Embezzlers, Highwaymen, Swindlers and Assassins Through the Modern Science of Alchemy.' I am afraid most of those registered have been drafted into the King's service."

"That is ill luck. Perhaps you can present it again next year."

"And you, have you made any progress?"

"Yes, I have uncovered the nest of our hillmen at an abandoned estate."

I heard a gasp and I turned to see Mahvan carrying two mugs of ale into the room. A wet circle on the table in front of me, the exact size of the mugs she carried, said I was now in her seat. She quickly covered her shock and continued across the room. I stood and motioned for her to sit.

"I must go scour the day's dust from me," I excused myself. "It has been an arduous day."

Olmsted noticed Osyani's gaze at his plate and he motioned for her to help herself. The harpling looked at me for direction and I nodded approval. She hopped to the table, delicately gripped one strip of deep-fat fried snapper and turned to roost on the back of an empty chair.

I left the small group to climb the stairs and follow the narrow hall to my room. Rummaging through my traveling pack, I pulled out a clean, if not wrinkled tunic, and a pair of cotton leggings. The servants had left a tub of water in the corner and though it was not warmed as at the Duke's lodging, it looked clean.

I was pulling my dirty tunic over my head when I was slammed with great force from behind and fell face down on the bed.

Cold iron was pressed to my throat before I could struggle and a familiar voice said, "Do not tussle with me, Master Jak. for I would not enjoy cutting your throat."

"Ah, I do not suppose you are here because you would like to bathe with me?"

"No."

"Bed sport?"

"No."

"You heard me tell Olmsted I had found the hillmen's warren?"

"Yes."

There was an uneasy minute of silence. I was pinned down in an uncomfortable manner, arms tangled in the tunic, and my face covered.

"Now what?"

"That is the query," admitted Mahvan. "I have come to like you, ferret..."

"Private inquisitor."

"I have come to like you, Master Jak, and I am faced with a quandary. You have saved my life and we have been trail companions, but I cannot let your information reach the ears of the king's agents. How many others know of this?"

"Dozens. It is all over streets. How else would a blundering private inquisitor like me hear of it?"

"I do not believe you."

"If you are going to kill me, at least let it not be like a bound hog," I tried asking in a steady voice.

"You deserve that much, but I was told by a classmate of yours, Ferred Kloppenhorsh, that you are all trained in the martial art of Kim Chi and must register your thumbs as weapons. I would be a fool to unloose you."

"He is a banty rooster crowing nonsense," I argued as best I could with my face pressed against the mattress. "Besides, I almost flunked the course. I think I had the flu that fall. And, ah, my thumbs are too small. It is not something a man likes to talk about, especially to a beautiful woman, but..."

"Quiet."

Cool heads prevail. So taught my private inquisitor instructors, but once again I doubted they had ever found themselves in such a spot. A blade to the throat and a knee firmly placed in the small of the back does place a restraint on one's responses.

The bed creaked as I felt the blade and knee removed. Fearing the knife had been withdrawn for the fatal plunge, I curled then released my self like a taunt spring. The action flung me across the bed and I hit what must have been the headboard then dropped to the floor in a battered daze.

"If you continue as such, Master Jak, I will not have to slit your throat. I was letting you free."

I felt my tunic pulled off my face and looked up into Mahvan's beautiful blue eyes. They didn't look like the cold, hardened eyes of an assassin.

"That was just a ruse for a counter ploy," I replied and pushed myself up on still-entwined elbows to kiss Mahvan on the lips.

She froze then jerked her head back in surprise. "I should have known not to trust a man with small thumbs."

I sat up and completely removed the tunic.

"Master Jak, you play with rough company."

She was talking about the number of assorted bruises and scrapes covering my torso.

"You know what they say--no bruising, no improving."

"What am I to do with you?" Mahvan inquired as she sat on the bed and looked down at me with hands folded over the knife in her lap. "Do you know who I am?"

I stiffly stood and sat next to her. "You are an Ayerian who plans to kill the King. Those hillmen are your kin."

She smiled sadly and traced a yellowing bruise on my shoulder with a fingertip. I looked with suspicion at the dagger.

"Do not worry, I could not kill you. Though I may still be forced to take some action to prevent your news from spreading."

"Is this but some sick excuse to tie me up? I have heard you hill maidens are into that kind of sport. But tell me, how is that oafish Lost Elf involved in this?" I asked.

She laughed. "Still jealous of an elf."

"Jealous of that twisted midget? Hah. I ask because I would know what business he had at the hillmen's lodging today."

"What?" Mahvan responded and pulled her hand back in surprise. "You saw this?"

"He was at the mansion today and met by the hillmen as a friend."

She rose and began pacing about the room, then turned to me,

"You have told no one of what you found today?"

"No."

"Why?"

"I did not relish being impressed into this service."

"And how long will this peevishness last?"

"How long do you want?"

"Do ferrets..."

"Private inquisitors."

"Do private inquisitors so easily ignore their duty to a client? Is there not some code of conduct you break?"

I leaned back on the bed, grateful to relax my aching body.

"We do when it conflicts with a previous patron."

"Who is this?" she asked in suspicion. "What other party has hired you?"

"Why, lady, you. Do not you remember asking for my service while we were on the road?"

"Aye, I do remember. But I also recall you gave no answer."

"You were most likely not listening close enough. I consider myself pledged to aid you."

She sat back down at the foot of the bed. "Am I a fool to trust you?"

"No bigger the fool than one who enters the cursed temple of Dorga to rescue an acquaintance of only several days."

"There be that. You know but little of me. I wonder if you would still serve me if you were aware of all my secrets."

I hesitated before I spoke. I have found out, as with those thieves who left me dangling in the wind, that it is sometimes wiser not to reveal all of what one glimpses. I had deduced much of Mahvan during these past few minutes.

"I know you are yourself royalty--probably very close kin to the queen, that you are unaccustomed to the social company of men, and yet you spent your early years around many. You began your training at a young age, yet sometimes question the path you now travel. And you are here against the wishes of the other Ayerians to the point you could possibly be a criminal."

"And I know," I continued, "that I do not particularly like the way you now trifle with your blade."

She looked down at how she was restlessly rolling the knife in her hand.

"Maybe it is unwise for me to remain too long in your company, ferret... Yes, I know, private inquisitor. You see too much. At first I doubted your skill because you flaunted the role of a witless scoundrel, which I now can see it is a charade for you to hide behind."

I didn't know how to accept the praise, if that's what it was. Witless scoundrel? Charade?

"Ah, yes, I often do that. It is not to my advantage to let all know what fine skills of deduction and probing cleverness I possess."

Mahvan laughed and clapped her hands. "Oh, you do that so well. I could still almost believe you are but a foppish clown."

"It is a talent," I reluctantly agreed. Foppish clown?

"But you do not always keep your secret well covered--as with that harpling. I have watched you with the creature. It was partly because of your care for the orphan that I came to believe I could trust you. That and Jennair testifies for you."

"But tell me," she continued, "how do you know this of me."

I chewed on my top lip and paused for a moment. I should know by now not to explain my deductions since though I am always correct, I commonly reached these conclusions by erroneous routes. Jennair once said it was almost magical how I drew buckets of sound answers from the wrong well.

But this time, I hoped, the explanations were too obvious to be wrong.

"It was not difficult," I began. "Even one not trained as a private inquisitor would be able to reach the same conclusions. You carry yourself as someone of high birth and traces of court speech find themselves into your speech. Your right ear near the top still bears the pierced traces of where were once four rings--the placing and number common to a fad practiced several years ago by young members of surrounding royalty.

"Only one trained from early childhood moves and fights as capably as you. Some of your weapons are quite esoteric--such as the arched dirk of the Sippian Desert Tribe and the razor wire once common among death priests. These are not the weapons of a novice.

"I have also watched you among men and you appear uneasy when the occasion calls for affable interaction, finding it difficult to make the smallest of talk. But you are not intimidated by men. When you do converse, you stand closer than do women who have grown up in a royal court--as if you were a commoner--which I know you are not. But it is also a distance one soldier would unthinkingly stand before another.

"If you were here legitimately, you would have visited your kinsmen by now and know of the Elf. Why else would you not make yourself known to them?"

I had my fingers crossed and looked away to the window. I just knew she was going to tell me the pierced ears were curative practices of her village shaman or some such nonsense, and that she was a traveling muse before coming to Stagsford.

"Wonderful," Mahvan exclaimed. "You do make it sound so easy."

I glanced at her from the corner of my eye. She looked sincere.

"But tell me, how did you know I have doubts of my purpose?"

"That was the easiest of all," I said as I sat up next to her. "I could tell by the kiss."

This time she didn't jerk away. It was a strange kiss, both of us with hands by our sides. I was too fearful any move would frighten her away. We finally pulled apart to catch our breaths.

She looked at me solemnly, as if I were a riddle she couldn't unravel.

"Do you remember in the temple, when you asked me why we came for you?"

She nodded. "I said to not tell me some fantasy that it was because you were smitten with me."

"I..."

The door burst open and the harpling came flying through to plop on the bed then began bouncing just as a human child would do.

"Osyani, you must learn to knock, Come back here," laughed Lorenzo from the hall. The harpling flew to his shoulder. He then paused to look intently at me. "Geez, Mahvan. You should be a bit more gentle with our little private inquisitor. I know you warrior women like it rough, but this is ridiculous. He looks like a patchwork quilt."

I sighed and shook my head, too dejected by the interruption to say anything.

Mahvan's posture became rigid and she looked as if she could use the razor wire on Lorenzo. I watched with wonder as she slowly relaxed and even smiled.

"If you think my little ferret looks bruised," she said as she rose and went to the door to firmly shut it in Lorenzo's face, "you should see the teeth marks."

For the only time since I have met the mysterious wanderer, he actually looked surprised, though I doubt no more than I.

~ * ~

I was still sore when I woke, but for the first time in days I felt well rested. Osyani had awoken me and was sitting on my chest. I opened one eye to see her looking sternly at me.

"Jako, I had to sleep with Jennair. Why?"

"Ah, I think Jennair was lonely."

"You lonely? That why sleep with Mahvan?"

"Yes, well, that is sometimes done when you become older. You will understand this when you grow in age."

Osyani did not appear to be very understanding. She was still frowning. It made me think of Olmsted. Where had my half brother slept last night? I turned to see if Mahvan was still asleep and was grieved to see the warrior woman was already up for the day.

"I must bathe, Osyani. Go and tell the others I will soon be ready for breakfast. Tell them I said you may have what you crave."

The mention of food sent the harpling out the door in a burst of feathers. I quickly immersed myself in the tub, anxious to talk to Mahvan about last night. The life of a private inquisitor is not salutary to marriage, but I was ready to try. Let the patrons of the King's Wart Inn scoff at this sudden change in their drinking cohort, I thought as I pulled on the clean leggings. Their jeering would end soon enough when they saw her pull out the arched dirk of the Sippian Desert Tribes.

Jennair was in the hall as I reached the stairs. I cheerfully greeted her and went to pass by when she touched my shoulder.

"Jak."

I stopped and looked with curiosity at my half-sister. Her voice held a strange ring.

"Yes?"

"I woke during the night to see Mahvan packing her kit. She was of little speech and would not say where she was going. She wanted me to give this to you."

I looked down to see Jennair holding a bit of folded parchment. I turned and sped back to my room where I grabbed my canvas-cloaked scabbard from under the bed. I passed Jennair on my return and took the stair steps two at a time.

"Jak, do you not want to read it?"

"A private inquisitor has no need to read the obvious," I called back over my shoulder.

Time was of the most import. I rushed by the rest of my group as they took breakfast and was out the door before anyone could look up from their plates, except for Osyani, who darted from the table and caught up to me as I flew out the door.

"Go?"

"Yes."

I was about to order the harpling back to the inn when I realized how well suited her flying abilities would aid in the venture.

No stable hand was on duty and I saddled Hazel with a silent intensity. The old war steed snorted and looked at me with her large, brown eyes. She could tell something was amiss.

I knew the king planned to leave the capitol today because of a feared retribution by the Dorgians. Mahvan was obviously going to intersect with the departing group. I had to prevent the relentless maiden from taking her vengeance--which could only spell her own doom.

Hazel was obviously feeling coltish after her day of idle time. She trotted briskly into the street and her iron-shod shoes clapped loudly as I urged her into a faster gait.

It was a fine morning, one at any other time I would have enjoyed. A cleansing breeze from the mountains cleared Stagsford of its normal stench and the sky was a crystal blue. But I ignored all about me as I sped down the streets, heading to the Castle Raven, home of my illustrious king. I barely missed running down a very sluggish drunkard just stumbling from an alley. He cursed and waved his fist.

After riding several more blocks, I heard the stomach-twisting wailing of a constable's bugle. I looked over my shoulder to see a rather plump street patrol officer bouncing about on the back of an overburdened nag.

It was unlikely he could catch me, but if I took flight there was a risk of more constables joining the chase. I chose caution and reined Hazel to the side of the street, allowing him to pull up next to me.

"Do you know why I stopped yah?"

I eyed him in mock surprise. "You have forgotten already?"

"No, you be speeding, galloping in a trotting zone."

"I was only going as fast as the rest of the traffic."

He looked unmoved. "There be no traffic except you."

"See, they were so fast they are already gone."

"I would like to see your permit."

"Permit?"

"Riding permit."

I was nearing the end of my patience. While I dawdled here, Mahvan could be in dire danger.

"Since when do you need a permit to ride a horse?"

"Since last month. And you will need a commercial permit since that mare be at least 18 hands high. And what be that?" He was pointing at Osyani, who had landed upon a gas street lamp and was gazing down at us.

"A harpling."

"Do you have a permit for it?" he asked, taking a small ledger and chalk from his pocket.

"What are you talking about? A permit? Since when do harpies need permits?"

"It does not need a permit. You be the one needing a permit for a vicious and hazardous beast."

"Does she look vicious and hazardous to you?" I almost screamed at the dolt as Osyani watched in puzzlement. "And if you call her an 'it' one more time, I will take that slate you are writing upon and shove it somewhere most people would believe to be anatomically impossible."

"Keep speaking, you be only making it worse for yourself."

I slapped my forehead. Why was I wasting precious time with this oaf when I had the token given to me by Vil.

I fished about in my pocket and brought the gold medallion out and waved in it front of his face.

"See this? I am on official business of the King and this is a pass from the CIA. Now stop this blubbering and let me be on my way."

The patroller took a similar coin from his pocket and the two began glowing and pulsating in unison.

"It be real," he said in exasperation. "Why did you not show me this firstly than be wasting my time?"

I had a few choice words about wasting time, but I bit them back and nudged Hazel to be off. She went straight into a gallop and this time I pledged not to slow down for any more street patrollers.

Chapter Fourteen

The streets filled as the morning progressed and the castle drew nearer. I was forced to drop to a trot because of growing congestion.

Something was amiss across the river in the older section of the capitol. A stream of people was pouring across the wide, ancient bridge that linked old and new Stagsford. There were looks of worry in many faces, but no one showed signs of outright panic.

I urged Hazel onward and we were immediately surrounded by this river of humanity that crossed over the bridge rather than running beneath its stone arches.

"What happens that you flee Old Stagsford?" I asked an old man rushing past.

"The Dorgians are preparing to attack Castle Haven tonight or tomorrow. It is said they will come with wizards and battle priests, as well as their numerous followers," he huffed before being swept past me.

I looked ahead with despair. There was no way Hazel and I could make headway in this tide. Just as quickly my mood changed. I guided Hazel off the bridge and down to the river. The water looked sluggish enough and Hazel did not appear anxious as we stopped at the river's edge. Osyani hovered about my head.

"Go look for Mahvan," I shouted to the harpling then pointed to Castle Raven perched upon the top of grassy-sloped hill. "She may be about that castle."

"Castle?"

"Yes, castle. Like a very large inn. That one there."

"I look for Mahvan. I like Mahvan."

"Good. And return to me when you have found her. I will also be heading to the castle.

I watched as she crossed the river and again marveled upon the swiftness of her growth. Osyani now had the face of a six or seven year-old human girl and was as big as a large goose. She could no longer perch on my shoulder. Her rapid advancement, I knew, was due to the magical properties of harpies. It would not be long, it occurred to me, that there would be a need for proper clothing.

I was hoping Osyani had another apparent magical ability of harpies--tracking down people. How else had her mother found me? Thinking of the older harpy, I nervously glanced about the empty sky.

I sighed and ran my fingers through my hair. It seemed eons ago that I viewed Duburoake as a lusterless abode and had looked forward to the adventure of traveling to Stagsford. Adventures are not always that much fun, I decided as I considered the numerous aches and pains murmuring for my attention.

I urged Hazel forward and she began carefully picking her way across the river. The fording proved surprisingly void of incident. The water only once came to the large horse's belly, and I kept my feet dry by pulling up my knees.

A large park borders the river and I directed Hazel across it rather than challenge the crowded streets. I skirted a crowd of Dorga pilgrims also heading toward the castle, a ragtag mob good only for throwing stones or burning heretics. I came upon and tried circling another group of Dorgians, these more fierce looking and accompanied by warrior priests.

"That be he, the man at the door who left with Arch Priest Comft."

I turned to see the lard lad from the Temple of Dorga pointing at me. The heads of a dozen temple guards and almost as many priest snapped around in my direction. Yes, I was quite sure I abhorred adventures.

I rapped my heals against Hazel's flanks and she leaped forward, sensing my consternation. A couple dozen mounted Dorgians followed suit and the race was on. Hazel was in good shape, but she was an older horse and of a size not bred for speed. Several of the pursuers were swiftly closing the gap.

I burst through a small opening in a row of bushes to find myself once again on a city street. Hazel was forced to slow and chart a serpentine course through the maze of carts and people. One of the Dorgians was almost upon me, but heedless to that about him, he ran his horse into the side of a sausage vendor's pushcart. He tumbled onto the cart and slid to the ground where he screamed and tore at his tunic because of the hot grease.

I led Hazel down side streets in an effort to lose those still following. It didn't work. We abruptly pulled to a halt when a small street turned out to be a blind alley. Hazel spun about on her own to face the Dorgians, her lips pulled back in a ferocious grimace. She reared once as if to intimidate our pursuers by her sheer size and two of the following horses frantically braked and whinnied with fright. The others stopped at a respectful distance. I drew my sword.

"I warn you, we are both combat trained and you invite death to approach us," I admonished the followers of Dorga.

"Where is the Arch Priest Comft, you dog? Tell us or it will be you who greets death," bellowed a black-garbed warrior priest. His snarl almost showed as much teeth as Hazel's grimace.

I patted Hazel's shoulder in an attempt to calm the mare so she would not leap into the throng of attackers. It was unfortunate that there were too many of them for us to overcome.

"Ah, Arch Priest Comft. Why, he, ah, said he was tired of being a priest. Yes, that is it. Said he could not endure it anymore. He was going to run away and join the circus. Said he had some physical deformity that he kept hidden under his robe, but the abnormality would be quite fashionable in a freak show. His last words to me were, 'I be tired of living this lie. I crave to be me.'"

"To which fair does he journey?" asked one of the priests garbed in a brown robe, a slight fellow with yellowed teeth.

"Idiot," snarled one of Dorga's Hounds, who cuffed the lout along side of the head. "He lies as any fool can see."

The priest in black also motioned to several of the temple guards and they unslung bows and withdrew arrows from their quivers. "You must surrendered or we will shoot your horse out from under you."

It appeared as if I had no recourse--I knew it and they knew it--but Hazel did not. She was not pleased at being backed into a cramped corner by such puny nags. I was almost tumbled from the saddle when she reared forward, clipping the lead warrior priest's horse along side its head. The unnerved mount spun to the side, crashing into another horse. Chaos broke out.

The other horses were much more frightened of Hazel than I realized. I frantically clung to the battle mare as she plowed through the band, my pursuers too busy clinging to their own mounts to attempt stopping me. Hazel and I burst back into the street, almost bowling over a surprised street sweeper.

I turned onto another side street, then again and again, hoping not to find another dead end in the desperate attempt to lose the Dorgians. Occasional looks over my shoulder showed it was not working, but they were not able to close the gap due to the street bustle.

A narrow avenue abruptly opened into a pastoral landscape. It was the grounds surrounding Castle Raven. I at first gripped the reins to bring Hazel around and back into the maze of streets, but stopped and instead urged the giant horse onward. A column of Glavendale Cavalry was emerging from a nearby woods and I wildly waved a hand and yelled.

They wheeled about when they spied the pursuing Dorgians. Swords drawn, the horse soldiers came on in a mad gallop and rushed past me. The outnumbered warrior priests had no choice but to seek escape back into the teeming streets of Old Stagsford.

The troopers broke off the chase and circled back to where I waited for them. I held out the medallion Vil had presented me and a major sent a corporal to retrieve it for his examination. He then waved for me to approach.

"You be with the CIA?" he asked in annoyance. The officer was white in beard and gruff in voice with leathery skin that had seen too much sun and wind. He obviously did not think much of government snoops.

"I am a private inquisitor who has been asked to aid the royal agents."

"Hah, a ferret, Just as bad."

"A private investigator," I bristled back.

"Whatever. What did those Dorga devils want with you?"

"They know me to be on royal retainer and thought to gain information from me about King Kenton. I hear they plan hostile actions against His Majesty."

I wasn't about to tell him I had taken part in the Arch Priest's death while freeing a woman bent on the King's death.

"That rabble and their demon cleric may believe so, but before this week be over we will sweep them from the city and burn their temple to the ground. It be time that vile sect was driven from the city."

"I agree with whole heart," I replied. "Thanks be for the rescue. And now I must return to my investigations."

"Not so fast, ferret. You be returning with us to the castle. A call has gone out for such as you," the major informed me with little enthusiasm, probably wishing he was crossing swords with the Dorgian war priests rather than escorting some lowly private inquisitor.

"Ah, that is wonderful, but first I must track down one more tatter of lore then I can return for such a debriefing."

"The call is for your immediate trek to the castle," he said with a voice growing more bored. "No argument. Fall in along side the corporal."

Hazel was slightly winded from the chase, but kept perfect cadence with the other horses. She had been bred to carry heavily armored knights and therefore was much larger than these light-cavalry mounts, yet she appeared to enjoy once again being part of a cavalry formation.

I scanned the surrounding territory, trying to imagine how Mahvan or the Ayerians thought they could slay King Kenton. The small band was not up to storming the castle. Their plans must call for either entering the castle by guile or attacking the royal company as it left the fortress. This latest quandary might be a blessing in disguise, I thought, since I would soon be very close to the intended quarry--His Royal Majesty King Kenton.

The drawbridge began lowering as soon as the guards sighted our group. The horses thundered across the wooden timbers. We were in a large garden between the inner and outer walls. It boasted ancient elm trees and multitudes of flowering bushes. I was able only to get a glance at the rustic setting before passing through a second set of gates.

We crossed a large courtyard, also agreeably planted with a variety of foliage, before coming to a halt before a stone bridge crossing a second moat. It led upwards to the largest pair of doors I have ever seen, fit for giants. A soldier was assigned to see that I was taken to where the other private inquisitors were now billeted.

I was already thinking of how I would relate my visit to Castle Raven when I returned to the King's Wart Inn. It is a mythical edifice in Duburoake, so far away across the Megaoulas Mountains that few in West Glavendale have ever seen it, let alone gone beyond the front gates. I doubted the Duke of Duburoake had even been within the Castle Raven walls.

The hall I now traveled was impressive enough, with vaulted ceilings and velvet curtains framing the narrow windows cut through the thick granite stone. But it was not that much grander than in the Duke's castle in Duburoake.

Of course, this was a servant's area and the royal family's region would be almost beyond description--though I would try when I returned to my drinking mates. I would be handicapped by having never been allowed into that part of Castle Raven, but those at the King's Wart Inn would never have to know such petty details.

I was finally led to a large dormitory where a number of bunk beds lined one wall. The room was obviously used to periodically house soldiers and was now half filled with about a dozen civilians.

"Master Barley, I am so happy you were able to make the grade in receiving a king's commission--but from what I have observed here, they had need to scrape the bottom of the barrel."

"The bottom of a barrel--is that where you were hiding when we were attacked in the lift," I challenged Ferred Kloppenhorsh, recognizing his weasel voice without even turning my head.

"I would have rushed forward but was wedged in by the cowards in the lift," he huffed.

"If I remember right, just as big of a coward freed you from such an entrapment by forcing you to the front."

I ignored whatever feeble reply he had to make and continued crossing the room until I came to a bunk as far from Ferred's as possible. I lay down and wondered when they would feed us. My stomach was growling from having missed breakfast. With a guilty start, thinking of that hurried exit reminded me that little Osyani was now flying about by herself. I rose and walked to a narrow window. All I could see was a slit of blue sky.

"Master Jak Barley," called an official sounding voice. "You are wanted in the query room."

There was an elderly servant at the door waiting for me.

"Are not we first fed before we are questioned by some quill-pushing bureaucrat?" I complained.

The old man, garbed in the royal blue of Glavendale, slowed and turned to me. "You are not to be questioned by some bureaucrat. You will face Pater Ginn."

I stopped dead. "Pater Ginn? THE Pater Ginn?"

The servant was pleased with the reaction he had created. He smiled and answered, "Yes, Pater Ginn. The King has brought him out of retirement to direct the endeavors of the private inquisitors."

I could not believe it. Pater Ginn, the greatest living private inquisitor. A legend among all in the profession. As students, we were regaled with stories of his legendary skill. It is reputed that Ginn can pass a person on the street and with one glance know more about them than their own spouse or parents.

Pater Ginn, I repeated silently to myself almost like a prayer. Pater Ginn who solved the infamous Dwyjim murders and single handedly broke up the Fohm Family crime consortium.

The servant prodded me to step smartly and I continued to marvel that I was about to meet the fabled Ginn.

The servant gave me a sour look when I again stopped cold in my tracks. I was doomed. With one brief glance the master would discern everything about me--the knowledge I was hiding about the Ayerian soldiers and how I was staunchly aiding an enemy of the King.

"Oh, by the seven hellhounds of Brub, I think I am coming down with the plague," I cried, clutched my stomach then sank to my knees. "I see only darkness and feel about to swoon."

The servant was not impressed and he looked over his nose at me as I sprawled on the stone floor. "You be the third weasel..."

"Ferret," I snapped then corrected myself, "No, I mean private investigator."

"As I would say, you be the third weasel to collapse with some malady on the way to meet Pater Ginn," he continued.

"Egads, it must be an epidemic. I feel the black bile already tearing at my bowels. Such a vile contagion could easily rampage through the castle. Do not worry about me, save yourself and run for your life. I will try to crawl back to my quarters."

The servant remained unsympathetic. "Rise before I send for the guards and they be forced to drag you by your heels."

I staggered back to my feet, mumbling about the inhospitableness being shown an ailing agent of the king.

The servant rapped on a half-opened door and I was pushed into a dimly lit room. The windows were shuttered and only one smoky oil lamp was aflame. I squinted and waited for my eyes to adjust to the darkness.

"Leave standing there like a blinded bat and come forward," a dry, brittle voice commanded.

I slowly walked toward the light until I could just discern a bloodless, emaciated face hovering to the side of the flame. The closeness also permitted me to smell the staunch stench of cheap spirits, the same stature of rotgut served as the house wine at the King's Wart Inn.

"It is a pleasure to meet you, Master Ginn," I began, "You have always been a source of..."

"Make leave with the pig droppings," he interrupted. "You be Jak Barley?"

"Yes, Master Ginn. I am a graduate of..."

He impatiently waved his hand. "Have you gained any news of these Ayerian thugs?"

"Ah, I have not been able to espy any lore dealing with these ruffians. I have been to a number of Stagsford taverns, but I was rushed here before I could..."

"Tell me, Barley. Were you more engrossed in imbibing than spying for the King?"

I paused, worried he would see through my reluctance to be in his presence. I then recalled tenets supposedly attributed to Master Ginn himself. It is said--best admit and be beaten for a minor offense than exposed for a high crime and hung. The other was--the best shield be a striking sword.

"Yes, Master Ginn, I am a hopeless sot, addicted to the liquid reward of hops and wheat. They say confessing to this abhorrent foible is the first, most difficult step to recovery. I can say I have taken that first, arduous step, but it was at least ten years ago. It appears after that one I have stalled.

"As for yourself, even in this shadowed room I see the fissures and blotches covering your face that mark a life of lascivious actions and debauchery. It has aged you well before your time. Your rather garish clothes voice that you once considered yourself a ladies' man, but their current state of disrepair suggests...

"Quit your blabbering," he roared in a raspy voice and kicked out a chair from the darkness. "Hah, a rogue after my own heart. Sit and have a toast with me. Those other spineless worms come with empty heads and mouths gorged with sniveling excuses."

I was taken aback by this strange turn of events. He sat a bottle of wine and a goblet on the table holding the lamp. I cautiously took the seat and pulled closer to Master Ginn. I will admit my hands had slight tremors as I picked up the bottle.

I held the vessel to the flame before pouring. The label depicted a hound in the throes of a mouth-frothing convulsion. It was a particularly wretched juice known as Mad Dog, a wine best recognized for its prowess in causing projectile disgorging. It was with some reluctance that I filled my glass.

"Do not be a coddly babe on me," he said. "The only thing more favored by the gods than cheap wine is free wine. Salutation!"

I raised my chalice and tapped it against Master Ginn's goblet then took a sip and tried not to gag. It was only after I lowered the vessel that I clearly beheld the man's face. A cloudy stare declared his blindness.

"My eyes may no longer witness that about me, but I still have a sharp wit, nose, and ears. You have just detected my lack of sight."

"Ah, yes, Master Ginn."

"Do not let that affliction fool you," Ginn warned as he poured himself another glass. "I still be the master of private inquisitors. You are from Duburoake, a bastard, have a friend who works in a laboratory, and recently have been in the company of a harpy. Am I right?'

Pater Ginn was everything I had ever heard about him.

"Yes, but how could you behold that with no sight?"

He leaned back, momentarily fading into the darkness.

"Easy," he laughed crazily from the dark and slammed a hand down on the table, sending the lamp flame a sputtering, "Vil Hemloch told me."

I remained silent as he continued giggling, being rather

disenchanted with my childhood hero. I took a generous swig of the wine. Had he really degenerated into a drunken madman?

"So, now we pout?" Ginn said with wicked delight and leaned back into the light, his milky eyes gleaming in the flickering flame. "All right, Master Jak. You are in love and fear for a woman's life. You have recently been in the Temple of Dorga and most likely are connected with the Arch Priest Comft's disappearance."

I almost dropped the chalice but did choke on a gulp of wine. I coughed and had to wipe my lips with the cuff of my sleeve.

"And you are purposely withholding information on the hillmen. I would say it has something to do with the woman, but that is no great deduction since almost every thorn has something to do with a woman. You've been a busy lad, Master Barley. Oh, and you once had a dog named Phideoux."

"I will also give you one bit of advice," he whispered in a conspiratorial voice and leaned across the table. "Kill that asshole Elf."

I was fighting for speech. "How could you know of all this?"

He laughed again, knocked down the rest of his wine and said, "As with a stage illusionist, a private inquisitor seldom reveals his methods. Let us just say that I observe obvious signs an untrained eye will miss. Once explained, I am afraid my deductions would suddenly plunge from the realm of wonder to a more mundane plane."

I slapped my forehead and winced since I was still holding the goblet in that hand. Having uttered those very words for so long, I had almost come to think of them as my own. To hear them from the author's lips was overwhelming.

I refilled my glass.

"But, but how could you ever deduce I had a childhood dog named Phideoux?"

"Just a lucky guess," Ginn answered as he in turn opened another bottle of wine.

I slapped my head again, this time remembering to use the other hand.

The taste of the wine was improving. We sipped for a number of minutes and engaged in small talk.

"What will you do now that you know of my disloyalty to the king?" I finally had to ask.

"Who is disloyal to the king?" he replied with just the slightest slur to his voice. "I know of no one disloyal to the king. You must be mistaken. Here, take this."

The old man was holding a bit of parchment. Upon it was a royal seal and permission to leave the castle.

"Leave this city, Master Jak," Ginn said as he once more faded into the shadows. "This city is poisonous for the soul. Stay and you will end as I, an empty man about to leave an empty life. I hear before me the young man I once was. Remain earnest and be not blind to the one who loves you."

"Thank you, Master Ginn," I replied to the puzzling words. There was a slight catch to my voice since wine always makes me maudlin. "I have no intention of staying in Stagsford. My greatest desire is now to return to Duburoake. And even now I seek that lady."

"Stay one moment," Ginn unexpectedly ordered as I made to rise. I froze in surprise. The hero of my childhood stood on unsteady legs, either from the vast amount of wine or old age, and walked around the table.

He leaned into my face and said, "Did you know that just as a man separated from his own country will gain the slightest of foreign accent in a matter of months, just being amongst strangers can also subtly accent one's speech?"

I could hardly breathe because his stiff wine breath and his cloudy eyes were frightening, like eerie moons glowing during a foggy night.

"Ah, I have read of such in professional journals, but I..."

"It be true. Tell me, have you been of late in the company of a foreigner, one from a land beyond your knowledge?"

The wine had made me a bit dazed and his sudden intensity was disconcerting. Was he talking of Lorenzo Spasm? Would it be a betrayal to speak of him to Master Ginn?

"You have," roared Gin, at least as much as his raspy voice allowed. "His name be Lorenzo Spasm, am I not correct?"

My silence was no cloak to the master private inquisitor.

"Do not worry, Master Jak. I am no enemy of your friend. I only ask that you entreat him to visit me before he is again off on his wanderings. We met once many years ago."

I could tell Ginn was beginning to weary. He waved a hand in dismissal and tottered back to his chair. I paused at the doorway and looked back in more than just slight confusion. It had been a very peculiar discourse.

"Ah, Master Ginn. I would but ask one favor. Could you not give one hint on how you gleaned this knowledge of me?"

He looked up wearily from his table and smiled. "I will tell you, son, though I have not said this to anyone for many years. The reason I do not divulge this logic is that there be none. I have the blessing to be able to harvest sound answers like ripened fruit, but it is my curse that they are from the wrong vine. To explain my error-filled path of deduction would be to expose myself to ridicule."

He shook his head in self-mockery. "It is most difficult to believe, is it not?"

"Trust me, no. I guess we have more in common than you know. Of course, you now know this because you can deduct from my manner..."

"Please, Master Jak, be off with you. I need my rest."

I gently shut the door and stood in repose for a moment. Had that just happened? I am interrogated by Pater Ginn, legend, and he lectures me like a lost son? Maybe years of wine binges were taking a toll.

The wine on an empty stomach was making me feel a bit punchy. I decided it would be best if I filled that void with food. Clutching the pass given to me by Ginn, I started in search of the kitchen.

An occasional servant gave me odd looks as I meandered through the hallways, but they said nothing. Within minutes I was thoroughly lost.

Castle Raven was even larger than as seen from afar. As I traversed the numerous halls and stairways, I again considered the present state of affairs.

As long as the king was safely tucked away in his castle, I need not worry about Mahvan getting into trouble--I hoped. Would she attempt to enter the castle? It would be suicide, but was not she on a death errand? These and many other thoughts were twirling in my wine-sodden mind when distant voices snapped me from my reflections.

I cocked my head and held my breath. Were those faint voices echoing through the stone hallway familiar? I picked up my pace and soon found myself at an entrance to a large chamber encircled by mighty columns soaring to a distant ceiling.

The walls were encrusted with swords, shields, and tattered banners--most likely war trophies taken in bygone wars. Immense paintings depicted intimidating battle scenes with fierce warriors hacking, smashing, and cleaving their bloody way through waves of foes. Some artist had verily taken liberty with Glavendale's military history. As far as I knew, we'd lost every major battle of aggression and only preserved our national security because providence gave us mountainous borders, treacherous shorelines, and a land lacking in anything coveted by our more warlike neighbors.

My eyes finally fell upon a delegation crossing the alcove. I immediately recognized the portly figure of Baron Garsten Stee Hragen, Eli Smith, and a shrouded form that must be Chaatiguin. The Baron must be petitioning the King for the return of his family's trade route rights, while Eli and Chaatiguin were here to press the King on protecting the Gespe.

I bounded from column to column, staying concealed in the shadows. A retina of palace guards and royal ministers ignored the bantering Baron.

"I cannot believe I, Baron Garsten Stee Hragen, have been kept waiting this long without even a shred of sustenance. Is this what you call hospitality? I would whip my servants like dogs if they treated guests so."

One of the ministers finally turned and snapped, "Quiet. His Royal Majesty will soon be taking his throne and if you want to keep your blubbery gut in tact, you will silence that tongue."

We arrived at the end of the room where an opulent throne of gold and jewels was perched upon a raised platform.

"You will fall to your knees when King Kenton is seated," the group was told.

The Baron looked agitated at the thought, but only grunted. A door behind the throne opened and out poured a dozen of the King's guards dressed in silk court versions of their normal uniforms. They placed themselves at the bottom of the steps leading to the throne and froze with hands on the pommels of their swords.

"His Royal Majesty, King Kenton, Supreme Ruler of Glavendale is now present," shouted a page.

The King, of slight build and balding prematurely, made a swaggering entrance as everyone in the room dropped to their knees. I caught myself almost doing the same.

It was then I realized just what kind of situation I'd placed myself. I was for all intents and purposes spying on the king. With the castle on high alert because of the numerous death threats to King Kenton, how would it look if I were caught skulking about the shadows like an assassin? I hunched down and hoped the discourse would soon end.

The Baron spoke first in his usual flowery speech, but I could tell from the outset it was not going well. There was too much bluster to the Baron's speech. King Kenton was used to more groveling. He grew more impatient as his cousin continued.

"Yes, yes, Baron, enough. I will take it under advisement," the King interrupted in a bored voice. "And you, what do you beseech of His Royal Majesty?"

Eli, looking nervous as he twisted his odd hat in his hands, answered, "Your Majesty, I am here to ask that you right a wrong that has been done to citizens of your kingdom. They are being slaughtered and have no defense. I brought one of your inhabitants before you, that she might speak on her people's behalf."

King Trenton seemed more interested with the second half of the delegation, probably because of Eli's odd accent. He watched closely as Chaatiguin stood and dropped her robe. The sight of the fair Gespe maiden seemed to stun those present, even the stiff guards opened their eyes wide at the sight.

"She is a Gespe, Your Majesty," continued Eli, "and her people are being shamelessly butchered for their pelts."

"I ask, King Kenton, help my people," Chaatiguin appealed in her melodious voice.

I didn't like the way the King was eying the Gespe maiden. A lecherous leer grew on his face. I felt a shiver of dread and knew this would be of no good.

"Ah, a live Gespe maiden," the King almost purred. "I have been wanting one for some time."

Eli realized all was not going well and climbed to his feet, only to be grabbed by a pair of guards and forced back onto his knees.

The King snapped his fingers. "Guards, take my cousin and his friend to the dungeon until I decide their fate."

King Kenton looked to his personal guards and ordered them to escort Chaatiguin to his chambers. Eli tried struggling but more guards grabbed him, with one holding a knife to his throat. He watched in horror as the unresisting girl was led away, she clutching her robe in confusion. Then Eli and the Baron, surrounded by guards with swords drawn, were led in the opposite direction. I had expected the Baron to raise a howl, but he retreated silently, though scowling blackly.

I was bewildered as to what course to take. Both Chaatiguin and the other two were under heavy guard, making immediate rescue impossible. I finally decided to follow the Gespe maiden as she was in the more immediate peril.

I kept to the wall, partially concealed by the pillars until I was behind the throne and next to the entry the King had departed through. It wasn't locked and I slowly edged it open. The guards were down a long hall pushing Chaatiguin into a room.

"Please, my dear, you will find an assortment of garments in the closet more suited to such beauty than that rag you now wear. I will freshen up next door and return soon that you may enjoy my company," said the King in a voice more oily than that of a muskpig.

I watched as a guard locked the door. The King entered a second room and the guards marched off to disappear around the corner. I ran down the hall as quietly as I could, almost on tiptoe. I leaned down to examine the lock, pushing aside a cord that hung from a bell above the door. The lock was nothing special, probably at least 120 years old and a type I had practiced on while a student.

Pulling a small pouch from a secret pocket inside the bottom of my pant leg, I withdrew a number of metal slivers. Finding the one I wanted, I inserted it in the keyhole and began manipulating it about. My fingers trembled and I paused to take a deep breath. I was more taunt than I had suspected.

The lock finally clicked. I stood and gently opened the door and stepped through, only to have a porcelain plate smashed over my head. I fell to the floor in stunned surprise.

"Chaatiguin, it is me, Jak," I managed to gasp.

"Oh, I sorry," Chaatiguin cried and dropped to my side. "I sorry, I no know. I think king."

"I am all right," I assured her as I rubbed a new tender spot on my head. She helped me to my feet and I leaned against a small table laden with cheeses, breads, and sausages.

"We must get out of here quickly, before the King returns," I said while stuffing some of the food into my pockets.

I rifled through a closet looking for a dress suitable to disguise Chaatiguin, since she might be recognized in the robe as we made our escape. I found a fashionable riding gown that came with a hood. I urged her to quickly dress.

She hurriedly pulled the garb over her head and drew up its hood.

"Yoo-hoo, my Gespe maiden, are you preparing yourself for me. I will be with you in but a heartbeat," King Kenton's voice came through a door separating the rooms.

I quickly opened the door to the hallway, and closed it just as fast. The servant who had led me to Master Ginn was outside, most likely combing the castle for his lost charge.

"Here, take this," I whispered to Chaatiguin. "It is a pass to get out of the castle. Do not speak to anyone, just show them this and keep on moving. Go back to the inn and tell Lorenzo what has occurred."

I shoved her out the door and pleaded under my breath for whatever aid I could receive from whatever god I had not yet offended.

"I'm coming, my Gespe maiden," the King's voice grew louder.

I rushed to where Chaatiguin's robe was and quickly threw it on. The door opened just as I pulled the hood over my head.

"Ah, not versed in proper boudoir attire," the King murmured as he crossed the room. "That is agreeable to me. We shall have you in your natural pelt."

I turned away from the King and bent my head to shadow my face.

"Do not be shy, little one. You are about to be honored by the King. Step out of your robe."

I shook my head no.

"Do as your king says. Disrobe."

His voice was taking on a bit of impatience.

Again, I shook my head. I felt him place his hands on my shoulders.

"That will be fine. I savor a bit of roughness."

He began tugging ardently at the robe.

"Please," I said in a voice as high as I could pitch it, "You must not."

"And why, my little rabbit?"

Yes, why must he not? I racked my poor and bruised brain. "I be with child."

The King paused for but a moment then again began plucking at the robe. "It makes no difference what bread is in the oven as long as there is room for another loaf," he snickered.

And who said romance was dead? I was wishing to be once again hanging naked over the gorge. He surprised me with an extra vigorous tug and I fell to my back, the hood partially falling away from my face. The King looked down in stunned surprise.

"You be no Gespe maiden," he said accusingly.

"Yes, I be," I replied in falsetto.

"No, you be not."

"Yes I be."

"You have a mustache."

"All Gespe maidens have mustaches."

"Your face appeared smooth in the throne room."

"You be far away on big chair."

He then looked down at my feet which were now exposed.

"You have boots on."

"I find them in closet."

"There be no boots in that closet," he stated firmly, as if that was one thing he was certain of.

The King was growing angrier as we spoke. I climbed stiffly to my feet. He made to grab for the hood and I instinctively warded away his hands and brought both thumbs up into his sternum.

My gods, I thought in panic, what misdeed have I performed? In my panic and fatigue I had reverted to the deadly martial thumb art of Kim Chi.

The King sputtered and clutched his chest, his face first turning white then a pale blue. He was desperately trying to draw a breath, but my blows had struck vital nerves and his muscles refused to work. He sputtered one more time and dropped to the floor.

I was as if stricken myself by Kim Chi. I had just killed my king. I staggered back to sit on the bed. This was no time to loiter; had to make my escape before a hue and cry arose for the king's assassin. With shaking knees, I dragged the body across the floor and rolled it beneath the bed.

Running to the door, I stopped, changed my mind and headed back to the closet for a disguise. All the clothes were obviously those of the woman's and there were none left with hoods. I ran back to the door then spun away, knowing I would be stopped with no pass. But it was my only hope and I turned again for the door, once more to stop and turn. I was literally running in circles.

I forced myself to pause and take a deep breath. The king's wardrobe, I almost yelled aloud as the idea came to me. If Lorenzo could mimic the High Priest of Dorga, could I not be just as audacious?

The door between the rooms was still open and I rushed through it, frantically scanning the chambers until I saw a large oak wardrobe. Opening it, I found an array of royal wear. I looked for a male counterpart to Chaatiguin's riding garb. I finally came upon one and was just about to pull it over my head when the room went dark. Someone had silently entered the room and turned down the lamp. With the windows shuttered, it was as almost as dark as night.

"Oh, my King. I hear you have a new toy. I hope that does not mean you tire of me," a silken, seductive voice purred.

Just hearing the woman speak sent chills up my body. I listened as her light footsteps crossed the room. My back was turned to her and I felt two hands touch my shoulders in the same spots where so recently had rested the fingers of the corpse now under the bed. This embrace was by no means as repulsive.

"What odd garb do you wear?" the woman asked as she began unbuttoning my tunic, her warm breath caressing my ear.

As any good private inquisitor, I had taken voice lessons in Disguises 101. I displayed no dazzling talent at it, yet I had not been an apt student of Kim Chi and my blows dropped the King like a clubbed rat.

"I, ah, have taken a chill and put on warmer garb," I tried my imitation of the King with a hoarse voice.

"Oh, let me fortify you against the malady, my lord. Forget that Gespe child. Perhaps later I may join you in bedding the creature if she be as comely as they say."

This woman was no innocent maid, I thought as I struggled to find some way out of this calamity waiting to happen. The King and I are of the same build, but no woman, no matter how dark it be, would mistake a stranger for her lover.

She came around to the front and ran her hands down my bare chest then slipped the tunic from my shoulders. I felt her lips where her hands had just been. I only hoped she did not run her fingers through my hair since I had some where none grew upon the King's dome. I was thankful he also had a mustache when she kissed me on the mouth.

"Oh, what be this? You feel bigger," she exclaimed as she ran her hand down the front of my leggings.

"Ah, I think it be the fever and I swell from its poison. You best take care in case it be catching."

"I have just the cure, my lord," she said, her voice taking on a strange timbre. "It be cold steel."

If you're going to kill someone, an old instructor had once warned, do not chatter first. She gave me just enough warning that I managed to twist from her hold. She must have planned to stab me in the back and I felt a searing pain where the blade raked me down the side.

The woman pulled away to strike again and I wrestled her to the bed. I was in luck that I managed to grasp both her wrists. I had taken a class in fighting in the dark, but it pertained to stalking stealthily through the night, not grappling with a homicidal maiden bent upon sticking a dagger in my back.

She suddenly went limp. I kept a firm grip in case it was a ploy.

"Ah, was it something I said?" I asked, entirely confused as the abrupt turn of events.

"What do you wait for? Do you not feel well enough to rape me again? Why not call for your guards and have them assist as you have had need for in the past, though I would as soon you take this knife and drive it through my heart," she answered in anguish.

Now I was confused.

"Well?" she asked when I did not reply.

"I, ah, do not believe any of that is called for."

He body tensed again. I had answered in my own voice.

"Who are you that you are in the king's chamber?"

"I am a friend."

"I have no friends in Castle Raven."

"You do now. Just for argument's sake, if I were to release you, would you still endeavor to impale me with that knife?"

"What are your intentions?"

"I have none at the moment, except to be away from this castle as quickly as possible."

"If you speak the truth, you have no fear."

"Not that I do not trust you, but I would feel better if you would release the dagger."

There was a moment of silence before I heard the knife drop over the side of the bed and to the floor. I cautiously released her wrists and rolled off the bed. Tripping once over a footstool, I made my way across the room and turned up the lamp wick.

Even by faint lamplight, her comeliness made me catch my breath. Waves of black hair flowed off her shoulders and across her full breasts. Her pale face was that of an angel, though it now was marked by a fierce scowl. She could only be Queen Elay.

"Who are you?" she again asked.

"My name is Jak Barley, your highness, I am a private inquisitor who finds himself in a very tangled web from which he is actively trying to escape."

Her alluring dark eyes carefully examined me.

"Much a web it is if you are an unwelcomed guest in Castle Raven. But where be the King?"

"Ah, he is indisposed at the moment."

"Indisposed?"

"He is, ah, resting."

"Resting, where?"

"In the other room, your highness."

Queen Elay's eyes widened and they turned downwards to frantically search for the knife.

"But I can assure you that he will not be bothering you at this moment."

She stooped to pick up the dagger and replied, "Swines are light sleepers, Master Jak. I have tried taking the beast unaware before."

"This time he indeed will not be easily disturbed."

"You have drugged him?"

There was no mistaking the joy in her voice. She gripped the knife even tighter and began with determined strides to the door.

"That will not be necessary, your highness. King Kenton is dead."

She turned to me and her mouth silently shaped the word, "Dead?"

I leaped to catch the queen as she dropped in a dead faint. It was no chore carrying her slight form back to the bed. I waited until her eyes flickered open.

"Your Majesty, if we are to safely flee, we must make haste. I will help you escape."

I looked down at the almost transparent gown she wore and cursed the events that made me say, "You must go dress in something more appropriate for riding. There are suitable clothes in the other room."

She continued to tremble after I helped her to her feet.

"I will not wear the garb of the king's concubines. Wait but a second for me. I must put on my own attire," she ordered and was out the door.

I took a deep breath. This latest encounter had been the most stressful, though for entirely different reasons than the other perils. I had been unable to ignore the passion she roused in me. No wonder the Dorga priests had wanted her, and the King was unable to let her go.

What was I to do now? I rushed back to the bed and pulled on my tunic. I reached for the riding wear and again began pulling the soft green fabric over my head.

This time the silent intruder did not fool with the lamp. I was slammed down across the bed, the riding apparel still covering my face. Two knees pinned down my shoulders and I felt a knife pressed through the fabric against my throat.

"If I have need to kill you, I will King Kenton, but your miserable life will be spared if you give me what I want. Do you know what that is?"

I recognized the voice. It was difficult to speak with my mouth pressed against the bed, but I managed to mumble, "Ah, I do not suppose you are here because you would like to bathe with me?"

"No."

"Ah, bed sport?"

A firm "no" was accompanied by the knife pressing harder against my throat. "I want the bitch queen. If you..."

Her voice faltered. "What say you just now?"

"Ah, bed sport?"

With a ripping sound, I felt the garb cut away with one clean slice. Two strong hands roughly flipped me over and I was looking into the shocked face of Mahvan.

"Surprise."

"Jak, by the blood of Jyst, what are you doing in the King's chamber?"

"One might also ask the question of a young maiden. Are you going to let me up?"

She slid from the bed while retaining a tight grip on her knife. She looked about the room and asked, "Where be the King?"

"Ah, he is indisposed at the moment. I was just about ready to depart when you so tactlessly undressed me."

"Indisposed, what do you mean?" Mahvan was obviously feeling strained. Her breath came in nervous gasps.

"He is not feeling well and is resting in the next room," I answered, feeling as if I had just had this conversation.

"He is here?" she gasped and brought forth a second knife as she retreated across the room to the open door.

She looked at me with suspicion. "He is not on the bed."

"Ah, he is resting under the bed."

This time her expression was that of someone conversing with a madman. "Do not jest with me, Jak. Where be the King?"

I sighed and shrugged my shoulders. "Take a look."

Mahvan acted as if she feared turning her back to me and sidled uneasily across the room. Dropping to one knee, she lifted the bed covering with the knife in her left hand.

"It is the King. He is under the bed!" she exclaimed in amazement.

"Oh, really?"

"Jak, what is the King doing under the bed?"

"Resting."

She prodded one leg with the knife. "He be not resting, Jak. He is dead."

"Dead, resting, whatever pastime King Kenton is now pursuing, I believe it wise if we make a hasty retreat."

Mahvan stood. "Jak, tell me what occurs that you are here in Castle Craven with a dead king. Have you been playing me for a fool? Are you an assassin?"

I crossed to Mahvan and meant to place my hands on her shoulders, but she placed both knife tips against my chest.

"Jest not? I have need of the truth, Master Jak."

"Mahvan, I did kill the King, but it was by accident."

"How does one kill a monarch by accident?"

I held up my thumbs. "He was trying to disrobe me and before I knew it, I had Kim Chied him."

She looked skeptical. "Why would King Kenton desire you disrobed?"

"What? Do you not think I have a cute butt?"

She lightly pressed both knives against my chest.

"He believed I to be Chaatiguin."

"And why...?" She shook her head. "This be too much for me. I have other duties that call and you only muddle my thinking. Go, Jak, escape now."

"Are not you coming? The King is dead, we can leave together."

"No, Jak, it cannot be."

I remembered her speech from the bed. It was not the King she had wanted, but some bitch queen. That could only be Queen Elay.

"But why, Mahvan? Why do you desire the death of your queen?"

"Because she is a traitor to our country. She became King Kenton's whore. She has sullied the Queen's Guardsmen who died for her and those who yet seek to rescue her."

"So this why you have avoided your kinsmen," I said, still bewildered by this mad twist of events. "They seek the King's death and to save the queen, while you want her dead. But Mahvan, it is not the queen's fault she was kidnapped and abused by King Kenton. She is a victim."

Mahvan had hidden her knives and took my hands. "Jak, you did read my book flawlessly except for the chapter where I must kill Queen Elay. The lone surviving Queen's Guardsman is my brother. We both trained together, I someday for the new king's guard. I will not have him die for that whore."

"But you will be captured and punishment for such is the axe. Her life is not worth your own."

She smiled sadly as she put her knives away and ran a finger across my cheek. "It cannot be. She must die.

"But first we must rid ourselves of the king's body. It will give us both more time if he is not promptly discovered," she quickly change thoughts.

"The wardrobe or under the bed?" I asked.

"They be the first place to look. Quick, help me wrap him in a bed cover."

Mahvan pulled the cover from the bed and spread it on the floor. I helped drag the corpse to the cloth, then rolled him up in the cover.

I stood back. "I fear this is not a good camouflage."

Mahvan ignored me as she pulled cords from the velvet curtains and began winding them about the corpse then proceeding to tie a large metal chamber pot to its feet.

"That did not help," I observed. "It still looks like a corpse in a blanket, only now fettered to a chamber pot."

The room was suddenly flooded by light as she tore the curtains away and threw open the shutters. I blinked and threw up a hand to shade my eyes.

"Help me cast King Kenton out the window and into the moat," she ordered.

"You cannot toss the King out the window in wide sun. He will be seen as he falls."

"From the gossip I have heard, it is not that uncommon a practice for the King," countered Mahvan. "They will think it but another of his former distractions."

I grudgingly grabbed one end of the cocoon and hoisted it to the window. Together we slid the former king of Glavendale over the sill and watched him tumble down from our lofty perch.

"Oooh," I groaned as the cord connecting the King and kettle snagged on a gargoyle's ugly snout and jerked the corpse to a rough stop.

"The king has disappeared, but there is a body hanging beneath his window. Even the most dense of the king's guards will be able to decipher this puzzle," I commented with the slightest of reproach.

"They may not see him."

"Yes, who would notice a bright pink bundle against the black of the castle wall?"

"Stop your grumbling," Mahvan said as she turned from the window and me. "We must make speed if you are to escape and I am to finish my task."

She struggled but for a few seconds, frantically grabbing at my wrists in an attempt to pull them from her throat. I had used the Hudren death grip.

I let her limp body slide to the floor before her heart actually stopped beating. She was right. I must make speed if I were to escape. I ran to the closet and grabbed a roll of goose tape. The strips of cloth with goose fat glue are used whenever a mending or binding job needs hastily performed. Some say civilization would collapse without goose tape. I gently pressed a piece over her mouth and bound her hands and feet.

Following Mahvan's own cue, I rolled her slack body in another of the bed's sheets and tied it with more cord.

"Is etiquette?"

The unexpected voice sent a jolt through my body and I spun around with a gasp. It was Osyani, looking a bit tired and weary from her search.

"What?"

"I search for Mahvan. I find Mahvan. You put Mahvan in blanket. Is etiquette?"

It was difficult to believe the swiftness of Osyani's development. She looked another two inches taller and her face was loosing its baby fat. And she was speaking in sentences.

"Ah, yes, it is?"

"How?"

I could tell she wasn't believing me. "Osyani, it is something that must be done. It may be difficult to understand, but I do this for Mahvan's good. If she were to stay in this castle, she would be killed. It is the only way to see her to safety."

There was still puzzlement on Osyani's face, but she was distracted by the sight of the food on the table.

"Etiquette?" she asked wistfully.

I had to laugh. "Go on. I doubt the King will contest you dining."

She glided effortlessly across the room and landed on the table. Osyani began eagerly feeding from the plates. She was tidy about it and would occasionally glance at me as if seeking my approval of her good table manners.

I walked to the table and also began snacking.

"Osyani," I said between bites, "Chaatiguin has fled the castle and is now trying to find her way back to the inn and Lorenzo. Can you find her and help the Gespe home?"

The harpling looked up with a hurt expression. "I want stay here by you. Why, Jak, why I go all time?"

I ran my fingers across her cheek and sighed. "I am sorry, Osyani. I promise when these adventures are over, I will not dispatch you on these errands."

This brought a smile to the harp chick and she nudged my hand with her head. "I wish I have hands. I wish I am like you and Mahvan."

"But you are special, Osyani," I replied. "You can fly. Many humans would gladly trade their arms for wings if they could soar among the clouds."

"Am I pretty?"

"What?"

"Am I pretty or only humans pretty?"

"Yes, Osyani, you are very pretty," I assured her, once again noting that soon I would have to find some attire for the harpling. Her face was maturing and soon her upper body would begin changing into that of a young woman.

We ate in silence for a few more minutes until I brushed my fingers across the table cloth and said to the harp chick, "Osyani, we must be off now before I am found out. I am going to escape the castle dressed as the King. I can only hope it works. You must look for Chaatiguin and help her to safety. You must also be careful of your own safety."

She flew to the window then turned to me. "Is etiquette"

"Is what etiquette?"

"You hang King on castle?"

"Ah, probably not, but we will speak of it later. Now be off with you."

She flexed her legs and launched herself into the blue sky.

Poor Osyani, I thought. What will become of her when she is a grown harpy? Will she be happy living among humans?

Chapter Fifteen

"Be you ready?"

It was Queen Elay.

"More than ready, Your Majesty."

"Please, we are now questmates; call me Elay. And may I call you Jak?"

"Certainly, Your...ah, Elay."

"What is this?" she asked while examining the trussed Mahvan.

"That is, ah, the Gespe maiden."

"Why have you bound her so?"

"She is timid and might give us away."

This was perhaps the most shocking event of the day. A queen asking a commoner to be on a given-name basis. I could see why even an animal like King Kenton could not bear the thought of giving her to the Dorgians.

And now for the arduous part. After disguising myself in another riding attire, this one red with gold trim, I opened the door and tugged the cord to the bell. As I pulled up the hood, I could only hope the bell was for calling servants and not a fire alert.

The servants came running from one end of the hall and the soldiers the other.

"Bring the new prisoners to the stable. I want them there immediately," I said to the soldiers then turned to the servants. "You, see that their horses are saddled, as well as an extra one for the Gespe maiden and Queen Elay. In the stable is also a large warhorse brought by one of the ferrets. I am confiscating it. Bring it along."

"And you," I said to a burly servant, "carry the Gespe girl. We will make peace with the priests of Dorga by giving them a sacrifice."

I tried keeping my speech brief. They did not seem puzzled by the King's odd actions, more likely that by now they have grown accustomed to their ruler's erratic behavior. The servant kneeled and lifted Mahvan. I motioned the remaining servants to lead the way.

We descended a number of stairways and traveled through large, ornate rooms and endless hallways before we were beset by one of the king's ministers.

"Your majesty, where are you going? Shall I gather an escort for you?"

"I am on a mission," I waved him away, wondering when someone would finally see through the disguise. "I need no escort."

"But your majesty, you are leaving the castle while those Dorgian dogs are about," the minister replied as he wrung his hands and sweat glistened on his forehead. "That is very dangerous, Your Highness. Could not we send some other to do this task?"

"No. Be off with you. I am the king and I shall do what I desire."

I waved him away, though he paused in the middle of the hall to watch us leave as he continued to wring his hands.

Baron Garsten Stee Hragen and Eli Smith were waiting at the stables when I arrived. Everyone appeared either bewildered or distressed. The Baron and Eli looked at me with suspicion and at the Queen with outright amazement as I waved them to mount.

"Where is our destination?" asked one of the soldiers.

"I go alone with these two men, the Queen, and the Gespe who will be an appeasement for the followers of Dorga."

"This cannot be, Your Majesty, it is too dangerous. We must..."

"Silence," I tried speaking in a forceful tone. "I am the king or do you forget?"

The soldier paled and snapped to attention. "No, Your Majesty."

No one wanted to argue with a demented king nor did they seem surprised at my illogical actions. I wondered if some of those about me were even secretly joyful that the King was about to place himself in danger. With no children, who would reign next? There would probably be numerous coupes and murders before Stagsford again settled into its indolent ways.

Mahvan had regained consciousness. She was lying across the horse and was now squirming and trying to curse through her taped mouth.

"Ah, the Gespe maiden does not want to visit the temple of Dorga," I observed while trying not to appear nervous. I should have disarmed the warrior maiden before bundling her in the blanket. There would be trouble if she somehow reached one of her wicked blades.

I could tell Eli was having a hard time hiding his surprise as I mounted Hazel and she did not object. He peered closely at me, as if trying to see beneath the hood.

I motioned for a servant to open the stable doors and urged Hazel out to the inner courtyard. The horse carrying Mahvan obediently followed when I pulled on its rein. I was slightly confused about my location.

"Baron Garsten Stee Hragen, lead the way back into the city," I commanded.

I was surprised by the Baron's unusual silence as we passed out of the defenses of Castle Raven. I once looked over my shoulder to note a tiny pink dot hanging halfway down the castle's wall.

It wasn't until we were a good hundred yards free of the castle that both of my companions pulled their horses to a stop.

"I don't think I would believe it," Eli said with a shake of his head, "if it weren't for Hazel. I know she lets only one person ride her."

"I find it astounding, myself," the Baron chimed in. He bowed slightly in his saddle to Queen Elay and turned to me. "Just how do you come to wear the King's attire. And most important of all, where is the King?"

I turned and pointed to the castle looming above the walls. "See that pink speck just below the gargoyle? That is His Royal Majesty, King Kenton. As you can see, he was of no hindrance to my borrowing a riding outfit."

Both looked at me in astonishment.

"Is this true?" demanded the Baron urgently. "The King is dead?"

"Deader than the gargoyle he hangs from."

"By whose hands did he die?"

"Ah, it was really by thumbs, but it was an accident," I uneasily admitted.

"I must return to the castle."

It was my turn to be surprised. "Wait, Baron, what are you doing? Castle Raven will not a prudent place to be when the King's death is discovered."

The Baron had barely time to shout over his shoulder, "I must see some affairs put in order, Master Jak. I will remember this good fortune that you have sent my way."

I looked at Eli. "Do you know what this is about?"

"I've been confused my entire stay here in your world, Jak. What say we ride over to those trees and cut Chaatiguin free?"

"Ah, we have a small quandary here, Eli," I replied.

"What problem could that be. Jak? No one from the castle can see her from there. The trees will hide us."

"That is not the problem. You see, Eli, ah, this is not Chaatiguin."

"What?"

"No."

"Then where is Chaatiguin?"

"She escaped a couple hours ago. I have sent Osyani to see her safely back to the inn."

Eli looked down at the wrapped figure on the horse. Mahvan was again fighting against the bondage and she looked like a belligerent butterfly attempting to escape from its cocoon. "Then who is this?"

"Mahvan."

"Mahvan?"

"Mahvan."

Eli was eying me from under his strange hat. "Then why don't we cut Mahvan free, Jak? You're confusing me, pardner."

"Because Mahvan would then kill me."

"Really?"

"Truth."

Eli reached under his hat to scratch his head. "Why would she want to go and do that? I thought she was sweet on yah."

The Queen was now listening on in confusion.

I took a deep breath. "Well, it is like this...."

I described my rather heavy-handed invitation to Castle Raven and how I chanced to come upon the three of them. Eli scowled and restlessly played with the handle of his strange weapon when he heard of the King's attempt to molest who he believed to be Chaatiguin. He smiled and relaxed when hearing of King Kenton's ensuing death.

"Queen Elay's eyes widened when I described my confrontation with Mahvan.

"I bid you, Mahvan, know that I was not the king's bed guest by my own will and tried more than once to end his life," she spoke to the rug-bound maiden. "You may fault me for not taking my own life, but I lived so that I could see the beast die by my hand. Yet, I forgive Jak for robbing me of that joy."

Eli gave me a sideways glance at the Queen's informal use of my name.

"You know Mahvan?" I asked.

Elay sighed. "Yes, her training was by the suggestion of my ministers. She comes from a family line that has long guarded the queens of Ayeria. He thought my future husband should have such protection and Mahvan was chosen to see how a woman would fare under such training."

All too well, I thought silently.

"Yup, you gotta a problem there, pardner," Eli drawled as he twirled one end of his mustache and contemplated the bundle. "Whatcha going to do? It don't matter if you cut her loose now or next week. She's still going to come at yah with those wicked blades of hers. You gotta bobcat by the tail, there."

"Set the valiant maiden free," Elay ordered. "She has risked much to undertake what she believes is justice. If Mahvan still seeks my life, perhaps her judgment is worthier than my own."

"Don't look like there is time for that," replied Eli. "It looks like we're about to get company."

I looked first to my right toward the castle then to my left toward town. I saw no one. I wheeled Hazel about and stopped when I gazed toward the small stand of woods. Pouring from the woods were a couple dozen black-robed warrior priests of Dorga. Others had already begun circling to cut our retreat to the castle.

Elay spun in her saddle to view the Dorgians and her sudden move spooked her horse. It reared back, catching the mountain queen off guard. She tumbled backwards and struck the ground flat on her back. She lay as if stunned, fighting to catch her breath.

"Pronto, Jak. We have to high-tail it out of here."

I didn't understand Eli's idioms, but there was no mistaking the urgency in his voice. I started to dismount to aid Elay, still clutching the reins of the horse carrying Mahvan. The pack horse was unnerved by the excitement and leaped forward, yanking me from my own saddle

Stars spun before my eyes. A mass of old aches was provoked by the fall and a few new pains joined the chorus. I tried lifting my head, but a wave of dizziness flattened me back to the ground. I looked to the left and saw the queen's crumpled body only a few feet away.

"Jak, get up. They are almost here."

"Eli," I gasped. "You must, you must see to Chaatiguin. Be off. Find Lorenzo, tell him all what has come to pass. Make haste. You are our only hope."

Through a tunnel of darkness appeared a spot of light. In it was blue sky and Eli's worried face looking down.

"Eli, think of Chaatiguin."

There was no sense of us all being captured and I knew the only way to make Eli flee was to play on his love for the Gespe maiden. I succeeded. With a curse, he and the horse spun about and the fading sound of pounding hooves told of his escape. The same sound grew from the opposite direction and I blinked several times to see a number of evil grins peering down at me.

"So, we have the King. Dorga takes revenge in miraculous ways," one of the priests laughed.

I was roughly jerked to my feet.

"And what have we here. Queen Elay? This be almost too much marvel to ponder."

Several warrior priests had pulled Elay to her feet and she glared back at them.

"What is this strange baggage?" one of Dorga's priests asked of the fettered Mahvan.

"It is a plague victim," I quickly answered. "We have covered her so she will not spread contagion."

"Then she must be burned."

"No, it is a Gespe Maiden," Elay countered as one warrior priest drew his sword.

There was some muttering among the priests.

"She will make a second sacrifice to Dorga for the offense that has been given him. It is not often we have such a gift," approved a priest.

It was obvious that many Stagsford residents were already aware of the horrible trade in Gespes.

A taller priest of the group appeared to be the leader and he said after contemplating the horse and its burden, "I will examine her."

"No," I cried before thinking.

"I mean, that would not be wise," I added more in the King's tone of voice. "This bright light of day could damage her eyes, making her an imperfect gift to Dorga."

The priest looked at me with suspicion. He had a fish pale complexion and ice blue eyes. When he had smiled earlier, I observed his teeth filed to sharp points. He would have stood out as an exceptionally vile individual even among the scum and human refuse of the King's Wart Inn.

He approached me and put his face close to mine. His eyes half closed and he spoke, "There be something amiss here."

With that, he grabbed my hood and threw it back. I heard Queen Elay gasp as if in surprise, "That is not the King."

"No, it is not," the priest agreed. He stared intensely into my eyes then stepped back for a second inspection.

"That be the rascal I chased earlier," one of the other priests shouted. "The lard boy said he be the one who left with Arch Priest Comft."

"It is plain we have a mystery here," their leader said. "We will take them all back to the temple where our inquisitors may seek the truth. Mount up."

My stomach was twisting as my hands were bound behind my back. Their inquisitors were infamous for their odious methods of gaining what they called the truth. Hot irons, whetted blades, and wicked hooks were their toys.

I rode in silence, furtively scanning the sky for Osyani. I hoped she would not return. With her small brave heart, she would only take one of the arrows carried by several of the priests.

I had pondered the slim chance of rescue by more of the king's guardsmen, but none were spotted. It appeared as if most had retreated to the castle as the evening neared.

My heart sank as we dismounted at the palatial front of the temple. Huge pillars ran the length of the temple's front. I looked up to see the obese statue of Dorga leering down at me. I was shoved forward to be marched up a wide span of steps. Temple eunuchs opened the large bronze doors that depicted tortured souls screaming in rivers of flames and being rent by devilish creatures.

The leader ordered two of the other warrior priests to carry the supposed Gespe to a cell.

"Please, be gentle when you untie her, she be a delicate creature," I pleaded, though secretly pitying them when they unwrapped Dorga's present.

I was unceremoniously dragged in an opposite direction while Queen Elay had convinced the priest that she should be taken to the highest of the Dorga hierarchy for consultation.

It seemed we had walked for miles before coming to the end of a dark, dank hall, where they pitched me into a cramped cell. I tried making myself comfortable on a few planks filling in as a bed. Despite my hurts and pangs, I started drifting into an uneasy sleep with my thoughts wandering to Jennair and her search for our father.

I was jerked wide awake by a distant scream sounding from somewhere in the temple. The guards had apparently released Mahvan from her bonds. Would she come looking to gut me before or after she'd killed her queen?

Thoughts of being the target of one of Mahvan's many wicked blades made me edgy enough that it came as even more of a startlement when my name was called.

"Jak, you be all right?"

I looked up to see Osyani at the small window high above the bunk. She was perched on a ledge and had her worried face pressed to the bars.

"Osyani, did Chaatiguin find her way safely to the inn?"

"Yes, Jak. She be safe. I saw Eli. He say Lorenzo not there. I come find you."

I stood on the planks and reached up to brush her cheek. She continued to grow at an amazing pace. She now had the open, pretty face of a girl almost to enter teen years.

"Yes, Osyani, I am fine. Please try and find Lorenzo. Tell him he best conjure up something quickly or I will not be long for this world."

She shut her eyes and nuzzled my fingers.

"I will fly fast for you, Jak. I come back when I see Lorenzo," the harpling said before she leaped away in a flutter of wings.

Sometime later I was rousted from my troubled sleep when the door opened and two guards with drawn swords waved me out. We walked in grim silence down even grimmer halls until coming to a spiraling staircase. The climb took an eternity. Small windows showed we were in a large tower at one end of the temple.

I was finally shoved into a shuttered room lit by a duck-fat lamp and occupied by a spindly, grizzled old man dressed only in a greasy loincloth. His flesh hung in flaps from his upper arms and when he opened his mouth, I could see only yellowed stumps for teeth. He sat behind a small table with quill and parchment.

Motioning me to sit on a short stool, he asked, "Name?"

"What?"

He picked up a long stick and smacked me along side the head with an unexpected swiftness. I leaped from my seat and would have given him a savoring of his own medication if the guards had not reminded me of their presence.

"Name?"

"Tijfver Styxlaquo."

He looked like he wanted to reach for the stick again.

"How do you spell that?"

"Just as it sounds."

He grunted and scratched something down.

"Age?"

"26."

"Place of birth?"

"Ah, what is this about?"

"You are being processed for the terrible chambers of torture from which no one returns. Now keep your tongue from wagging idly or it will be the first fragment you lose. Place of birth?"

"The Glades of Besffial."

He paused before he transcribed the answer and looked up crossly. "You have no Besffial accent."

"Yes I do."

"No, you do not."

"Yes I...ouch."

He put the stick back down and the quill point scratched across the page. "Occupation?"

"Harpy trainer."

"Just for what purpose would one want to train a harpy?"

"Ah, for a messenger service. That is why I was coming to the castle, to inquire if the priests of Dorga would like such a service to maintain quicker contact with their outlying temples. And then I was treated shamelessly by being imprisoned. Wait until Arch Priest Comft hears of this outage. Heads will roll."

The jailer shuffled parchment about then said while squinting at one scrap, "It reads that you were apprehended while disguised as King Kenton and in the transport of a captive Gespe."

"Hah, that be a good one," I laughed. "He was the mad man down the hall. I see it now. Just a case of mistaken identity. You can release me and I vow I will not mention a word about this mishap to the Arch Bishop."

"And be that the customary garb of a harpy trainer?" he asked.

I looked down at the bright royal red riding attire with gold trim. "What, this old rag? It is just something I threw on...ouch."

I was getting tired of the stick, but it seemed the jailer was more tired of me. He waved at the guards and they herded me out the door.

"This is a very unusual torture chamber," I noted as we again began ascending the stairs. "Are not such abodes of pain traditionally in dark and dank dungeons?"

"The Arch Priest Comft could not hear the screams from his sanctum," volunteered one of the guards. "He moved the chambers to below his den where he could listen to the faintest of moans and sobs even when he rested."

"Such dedication is most admirable," I acknowledged. "It would be a shame to waste my screams when he is not about to relish them. Perhaps we should postpone this session until he returns?"

"Be not worried on that point. The Arch Priest Comft returned this vary day. It is said he was upon a secret quest. He went to his chambers but hours ago."

Comft returned? How could that be? My spirits suddenly lightened. There could be but one answer--Lorenzo was once again masquerading as Comft. It was a dangerous game he played, but a bit of good luck for me.

I was met at the chamber door by an apprentice torturer, a lank lad with a swarm of pimples about his face like red ants pouring from a disturbed nest.

"Bring him in and chain him over there," ordered the apprentice in a bored voice. "I be still heating the irons and have yet to clean and polish the tools from the master's last task."

"I must say one thing for you torturers," I told the apprentice after the guards had left and my hands were chained to an iron ring on the wall. "No cobwebs, rats, or rotting skeletons lying about here. Everything looks spotless. I am sure your mother must be very proud of you."

The apprentice was busy at a sink washing an assortment of knives, hooks, pliers, and clamps.

"Shut your mouth, dead man," he snapped in ill humor. He turned to face me and pointed to one of the many strange contrivances that furnished the chamber. "See that? It be a spinning jenny. Just got 'er in. She slices, dices, chops, and grates."

"Seems like a lot of machine just to make a salad."

He laughed, but it was not the kind of chuckling to bring joy to anyone's heart.

"That be right, dead man. And you be the carrot."

He went back to washing the tools of his trade. I prayed he would continue with his back to me. As quickly as possible when one has both hands chained, I propped a foot against the wall and fumbled for my pouch of metal slivers. It took but another second for me to pick the simple lock.

On the wall not far from where I had been chained was a rack of oddly shaped knives. I carefully removed a blade and silently made my way to the apprentice.

"Do not move, my young torturer, or it will be your own blood that must be scrubbed from the floor," I ordered as I placed the blade against his throat. "Do what I say and you will live to burn and batter another night."

I led the lad to the rather whimsical device of gears and springs that he called the spinning jenny. It also came with manacles.

"You will never escape from here," he said as I firmly secured him to the contrivance. "And when you are returned, I shall ask the master if I may personally work on you. First, I will insert slivers under your nails and drive needles into your eyeballs. I will..."

"Put a cork in it," I ordered as I waved the knife under his nose, taken aback by the youngster's villainous outburst. He was glaring at me like a taxman who had just had his nose hairs plucked.

"I will have you begging for death, though it will be meaningless mumbles after I have cut the lips from your face," he began again.

I sighed and leaned forward. "One must not make such promises when one is tethered so."

Something clicked. Looking down where I had been resting my hand, I saw that I had moved one of the several levers. I pulled away.

"No, you blockhead," screamed the apprentice.

"What did I tell you about such language?" I said and rapped him in the head the knife handle.

"Pull it back, pull it back," the lad was now begging.

I looked down. Which one had I pushed? It seemed to me it had been the third one to the right. I pulled it and suddenly there was a whirring noise. The contraption began a slow bending at odd angles.

"No, the other one, the other one," he was screaming again.

Now I was becoming nervous. I yanked on another lever and suddenly from the sides of the engine of torture emerged a whirling fan of blades. Pushing the lever in reverse failed to stop anything. I was now desperately shoving and pulling the levers. It was hard to think with him screaming so.

The apparatus was a clever device. Who would have guessed there were all those spinning screws and twirling blades tucked out of sight? I had to jump back when the blood began flying. It was a sight too horrible to contemplate. He was lucky in that I had activated so many of the machine's accessories at one time so it was a quick death by slicing and dicing.

There was blood on my royal riding garb, though it barely showed against its crimson hue. Still, I didn't like the smell. Pulling it off, I tossed it over the poor apprentice only to have the ongoing manipulations of the machine shred it to ribbons.

I tiptoed up the last flight of stairs and pressed my ear against the only door. This had to be the Arch Priest Comft's lair. I again resorted to my small pouch of picks and unlocked the door.

It was a spooky room. A human-size statue of Dorga dominated one end of the domicile. The room smelled of cat urine and incense and a number of stuffed animals crouched about the place, including that of a ferociously scowling griffin.

I realized the griffin wasn't stuffed when it opened its mouth to show a number of wicked teeth. I hate adventures.

"Ah, nice griffin. Good griffin. I was just about to leave."

The muscles tensed under the yellow fur as I took a step backwards, it appearing ready to pounce. I froze as if I were one of the mounted specimens watching on with glass eyes.

It is said that it is unwise to stare directly into the eyes of a wild creature in that they take it as a challenge. I nervously gazed off to the side, still keeping the griffin in the corner of my sight. It was then my eyes fell upon the torn and bloodied remnants of another unlucky visitor-- diced, sliced, and shredded by the griffin as efficiently as any spinning jenny.

I gasped, momentarily forgetting the monster. What remained of the man was garbed in the tattered robe of the archpriest. My only relief at the gruesome visage came about because I could tell it had not been

Lorenzo. Some priest, deciding to take a try at aping his master, had not been able to fool Comft's pet griffin.

I returned my gaze to the creature to see it licking its lips as if in anticipation of dessert. Racking my poor brain, I could not remember any past guidance given by my instructors on what to do when face to face with a hungry griffin.

"Jak, what be that? Is it fun?"

The griffin was just as surprised as I. It spun to see Osyani sitting in a window. A deep growl rumbled through its body. I shuddered at the thought of the harpling winding up like a sparrow in a cat's taloned grip.

"Not all that much fun, Osyani. It is a griffin, a very cruel and dangerous beast."

"Then why are you playing with it?"

"That is a very good question that I will answer at a more opportune time." I answered softly so as not to provoke the archpriest's sentinel. "Make no sudden moves or it will attack."

She cocked her head, then smiled. "I want to play. Here griffy, griffy."

She hopped about the sill, boldly flapping her wings. The capering was too much for the beast and it bounded forward with its last leap carrying it straight to the harpling.

"Osyani," I yelled, "do not..."

I closed my eyes, not able to watch the young harpy's untimely demise.

"Oh-oh. There goes the griffy."

I opened one eye then both. Osyani was hovering right outside the window with her face turned down. My legs were shaking and I used several pieces of furniture as handholds as I crossed the room. Standing on tiptoes, I stuck my head out the window and followed her downward gaze. The griffin's small wings were apparently just for ornamentation.

I raised my head to come nose to nose with Osyani.

"Etiquette?" she asked then smiled innocently.

The harpling was developing a sense of humor.

"Osyani, you almost gave me a heart convulsion," I said then paused to examine the harpling.

She was wearing a sleeveless tunic. It was of a simple design and adorned with embroidered roses. Osyani's smile broadened when she saw me looking at her attire. The harpling returned to the sill where she could strut back and forth in front of me.

"You like? Jennair gave it to me. Am I beautiful?" She gazed at me with expectant eyes.

"Yes," I admitted. "You are beautiful."

What was I going to do? As her magically-fast maturing continued, it gave me less and less time to find an answer to what I would do with the harpling. It would be cruel to keep her in any human city where there are always spiteful thugs who would like nothing more than to kill or maim such a creature. Those less violent would still be armed with cruel words and looks. As a bastard child, I knew only too well about the bullies of the world.

And yet, it would be even crueler to loose her unprepared upon the wilds where she would easily fall prey to the many beasts and monsters. Used to human friends, she might even pine away from lack of companionship.

But there were other pressing problems at the moment.

"Did you find Lorenzo?"

"Yes, Lorenzo said he would meet you here."

"Meet me here?"

"Yes."

"Meet me here? What does he mean by meet me here? Am I to wait in front of the Dorga statue with a pink daisy pinned to my tunic or greet him at the punch bowl during the reception following the sacrifices?"

Osyani sternly stared at me and stuck her button nose up in the air. "I be only the messenger, Master Jak."

We locked eyes and I tried to maintain a dour expression but quickly surrendered. We both broke into grins. Osyani had perfectly mimicked Jennair.

"You little tart, are you sure that was all Lorenzo said?"

"Yes. Now I must go."

"Go? Where are you off to?" Her volunteering to leave took me by surprise.

"I help Jennair find your father. He be at the castle. Are you excited?"

I sighed. "Any other time and I would be overwhelmed, Osyani. But there is something about being trapped in the Temple of Dorga and having more bruises than a month-old tomato to dull one's sense of awe and wonder. Go on with your chore and we will talk later."

She darted in and kissed me on the forehead then almost magically vanished in her familiar blur of wings. I was glad Osyani was on a less dangerous task than rescuing me.

I took a deep breathe before readying myself to continue this absurd saga in which I was trapped. I abruptly jerked up my head. Did she say my father was at the castle?

I have wondered what possessed some highwaymen to become so bold that their increasingly extravagant exploits inevitably lead to capture and the hangman. Now I know. With each more outrageous act, life seems more unreal--it becomes theater and the worse thing one can do is bore the audience--even if it is only yourself.

Therefore I tore through the Arch Priest Comft's closet with barely a thought to what I was doing. I carried several hooded robes to a mirror between a row of mummified heads and a suit of eerily molded armor that could never be worn by anything remotely human.

"Hm-m-m. Do I want the black robe with scarlet trim and gold stitching? Or maybe the black robe with silver stitching and gold trim?" I asked my image in the mirror.

I decided upon the scarlet trim and gold stitching, similar to the one Lorenzo had liberated from Comft's body. I had just pulled on the robe when a knock came at the door. Now was as good as any time to try out my latest masquerade. Pulling the hood over my head, I was walking to the door when I remembered the remains of the priest. I gingerly grabbed one edge of the tattered robe and dragged the body behind a stuffed albino crocodile. A finely woven rug made from the hair of woolly dire rats was quickly thrown over the bloodstained floor.

"Your Archness, we bring you the Gespe maiden," one of four badly battered warrior guards announced when I opened the door. "Whatever a Gespe be, they are fighters. She killed three and wounded another score before we could quiet her."

Mahvan was just as badly punished. One eye was swollen almost shut and there was dried blood beneath her nose. Mahvan hung limply in their grasp, her hands bound behind her back.

"Ah, put her over there," I ordered and waved to a chair. "Then you can go."

The men dragged her across the room and dumped her on a high-backed seat of polished wood, gems, and brass. They looked nervously about, most likely wondering where the griffin was hiding. It was then I noticed a detached, bloodless hand lying in the middle of the floor. I gave it a quick kick and it flew to land upon the head of a mounted butterfly bat.

They turned at the sound, looking anxiously about.

"What was that?" one of the guards asked warily, then spotted the pallid hand against the vibrant reds and blues of the bat pelt. His eyes bugged.

I sighed. "Griffins be such messy eaters. It is impossible to make them forgo playing with their food. Now be gone. I must question this Gespe."

One hesitated at the door, as if worried about leaving the dangerous Gespe alone with their leader. I waved them impatiently along and shut the door firmly behind them.

I returned to gaze down at the warrior woman. One must give credit to Mahvan. Beaten and bound, she remained defiant. She peeled back her lips as if to lunge and attack me with the only weapons remaining--her teeth.

"So why not cease this sport, monk, and kill me now," she growled. "I am no longer a pretty offering for your god. Or do you plan to continue your entertainment in your chamber below, as you did with the ferret?"

Ferret? Had the Dorgians captured a fellow private investigator? Then her words grew in meaning. The poor wretch on the spinning jenny! I had thrown the king's attire upon the apprentice torturer. She must have been to the chamber and believed the boy to be me.

"He was of no great matter," I muttered in a deeper voice. "A bothersome fly to be swatted."

"Master Jak was of more worth than you and all your sodomist priests combined."

I was half mindful to continue in this line of intriguing speech, but Mahvan would be in even fouler humor if I played her the fool. To escape, I would have to cut her free and I was not all that keen at testing her temper the way it was.

"I am told you and the ferret had a falling out, that your own blade sought his blood."

She clamped her mouth firmly shut and turned away. I sighed and brought out the knife I had earlier held to the apprentice's throat. Mahvan calmly examined the blade, showing not the slightest trace of fear.

"I would take your weighing my worth above those of the Dorgians as a good sign if I was not aware of how poorly you hold them," I said in my own voice.

Mahvan opened her mouth for a retort then froze. Her beautiful blue eyes, or at least one of them, widened. I threw back my hood.

"What be a nice maiden like you doing in a temple like this?"

"Argh-h-h" she screamed and hurled herself from the chair, head-butting me in the stomach.

I doubled over and stumbled backwards to fall on my already bruised arse. Mahvan landed on top of me and I quickly rolled in case she had plans for me and her teeth. We both lay on the floor gasping, heads turned to each other. Her hands were still bound behind her back.

"I take this to mean you still feel ill will toward me," I managed to choke out while rubbing my stomach.

"You, how could you lead me on to believe you dead?" she snapped.

I sat up. "Why? Were you disheartened to find someone had beat you to it?"

"It is never too late," she reminded me.

"Ah, but you are bound and I have the..."

I looked around. Where had the knife gone? When my gaze returned to Mahvan, I uncomfortably observed goose tape dangling from her wrists and the blade securely gripped in her right hand.

"I would not do anything drastic," I urged the maiden. "I can understand why you are irate with me..."

"Irate? Irate? You wrap me up like a gutted fish and deliver me to the Temple of Dorga and you believe me to be irate?"

"Ah, angry then..."

She gave me a fierce look.

"All right, very incensed. But I did it only to save your life and to prevent you from making a grave mistake I believe you would later regret. I had hoped hearing the Queen's speech would have tempered your resolve to kill her."

"I have spoken furthermore with her," Mahvan said in a cold voice that sent shivers through me.

The image of a diced and chopped Elay was so disheartening that I felt as if I were suffering from the plague, my limbs suddenly weakened.

"But since I did not slay the bitch queen, I believe I might as well spare you, ferret," she added with a nasty grin. "There, we be even."

"She lives?"

"Yes, if but only for the next several hours before the sacrificial rites. After dispatching those knaves who unwrapped me, I found my way to her cell."

"But you spared her life?" I asked again.

She looked down at the blade she gripped and rubbed her thumb along its edge.

"I heard her speech with you, yet might have slain her still but for the arrival of two more guards. She begged them to let me go free and she would gladly meet Dorga. These, too, I did dispatch. The priests of Dorga be a gutless lot good for only torturing helpless captives and faint-hearted girls."

Mahvan climbed wearily to her feet and reached out a hand to me. I gingerly took it and she pulled me to my own feet.

"I was never eager to kill my queen and am now convinced she had not betrayed our people," Mahvan said as she straightened her bloodstained tunic. "I was attempting to break her free when more guards arrived, this time too many for me to overcome. And you, how do you come now to be the Arch Priest Comft?"

She eyed the hand. "Is that Comft?"

"No. I believe it be the remnant of some priest who would be the Comft, but for failing to convince the griffin," I answered.

"And you, the master ferret that you are, fooled the beast?"

"It is private inquisitor. No, I fear the griffin met a demise not by my hand. It made to snack on dear Osyani, but missed, and now lies on the grounds below."

She walked to the window and stretched to peer down at the griffin. She spoke over her shoulder, "Though it is I who am supposedly the assassin, it seems that the carnage follows more closely upon your heels."

Mahvan turned to me and cocked her head. "Let me count. There is the Arch Priest of Dorga, the King of Glavensdale, the unfortunate wretch who must be a torturer below our feet, and a frightful griffin. And I have heard rumors of missing CIA agents and Ghennison viper mages. Quite an assortment for just a lowly ferret."

"It is private investigator," I said, "It would appear as if misfortune has fallen upon some of those about me."

"Misfortune? I would guess hanging in a pink rug from a Castle Craven gargoyle is a misfortune," she agreed.

"Maybe you fear to continue in my company?" I said as I pulled the hood back over my head.

She laughed and walked across the room to straighten my robe like a mother readying her child for school. "As long as the misfortune falls upon the likes of Kenton and Comft, I believe I feel safe enough. Now what are your plans?"

I was surprised the warrior maiden would look to me for a plan of action. I chewed at the edge my lip and stared at the floor.

"I will take a notion from Lorenzo, who says the best plans are the simplest. I say we free Queen Elay and leave the temple before the sacrifices begin. Then we can gather the rest of our group and as I once heard Eli say, 'Get out of Dodge.' I would like you to see Duburoake."

Mahvan placed both hands on my shoulder and looked into my eyes with a sad smile. "It sounds like a good plan, Master Jak, but I will not be able to travel to your home city. My duty is with Queen Elay."

I have been sighing too much lately and tried holding the latest one back. I wanted to kiss the maiden, but for her sorely bruised lips. I shrugged again.

"We must make haste if we are to be free before the sacrifice."

We exited the den to find several guards loitering in the hall. They silently followed at a respectful distance in puzzlement. Mahvan led the way back to the queen's cell. There were no guards at the door--a very bad sign. I looked through the small window to find the cell empty.

"This does not bode well," I announced softly to Mahvan. "I held hope that this would be a simple task, but as with the past couple days, it appears the gods still enjoy toying with me."

Mahvan just shook her head and began purposely marching away.

"Where are you going?" I asked after catching up to her.

"Come, Master Jak. Griping will not save the Queen," she said low enough that the guards could not hear. "We must be off to the sacrificial hall."

I guess there was no use arguing with her. Determined as she was to kill the Queen, Mahvan was now just as resolute to save her.

We met no priests. They must have all gone to the ceremony. Several times we passed servants and they gazed down in fear as we passed. Mahvan finally stopped at a pair of large brass doors.

"This be it, Master Jak. Are you ready for your performance?" she asked with a smile lopsided by her beating.

My stomach was churning and any second I believed my teeth would begin chattering, but I waved her to lead the way. She opened the door and we entered the giant, roofless chamber.

It appeared much larger by daylight. We entered by a side door and the crowds of priests looked in astonishment as we pushed our way through them. They hastily retreated to each side until we made our way free of them into the center of the hall. I headed toward the statue of Dorga with what I hoped was a stately stride. A low din of confused murmurs filled the air. I soon found out why. I reached the feet of Dorga and turned, only to find myself looking up at two figures on the sacrificial platform. One was a bound Queen Elay and the other my twin--a priest garbed in the robe of the Arch Priest Comft.

"This does not bode well, ferret." whispered Mahvan.

"No shit," I found myself quoting Lorenzo.

"Seize that impostor." I decided to act before the other Comft reacted. "He is a fake. I am the Arch Priest Comft who has just come from my den where no other may dwell because of my griffin."

"This is so," spoke up one of my guards. "We have just come from the High Arch Priest's sanctum."

I waved a small group of guards to follow me and in single file we climbed the narrow ramp of carved rock. Several guards grabbed the impostor priest and held him as I strode to his side.

"See, this be my false double," I yelled as loud as I could, my voice echoing from the massive stonewalls. I yanked down the hood to find Lorenzo staring back at me with the look of a mother when her child has done something very stupid.

"Another fine mess you've gotten us into," he observed.

"It is your fault. You did not tell me where to meet you," I hissed back.

I felt my own hood being wrenched from my head and a loud gasp swept through the crowd. It was the warrior priest who had captured me earlier.

"They be both fakes and will now taste Dorga's vengeance..."

He staggered back and fell from the platform. I turned to see Mahvan standing with a bloody blade.

"I never did like him," she stated before wheeling and shoving two guards from the platform.

Lorenzo threw back his robe and withdrew his lean sword. He quickly dispatched two more guards. Between the warrior maiden and Lorenzo, they speedily cleared the platform and stood guard at the only way up to the sacrificial dais--the narrow ramp.

The assemblage roared in outrage and beat back and forth against the foot of the platform like a stormy sea. I looked down into a mass of savage, twisted faces. No individual voice could be heard above the deafening clamor.

"This does not bode well," I repeated to Mahvan.

"No shit."

"They do seem overly excited," admitted Lorenzo.

One by one the warrior priests tried gaining the platform, only to be pierced by the point of Lorenzo's swift sword. Mahvan continually circled our island, slashing at the few who managed to climb the backs of their fellow priests to grasp the edge of the platform. I tried to aid as best I could by stomping their fingers.

"What be your plan now, Lorenzo?" I yelled above the din. "I would truly like to hear it."

"It appears I may have to devise a more intricate scheme. You know, I'm really beginning to dislike these Dorgians. They are a tiresome bunch."

I heard a moan and turned to see two priests had gained our refuge. One stood over a lifeless Mahvan as the second advanced with a drawn saber. He reeled as he advanced, blood dripping from a side wound. The sight of the downed warrior woman sent me into a frenzy. I had been instructed never to fight while angry, but all cold logic flew away.

I charged the priest and dipped under his weaving blade to thrust one thumb into his left eye. He screamed and clutched his face as I followed with a kick to the crotch. The priest tumbled over the side and I turned to the remaining villain who was armed with just a dirk.

Deciding not to employ too close of combat, he pulled his arm back to throw the blade. He failed to follow through. A feathered shaft miraculously bloomed in his chest. I spun to see at least a hundred Ayerians silhouetted high above me against the windows circling the room beneath the ceiling. Some were already swiftly sliding down their ropes.

These latest interlopers, if it was possible, seemed to enrage the mass of Dorgians even more. The roar of the crowd made me cover my ears as I ran to Mahvan. She was still conscious; the sight of her fellow Ayerians bringing a pained smile to her woefully battered face.

I pulled her into a sitting position and held her in my arms. We both watched as the warriors dropped to the floor with blades swinging. Among them was the scarlet uniformed figure of the apprentice Queen's Guardsmen.

I at first believed they would actually succeed in making the platform; they fought with such courage and resolve. But the horde of furious Dorgians slowed their advance until the Ayerians were surrounded by the warrior priests. I watched with dismay as they were pulled down one by one. I could see the face of Elfshold, his eyes riveted to the figure of his queen.

From the corner of my eye I detected another disturbance. The giant main doors to the hall had been thrown open and forcing their way in were Glavendale soldiers. They numbered many more than the Ayerians. Even so, their progress was thwarted by the large numbers of Dorgian priests and followers.

Another warrior priest had gained the platform. I jumped to my feet with thumbs before me. My luck ran out. The man was obviously well experienced in battle and he easily dodged my thumbs to thrust his sword into my side. A cruelly hot bolt of pain drove me to my knees.

He was pulling back for the killing blow when Osyani came swooping down, hurling herself against him. She was now the size of a young woman. The warrior priest backhanded the harpling and as she stumbled back, drove his blade this time into Osyani. Lorenzo appeared and cut the villain down before he could pull his own blade free.

I fought to maintain consciousness, crawling to the lifeless form of what was now almost a full-grown harpy. Mahvan limped to my side and kneeled by Osyani. She pulled away the cloth to reveal a horrible wound from which blood furiously spurted. The Dorgian had hit an artery. I tried pressing my hand against the injury, but her blood continued madly pumping through my fingers. The last thing I remembered before the darkness rushed in was sobbing uncontrollably.

~ * ~

I woke to pain. It lanced through my side as I breathed, it wracked my head as I opened my eyes, it plagued every part of my body.

"By the gods of Fryrf," I muttered through dried lips, "That must have been one hell of a night at the Kings Wart Inn."

"You are suffering from more than just a hangover," a strange and yet familiar voice intoned.

I turned my head to see Lorenzo sitting by my bed. The sight of him brought back memories more painful than my wounds.

"Where am I?"

"In the king's infirmary. You've taken quite a beating, but the doctor tells me you'll live. He was quite angry with me when I wouldn't let him bleed you, but I remembered how disagreeable you found the treatment."

The thought of bleeding brought back my last glimpse of poor Osyani's slender body. I closed my eyes to keep from crying.

"He is awake," another voice called from behind me.

At the door was Jennair, who entered the room followed by what seemed like a crowd of people. I watched as they trooped in--Olmsted, Eli, Chaatiguin, the Duke, Mahvan, Queen Elay, and a young woman who must be my nurse.

"We wondered if you would ever quit your indolent ways and awake, me brother," Jennair jested, though her gentle touch on my arm spoke of her concern.

"I have commanded my healers to give you nothing but the best of treatment," said the Duke.

"Your healers?"

"Why, of course. I am now the king of Glavensdale."

I could only stare at him in dumbfoundment.

"Your 'accident' with Kenton left me to claim what was rightfully mine. I am of the royal line, though it did no harm to already have supporters within the court."

I looked to Chaatiguin. "This means the hunting of Gephs will stop. Your people should now be safe."

"And I will return to make that a certainty," Eli spoke as he put his arm around her. "The King said he will send an army packing with me to wipe out them varmints."

I tried sitting up but almost fell back before the nurse steadied me and slipped several pillows under me.

"And you, Mahvan, will be returning with Queen Elay."

"Yes, Master Jak," she replied as she sat on the edge of my bed and took my hand. "It is my duty. But I will never forget my ferret."

"That is..."

"Yes, I know. I will never forget my private inquisitor, though I will always think of you as my ferret."

"The people of Ayres owe you much, Master Barley," Elsford, the young Queen's Guardsman, interjected. "You will always be welcomed."

"Though my guardsmen should not so easily speak for his queen, he speaks what is in my heart. And when you visit, you will call me Elay when we visit in private."

"Everyone seems to have gotten what they most desired. Even Lorenzo, who said he craves adventure. What about you, Jennair, did you find our father?"

She smiled. "That I did, me Jak."

I craned my head. "Where is he?"

"He be in this room."

"I do not see Pater Guinn."

"Who?"

"Peter Guinn, the Master Inquisitor. I deduced from our conversation that he was our father."

"You do not always guess correctly, my befuddled brother. This be our father." She stood up to walk across the room to take the arm of the former duke and now king.

For the second time in but a few minutes I was tongue bound.

"You are our father? You?" I declared in disbelief.

King Garsten Stee Hragen looked momentarily abashed then grinned. "I was not always so stout of girth, Jak. As a young man, I cut quite the bold figure. Though I have slowed down since then."

I shook my head in amazement. "Then I am now a prince."

Jennair's silver laugh followed my declaration. "You and half of Glavensdale, me brother, from soap makers to hide tanners. You would have a long line to wait in to someday claim the throne."

"Though you could always join the CIA," broke in Vil Hemloch. "I believe Ferred Kloppenhorsh would be overjoyed to hear that you were now a prince and an agent assigned to fraud."

It was my turn to laugh, even if it were with half a heart. "I do not believe so. I find myself growing homesick for Duburoake. I am through with adventures."

"I believe Jak is in need of more rest," declared Queen Elay in a royal voice that brooked no opposition. "We can visit his beside again when he is more sound. He is still too pale of face."

They gave their goodbyes until only the nurse and Lorenzo

remained.

"What about that damn Elf," I wanted to know. "Where did the little bastard fit in?"

"I'm not sure. No one has seen him."

"That is queer. He is a mystery unsolved."

"This is not a troubadour's reciting, Jak. It is not some adventure in a book. There are always mysteries in life."

There moment of silence, the Lorenzo asked, "And you, Jak, did you find what you were looking for?"

I thought a moment. "I thought I had. I believed Jennair when she said my quest was of the heart. I thought it might be Mahvan, and yet though her departing saddens me, I find myself not heartbroken. I believe my sister was finally wrong."

"Yet you sound heartbroken," my friend observed.

"I cannot help but grieve for Osyani. She was an endearing creature who deserved better. Harpy or not, I will miss her."

The nurse laughed. "Miss a harpy, what fool claim is that?"

I turned angrily to the young woman. "She..."

It was only now that I viewed my nurse's face.

"What poor joke is this?"

"It is no joke, Jak," the nurse said as she sat on the edge of the bed and arranged my pillows.

I looked to Lorenzo for an explanation then turned back to the human girl with the face of Osyani.

"Though you said many would give up their arms to fly, I find I like them better. How else would I be able to feel your face as this?"

The girl brushed her slender fingers across my cheek.

I turned again to Lorenzo.

"It seems the king's surgeons could sew her wound, but she had lost too much blood to survive. I instructed them of a medical practice from my world, that of transfusion. It seems not only is my blood compatible with Osyani, its properties of dispelling magic worked other changes on her. Only magic could continue harpy lineage generation after generation of breeding with human males. My blood broke the enchantment and Osyani became as you see her now.

"But the queen is right. You need your rest. We will all speak of this again when you have regained more strength."

I watched in a daze as they left the room, Osyani pausing to give me one last smile. I struggled to keep awake to contemplate all that had just befallen, but my eyelids betrayed me.

ABOUT THE AUTHOR

Dan Ehl has been a journalist and editor at both weeklies and daily newspapers in Iowa. The winner of numerous journalism and photo awards, including first in humor from the National Society of Newspaper Columnists, he enjoys breaking out of dryer newspaper writing to pen fantasy novels.

He served in Germany as an Army photographer during the Vietnam War.

"Knowing that a lot of Vietnamese people were digging pits with sharpened stakes at the bottom meant I wasn't really wanted, I didn't want to be rude and show up anyway. Being from Iowa, we always try to be polite. And Germany during the early 1970s was interesting enough with the barracks always smelling of beer, vomit and hashish every weekend."

His favorite hobbies are hitchhiking and hopping freights.

VISIT OUR WEBSITE
FOR THE FULL INVENTORY
OF QUALITY BOOKS:

http://www.roguephoenixpress.com

Rogue Phoenix Press
Representing Excellence in Publishing

Quality trade paperbacks and downloads

in multiple formats,

in genres ranging from historical to contemporary romance, mystery and science fiction.

Visit the website then bookmark it.

We add new titles each month!

www.ingramcontent.com/pod-product-compliance
Lightning Source LLC
Chambersburg PA
CBHW060422180626
46817CB00007B/2621